SMALL TOWN REBEL

MARION MEADOWS

DESCRIPTION

A segregated small town. An illicit interracial affair.

Roadside trouble throws Minnie Brown into the path of the allegedly racist McCall brothers.

Can she resist the hot mechanic who promises to fulfill her every dark desire — a man who is her enemy?

The McCalls might control the mountain, but they'll never control Rebel.

When he sets his eye on the beauty of Black Florin, he's determined to have her.

The sons of Duke McCall, heirs to a criminal empire, find themselves at the head of a civil war.

In the restless hills, a darker trouble is brewing...

CONTENT WARNING

This book deals with adult themes about race and gender that some may find potentially offensive.

While a love story, *Small Town Rebel* aims to stay true to the spirit of its setting. Some readers may find certain content and language objectionable. This book is about a steamy and controversial romance. Please be advised.

CHAPTER 1
BEN'S HOT CHICKEN

Sunday morning at Ben's Hot Chicken had become an ordeal for Minnie Brown since she moved back to the mountain.

"Minnie is too picky," her mother told the table of church ladies. "Pushing thirty and she still never had one boyfriend. Got me wondering if she's a lesbian."

"Don't be so hard on the girl," said Ms. Greaves, a plump woman with kind eyes. "I'm sure she'll settle down with a nice brother soon. But don't wait too long, baby." She patted the young woman's hand. "Before you know it, it's gonna be too late!"

"I'm just focused on my career," said Minnie in her usual refrain. "Even if the practice is so small, it's hard to find the time—"

"Picking fleas off dogs and cats ain't a career." Ms. Brown gave her daughter a hard look. "I'd like to see some grandbabies before I'm cold in the grave!"

"Listen to your Mama, Minnie," said Mrs. Victor, the third woman at the table. Of all the women at the table, only she was married, so she had authority on the subject. "You're nearly on the shelf. Nice Black men ain't marrying no old girl. Especially with the way these young heifers act. Sluts and whores all over the place."

Minnie stabbed a wandering tomato in her salad and stifled a sigh. Every Sunday, after she took Mama to church, she treated the ladies to a meal at Ben's Hot Chicken. After they gossiped about everybody who had come to church, and everybody who hadn't, the older women turned their sights on Minnie and started digging at her nonexistent love life.

The ladies meant well. Even Mama, she supposed. But did any Black women get married these days? In a town like Florin, where farm labor was drying up and the menfolk found their extra hands unwanted, they deserted in droves to live in Rowanville. What was she supposed to do? Chase after them? Even there, they weren't exactly rushing sisters to the altar.

But of course, women of her Mama's generation never blamed men for anything. And yet, Minnie could count on one hand the number of women in her church who had husbands.

Meanwhile on the white side of Florin, it seemed like every Monday some nineteen-year-old was getting hitched. What did that tell you? Maybe nothing, maybe something. Minnie had her theories.

Not that she entertained the idea of white men. Please. They were dirty and mean, they talked to her rude, they drank and smoke and whored like every other male, but with the added sting of being racist. No, thank you.

Would she ever find love, then? Maybe not. She'd waited too long, and the thought of giving her body to some handsy, fast man who just saw her as a hole to fuck petrified her. Far better she spend most nights on her couch watching *Preacher Man* and eating ice cream.

Minnie glanced out the window as a pickup rumbled up the road, confederate flag stickers plastered across the bumper. She barely batted an eye; these sights were common. Sometimes she wondered what the hell she'd been smoking to come back here.

But if the truck kept going up the road it would soon hit the Forever Lookout, and see the reason Minnie had decided to return. Florin was simply beautiful. A place of lush forests and shimmering rivers, nestled in the very heart of the Blue Ridge mountains. While she spent the last decade grinding at University for her certifications, she'd ached for the quiet hills, the silence, the birdsong, the clean mountain air. She was a country girl at heart.

And she loved her Practice. Every small furry life she saved gave her a sense of purpose, and reminded her why God had put her on this earth.

For her part, Ms. Brown would never understand her daughter. She saw Minnie's faraway expression and her lips pressed tightly together in disapproval. The girl had brains, give her that, but not a particle of common sense. Minnie should have focused on getting a man before she ran off to that school. Then she wouldn't have to work all day covering herself in all kinds of nasty junk. Maybe she'd even make more money to take care of her Mama the way a good daughter should.

After all, that was what Minnie's half-sisters had done. That lying bastard's "legitimate" children. Ermina, Delphina, and Serafina. Nonsense names, but what did you expect, with a mother like that?

Minnie's father, an executive at Rowanville Bank, already had a family when he'd got Ms. Brown in a delicate condition. She refused an abortion, hoping it would make him see sense and leave that woman. Ms. Brown miscalculated. The man had cut her loose. He kept in touch for the child's sake, and paid for Minnie's school, but that was it.

Ms. Brown wouldn't forget how she and Minnie had been relegated to child support checks while Mister's meal-mouth wife and her brats lived in high cotton in Belle Hills.

But the insult didn't stop there. Minnie's half sisters all went to Spelman, married businessmen and moved to Georgia. While Ms. Brown's daughter went off to cut open animals and ensure she'd remain a spinster for life, Ermine, Dolphin and Slut-fina were preening themselves on piles of money.

Ms. Brown fingered her pearl necklace, staring at her daughter with resentment. Minnie's problem was her selfishness. She never thought about her poor Mama's struggles.

The girl might be a lesbian for real. Would she ever get married? If only she stopped fussing with those creatures. Get her nails done. Straighten that raggedy hair. Act more feminine...But she was a lost cause. Ms. Brown hadn't wanted a daughter at all. She'd never know what God was thinking, saddling her with a girl like that instead of a precious boy.

The tenor of conversation changed, and Minnie looked up from her salad.

"Girls," said Ms. Greaves, "Is that who I think it is? That's the Smith boy, right?"

Minnie glanced at the door. "The Smith boy" turned out to be a grown man. His silver watch caught the sunlight and threw dazzlingly into Minnie's eyes.

"It's him," breathed Mrs. Victor. "Lawrence Smith. Now that's a tree I'd like to climb."

Possibilities whirled through Ms. Brown's head. "He married?"

"Nope," Mrs. Victor.

The word was hardly out of her mouth when Ms. Brown raised her voice and waved him over. "Lawrence! Baby, is that you? Come over here and say hello."

"Mama," Minnie said, mortified, but Ms. Brown gave her a warning look and she fell silent.

Though Minnie concentrated all her attention on the napkin in her lap, she didn't miss Lawrence Smith's broad grin as he approached their table. Minnie put his age at thirty five, a little older than herself. She did recognize him from church, but that had been years ago, and he'd moved down the valley since. He was a lawyer at the

Queensbury firm, the only black man in that position, in fact.

Ms. Brown, Ms. Greaves and Mrs. Victor beamed like new brides and sat up a little straighter in their chairs.

"Afternoon, ladies."

"Lawrence," said Mrs. Victor, "What a nice suit. Your daddy had the same good taste." She eyed him like her last meal. "I do love a man in a suit."

"How is your mother, Lawrence?" Ms. Greaves butted in. "We didn't see her at church today. Is something wrong? Is it the shingles again?"

"Lawrence," said Ms. Brown loudly, and with a touch of impatience, "Have you met my daughter?"

"Only in passing," said Lawrence. Of course, he had noticed her immediately. Minnie Brown. Somebody had told him about the sister with the animal shelter on Bear Hill, but he'd never suspected the rumors were true. Lawrence had vaguely known the Brown girl growing up. Where was the shy thing with the bad relaxer and braces?

Gone. In fact, this puss looked like a completely different person. A sweet little piece of church tail. The type who didn't fuck on the first date, but might take it up the ass on the second. He licked his lips. Get her away from those old birds, he suspected, and she'd melt like butter.

"How do you do, beautiful?" he asked Minnie. The women exchanged looks.

"I'm fine, Lawrence. Good to see you again," she intoned.

"I forgot you had a daughter, Ms. Brown. I'd almost say she was your sister."

Ms. Brown raised her eyebrows. "I don't think me and Minnie look alike much. I was more slender when I was her age."

"How come I don't see you around much, baby?"

Minnie's speaking voice barely climbed above a whisper. "I work."

"Don't your man take you out sometimes?"

"Minnie doesn't have a man," her mother couldn't say fast enough.

"What?" Lawrence acted surprised. "I don't believe it."

Her annoyance only deepened his interest. He like a challenge.

Lawrence's tongue darted out to touch his lower lip as his eyes again dropped to her breasts. "Maybe we should get together, then."

Ms. Brown said, "That's a great idea. Minnie needs to get out more, I keep telling her that. You can show her- what, Minnie?"

Minnie glared at the corner of her napkin. "Nothing."

Lawrence chuckled. "Write your number down for me while I get my chicken, alright? We can work something out."

Minnie looked ready to refuse, but everybody was looking at her expectantly. Steaming with embarrassment, she gave in to the pressure. She scribbled her number down on a pad of paper as Lawrence picked up his order. He came back to collect the paper, standing so close Minnie could smell his bitter cologne. When he said goodbye he laid a hand on her uncovered back. The cold metal of his watch made her flinch.

"You're a real gentleman, Lawrence," said Ms. Victor. "I remember your daddy was just the same way."

"Who is that?" said Ms. Greaves.

A white man had just entered the diner. Every pair of eyes swiveled towards this foreigner. Engine grease smeared his clothes from top to bottom. A frayed fishing hat was crammed atop rioting gold curls, and he wore a toolbelt cinched over his narrow hips. Obviously some kind of mechanic, but among the starched church crowd he just looked like a ragamuffin. Rednecks never came to Ben's. They had their own chicken spot, which served the kind of dry-ass barbecue white people liked. To Minnie's horror, the white man made a beeline for their table.

"You the black Escalade?" he said to Lawrence curtly, in a very deep voice.

Lawrence straightened, removing his hand from Minnie's back. The men were even in height. "Excuse me?"

"Are you driving. The black Escalade," the white man repeated.

"Yes," said Lawrence. "That's my Escalade. Who's asking?"

"Some lady just keyed it."

"What?" Lawrence barked.

"If you hurry, you can catch her," said the white man. "Oh, and my buddy Larry does body work down mountain. I recommend him."

Lawrence all but sprinted out of the restaurant.

The white man touched his hat to the table of staring ladies in a passing gesture of politeness, then went up to Ben's counter and leaned on it with his elbows. "Hey, Ben!" He bellowed towards the kitchens.

"Comin'!" Ben Simpson called back.

Like everybody else, Minnie was now openly staring. She was not surprised to find she didn't recognize the man at all. Even in a small town like Florin, you couldn't know *everybody*. And White Florin was like another world, even for people like Minnie, who ran her hospital in their hills.

The stranger was tall, well over six feet. Minnie made a subtle adjustment in her position and checked him out. Broad shoulders, narrow waist, a round, firm ass encased in a pair of Wranglers...The man might be covered in grease, but he had an amazing body. She took a sip of lemonade, her throat suddenly dry.

Thoroughbred redneck.

Ben Simpson, owner of Ben's Hot Chicken, ducked his grizzled head out of the kitchen. "What you want?" Ben said gruffly.

"I ain't gonna shout it to you," said the white man. He had a deep drawl that meant he'd rarely left the mountain, if ever.

"He's one of them McCalls," Ms. Victor hissed, snapping her fingers. "Now I remember. I thought he looked familiar. He's the picture of Duke McCall, Betty."

"You're right," said Minnie's mother, eyes widening. "He must be one of the sons. How many are there?"

"Four," said Ms. Greaves.

"You're sure he's one of those people?" said Minnie, frowning. The McCalls were notorious racists. They owned most of the land on the mountain, and four trailer parks. The family was huge, some of them rich as Solomon, others poor as dirt, but every one of them had a nasty streak you didn't want to cross.

Ben dried his hands on a towel and came out to talk to McCall. The men spoke in lowered voices, aware that everybody in the diner was straining to eavesdrop. Ben shook his head at something the white man said, angry. They argued some more, then Ben took the man's order and stiffly handed him the receipt.

What's that about?

The white man stood off to the side and waited for his chicken. From the new vantage point Minnie could look straight at him. He really was tall. He looked to be on the tender side of thirty. Blonde stubble covered his cheeks. He was really handsome. No wedding ring.

He caught Minnie staring.

He winked.

Nobody saw it. The ladies were running on about Pastor Michael's wife, oblivious. McCall went up to the counter and collected his sandwich.

Ben took McCall's money and counted out the change.

McCall's hands made the sandwich look tiny. "It ain't poisoned, right?"

Ben shook his head. "Go on with yourself."

McCall grinned. His teeth were straight, and very white. "Always a pleasure, Ben."

The white man unwrapped the sandwich at the counter and began eating it as he walked out the door. He glanced at Minnie again, this time with a bold look of interest that couldn't be misunderstood. A flash of heat went through her, but he had already looked away. Luckily none of her companions noticed. McCall walked through the parking lot with an unhurried stride. He got into a red pickup and drove away, vanishing down the road. She wondered if she'd ever see him again.

CHAPTER 2
THE OLD MCCALL

The chicken sandwich was a strategic move. If he filled up first, his stomach wouldn't tempt him to prolong the encounter any longer than was necessary.

Rebel McCall's gaze wandered around the Blue Midge cafe. It was Sunday. After-church regulars squeezed around little tables, nibbling on bacon strips and buttery grits as they jawed about the usual safe subjects: the weather, cows, football.

Rebel had put his foot down about this place because it was neutral turf. While he was a confident brawler, he didn't like to start his Sunday scrapping with some by-blow cousin looking to gain the old McCall's favor. Or getting shot.

Stares passed over their table. Voices lowered from those nearest in an attempt to catch what Rebel and his father Duke were saying to each other.

The two men looked like different versions of each other, two of the same man, one at the peak of his vitality and youth, the other hard and lean, baked to a finish by the scorching sands of time. They had the same firm, long noses. Their hands were large and square-nailed, the hands of men who came from generations of timber cutters and yeomen, hands capped with scars from hunting or in Rebel's case, diving into the smoking innards of engines. Matching green eyes. Off the mountain, nobody would ever guess that Duke sat on one of the biggest fortunes in Southwest Virginia, a swathe of land so huge he had constructed an entire criminal empire just to pay its taxes.

Hostility radiated off the two men like the stink of hot metal.

Rebel rubbed his thumb against the inside of his palm over and over, staring at the door as if it would make time pass faster.

Five minutes. Five minutes.

"You look well, son."

"I eat my vegetables."

"How is the shop?"

"It's doing fine."

"Where have you been?"

"Working."

"The family needs you."

"That's too bad."

"You ungrateful son of a bitch."

"Right," said Rebel.

Whatever warmth Rebel lacked in his family, he'd found in the bellies of the mountain's beasts, in the sparking, roasting, belching churn of gasoline and metal. The machines freed him from the McCalls and the mercenary life his father had prepared him for. They huffed life into him the same way he'd done for them, raising them up from lumps of steel and copper to prowl among the hills. They gave him purpose, unlike his family, which only ever took.

A vein ticked in Duke McCall's jaw. "There's gonna be a war down the mountain, Rebel. Trouble's coming up from Rowanville. They want to stop our trade and they're sending in more men than we can deal with. We need the family together for what's coming."

"So you come to the only McCall bound to refuse you. It ain't the best idea you ever had, Pa."

Duke's eyes narrowed. "You act like I can't still cut you down, boy."

Green eyes held onto green. "Then try it."

"You don't care about your family."

"No more than they deserve."

"Well, I can't say I'm surprised. Look at you. You should have a woman by now. You should have sons of your own. You're a bare branch, a waste. I always taught you boys that family was the most important thing. You got nothing. No legacy."

"I got Katie."

"So? That girl is only good for lying on her back. I'm talking about boys. Sons."

Rebel had spent most of his life trying to escape the family God had saddled him with. He'd never been eager for another one. And of all people to lecture him about filial duty...

He said nothing. He sipped his coffee, though his hands shook with anger.

"You heard from Ross?" Duke asked.

"No. He's ashamed of us, so he don't call. I'm like to see his point."

"I heard he's seeing a nigger down in that city."

A couple heads turned.

"Is he?" Said Rebel.

"You heard about it?"

"I don't look where Ross dips his tackle," Rebel said. "Nor do I give a damn."

"You like them niggers too, I heard."

And that was five minutes. But before he could scrape back from the table his father grabbed the chair leg with his boot.

Long legs, like me.

Rebel jerked the chair back, nearly tipping his father out of his own seat. Unfortunately the old man still had a fighter's reflexes, and righted himself before Rebel could have the pleasure of seeing him topple to the floor.

"You just take care, Pa," he said.

Duke McCall straightened, seeming a little surprised. He glared up at his son. "Rebel. You might hate me, but I've only ever looked out for your own good."

"You want me to be your weapon."

"Is that what you think?"

"Running all that dope off Shy Hill must be costing you," Rebel said. "Especially with all that talk out East about making it legal. Yeah, I ain't good for reading, but I hear to the news, Pa."

"Lay it out, then."

"It's hard to keep all them plates spinning at once. Hard to find boys you trust. You're getting old. Ever since the feds locked up those boys in Charleston, you've been on a wire. You got to push more out of here than you can sell. And the fellas down in the valley don't care so much for you stomping through their turf. Fact is, business is changing too fast, and you feel like Roman will fumble it. You must be running scared, 'cause no way in hell or high water I'd ever work for you. And you done knew that."

"It should have been you leading the family. Not Roman. You had a better sense of people."

"Roman's loyal. He's smart. Strong."

"He ain't the one I need."

"Too bad. I ain't ending my days selling my ass for cigarettes to make you rich. You fucking sunuvabitch, you make me so goddamned sick."

He stood up.

"You tell Ross if he keeps seeing that whore he'll be picking up pieces of her from now 'till the rapture," Duke said coldly.

"Ross has a right to be happy," said Rebel. To avoid more curious stares, he sat back down, but on the edge of the chair. One leg bounced on the floor. "Pa, I mean it, I'm done with the operations. You got dozens of boys who know engines. Hell, some are surely better than me. I don't ask nothing of you. I don't *want* nothing *from* you. And I want nothing to do with the family stuff, you understand?"

"Nobody made you an outcast, son. You did that yourself."

THE OLD MAN'S WORDS STAYED WITH REBEL LONG AFTER HE left the Blue Midge. In the parking lot of the General Store, he smoked and watched the milling church crowd. Doubtless, if you scrolled back the clock sixty years, the scene before him would hardly change at all.

Sunday. All around him Church People licked fat ice cream cones and jawed in the shade of the General Store. A happy day, Sunday. A day for prayer. Families coming together. Rebel watched toddlers swinging from their parents' arms, girls in calico, boys in stiff jeans, roughnecks who'd packed their guts into button-downs, accompanied by plump, gossiping wives. Old men sitting on benches talking about the same things they talked about in Blue Midge. The weather, cows, football.

In the distance the church bell tolled. The smell of ham and biscuits floated in from *somewhere*. These people all seemed so sure of something, so certain about the steady pace of their simple lives. The past didn't concern them, nor did the future, though it promised nothing. For people like that, life was no more complicated than a straight road on a clear day. He wished he'd been born with what they had— whatever it was. Rebel watched for a while, then started his diesel truck and pulled out of the lot. His mind wasn't meant to dwell on these things. He just kept moving forward, on and on, and stayed away from the dark.

It wasn't always easy.

As he reached for the radio, his cellphone rang. He glanced at the caller ID and the fragile good mood he'd been trying to build evaporated. He answered it.

"Where are you?" Snapped his eldest brother. "Where the fuck is my daughter? I came back and she ain't here. I thought you were watching her!"

If Roman knew where his daughter really was, he'd probably lock Katie in a basement for the rest of her life. "She's with friends," said Rebel.

"She's ignoring my calls," Roman growled.

"I wonder why. Can I hang up now?"

Roman cleared his throat. "How did it go? How was Pa?"

"As one might expect."

"Did you talk to him?"

"I braided his hair."

"He's concerned about the affairs down the mountain with the Rowanville gang. Did he talk to you about that?"

Rebel's hand tensed around the wheel. "Concerned, is he? No, he didn't say nothing about that."

"I'll tell you later. I don't want to discuss it on the phone."

"I don't want to discuss it, period. And somebody should warn Ross, by the way."

"What? What's the matter with him?" Roman demanded. Say what you wanted about Roman, but he looked out for his brothers. "He in trouble?"

"He's seeing some Black lady and Pa's all bowed up over it. Threatened to kill her."

"Is that what he said?"

"Reading between the lines."

"You can't read shit."

"Yeah. Katie says I have dyslexia."

"Katie's just a kid. She don't know nothing," Roman scorned. Rebel heard a bottle clink against a glass. Roman drank too much and slept too little these days. Rebel's oldest brother added, "And if Ross is seeing one of *those*, then Pa's got a right to be mad. Ross should know better."

"Can I ask you a question?"

"Sure, Rebel. Ask me a question."

"There any particular reason you don't like 'em?"

"Thought we was talking about Ross," Roman deflected. "Don't give me your hippie bullshit, Rebel. I don't want my little brother fucking with some ghetto whore."

"Maybe you should pick a woman for him, since you got such good taste."

"Go to hell," Roman grated, and hung up.

Going over the speed limit, Rebel flew past a Florin Police car on the shoulder. But laws were more like suggestions in Florin, especially for McCalls.

The McCalls. A great big Scots-Irish clan as old as the town itself. On the mountain they all jostled for dominance, cheating and stealing and fucking and killing each other with no regard. If you wanted a body hid, you wanted someone pounded up, you wanted to turn dirty money clean or clean money dirty, or to taste the best damn shine in the world, your best bet was a McCall. Dirty rednecks with lots of fucking cash and land, and zero scruples. Rebel's kin.

Royalty. He supposed Pa was the King, then.

He passed a deer carcass thrown off to the roadside. It looked like the body was still twitching. Rebel stared, distracted. Jesus Christ. Could it be that—

CAR! His mind screamed a second before his body reacted.

. . .

Burning rubber scorched his nose as he slammed on the brakes, cutting the wheel hard at the last second. His truck slammed to a stop, roughly jolting the car in front of him. Rebel rocked back in his seat, teeth gritted, his heart pounding hard. "Fuck!"

He'd forgotten about that damned Stop sign. A split second too late, and he'd have sent the little car straight into the mountain. He moved his truck to the shoulder, turned off the engine and quickly opened the door. Like a butterfly emerging from a chrysalis, a Black woman in a pastel dress pushed her way out of the shotgun side of the gray sedan, and teetered awkwardly on the asphalt, recovering from the shock.

Rebel instantly recognized her from Ben's. And then, miracle of miracles, here came the girl in the mint green dress.

You got to be kidding me.

Not an hour ago he'd seen the girl sitting in Ben's chicken spot. She had skin the color of powdered cinnamon, and the smallest little curls hanging next to her ears. Those were the first things he noticed. Then her eyes. Right now, those big pretty eyes were squinting with fury.

"Mama? Are you alright?" The girl said, hurrying around the side of the car. Her voice shook, but it had a pleasant softness to it, her country accent slight.

Pig he was, he'd already started checking out her curves, which were packed into a dress that reminded him of his favorite dessert.

"I'm fine, Minnie. But look at your car!"

"Oh my God!" The girl gasped, seeing the damage.

The Kia's fender was dented badly, but it was nothing a couple hours in his shop wouldn't fix. His truck, of course, didn't have a scratch.

"Everybody okay?" Rebel asked.

"We're fine, Mister McCall," said the old woman in a deeply hostile tone. "A little faster and you'd have killed us, I'm sure."

He didn't know the woman, but she knew him, apparently.

He turned back to the young woman in green. She was gorgeous, even better looking in true sunlight.

"I'll need your insurance information," the beauty said. "Didn't you see the sign?"

"What sign?" he said, wanting to devil her.

"That sign above your head? It's nearly eye level to you!"

The older woman—her mother, maybe— lurched forward and grabbed Miss Attitude's arm, giving Rebel a frightened look. "Minnie! Stop hollering."

Minnie. He liked that name. The mole under her eye was like a very tiny button.

Minnie rifled in her purse and pulled out a notepad in the shape of a paw print.

"I just bought this car," she muttered to herself. She looked up at him darkly. "Your name and information, Mr. McCall." The hand holding the pen shook.

Rebel found his voice. "Hold up, before you go a-scribbling. I'm a mechanic, right? Me and my friend do body work. We fix up stuff like this'un all the time. My shop's over on Flat Hill. We don't need to get all this paperwork involved. I won't charge you."

Rebel hated paperwork. He preferred to do business with a word and a handshake, and he fully intended to give Minnie Brown the whole package. Shoot, for eyes like that he'd have the little pile of slag running sharp in no time. The car, that is.

Minnie faltered, but her mother shook her head. "No. He's just trying to get off with nothing. You better just leave him alone, Minnie. Look, there's the police!"

The patrol car from earlier crept down the road. Rebel fell back with a sigh and waited. After a minute Deputy John Daniel stumbled out of the vehicle, one hand clamped firmly on his hat, the other on his belt, as if he was trying to hold the pieces of himself together.

"Good afternoon folks," the officer sang. Fumes of whiskey rolled off his uniform. "Rebel! Hey, brother. Ain't seen you since the christening."

Rebel recalled that Deputy Daniel was married to his cousin. He had dozens of cousins.

"What's the problem here, Rebel?"

"This man—" began Minnie hastily, but the Deputy threw up a hand.

"Wait your turn, Miss! We can't all talk at once!" He chided. "Go on, Rebel."

"I missed the stop sign and hit 'em," said Rebel gruffly, annoyed that the woman was so desperate to report him.

"Missed the stop sign?" said the Deputy, his squiffy eyebrows lifting. "I don't blame you. You know, you're the fifth person this week? I don't know why the county put that fuckin' thing up anyhow. Mighty stupid place to stick a stop sign." He belched through his teeth. "You can go on ahead, Rebel. Nothing to worry about."

"Excuse me?" Minnie said, aghast. "I'd like to file a police report."

The deputy gave her a startled look, as if he'd forgotten she was there. "What? Why?"

"Because...because it's the law," the woman sputtered. "Surely you know that?"

"Put a 'sir' there when you talk to me, Missy," the Deputy scowled. " 'Surely you know that, *sir*.' "

Rebel took the man aside. "Deputy?"

"Yes, Rebel?"

"Can you kindly button it up?"

"Sure, Reb. Whatever you say. You talked to your daddy about giving me that raise, yet?"

"No, Daniel, I haven't. Give me a minute."

Rebel turned back to a furious Minnie. He snatched the notepad from her hand. He wrote his number in firm, bold strokes, then above it printed REBEL MCCALL. He shoved it back to her.

"Bring the car to my shop," he said.

She looked even angrier than before, like she wanted to rip the page out and stamp on it. "I really think–"

"Damn it, just say yes," he said impatiently.

"Don't cuss at my daughter!" Said the older woman.

At her loud voice Officer Daniel flinched. The man was jagged as a fence. "Well...Seems like you all got it worked out," he nodded, looking between a furious Minnie and an exasperated Rebel. "Just a little fender bender, missy. It ain't the end of the world. So if there's nothing you need me here for, I'll be— Woah!" He put his foot on uneven earth and nearly fell on his face. His hat tumbled to the ground. Rebel caught Daniel neatly and set him upright.

"Thank you, Rebel...Musta had more'n I thought...to drink." Officer Daniel wiped his nose. "Say, is it true Ross is seeing a nigger?"

The women recoiled, and for a moment it seemed like all the air had rushed off the mountain. Officer Daniel blinked out of his stupor, and saw Rebel's expression. He turned red as beets. He opened his mouth.

"Yes." Rebel said the first thing that came into his head, anything to keep the man from talking. "Yeah, he is."

It was the wrong thing to say. And likely the dumbest thing he could have possibly said. The older women just looked at each other, but those beautiful dark eyes pinned him down. "Bless his heart," said Minnie with the sugary *fuck you* of a true Southern woman. "Give your brother our congratulations." She put away her little book. "You'll be hearing from my insurance soon. If I can't file a report here, then I'll go to the station. Maybe someone there will be sober enough to hear a word I say. Have a nice afternoon, gentlemen."

She turned stiffly back to the car. Rebel was tempted to let her get away with that grand exit, but he had no intention of letting the most beautiful woman he'd ever seen prance off in a tetch, the words of a drunk bastard forever attached to him in her mind.

He quickly grabbed her arm. She froze, her gaze darting down in alarm, then widening with revulsion. Rebel realized his hands were filthy. *Fuck.* He'd stained her dress. *Double fuck.*

"I meant what I said," he said, quickly wiping them on his jeans. "The Car. I'll take care of it. I do good work. Flat Hill. Just bring it over, alright?"

"No, thank you," she said coldly. "I'm not that desperate." She turned her back on him.

CHAPTER 3
THE DATE

Safely in her trailer, Minnie got to her Sunday cleaning. She worked all afternoon, her hair tied up in an old shirt, dusting and scrubbing the small space until sweat trickled down her back and the afternoon sun was sweltering over Grace Hill. She aired out her small rugs, swept her porch vigorously, crammed linens into an ancient washing machine bought off craigslist, and dusted off every surface that couldn't take a strong polish with a rag. In the background she played old R&B. The cleaning frenzy helped take her mind off the giant dent in her car and how she was going to pay for it.

It also helped her stop thinking about a certain green-eyed man who was responsible.

She had completely forgotten about the date with Lawrence when he called.

"I want to see you tonight," he said. "I'm going back to the office tomorrow so it had better be tonight."

"Um, alright," said Minnie. "But I wasn't exactly planning—"

"See you tonight girl. I'll call you."

Minnie was tempted to call him back and tell him about himself and his inconsiderate behavior. What about the woman who had keyed his car? What would he say to that? But she decided just to give him a chance. Having dinner out with a stranger didn't seem so bad, even if she doubted Lawrence had good intentions. To be very honest, he probably just wanted her for sex.

Sex. She wiped her forehead. What was wrong with her? Maybe her doubts just came from insecurity. When was the last time she'd even been on a date? They were forgettable experiences except for the endings, when the men made blunt sexual passes at her that made her instinctively flee. She had the feeling it was not even her body that attracted them, but that these men were just happy for a willing hole to stick themselves inside.

In hindsight she should have just let them take her all the way. If she'd done that, she wouldn't be in this position, now considering offering her first experience to a man who reminded her of those men. Just to feel like she was still a woman. Just to be touched.

Minnie scraped the brass lamp Mama had given her with force. Just to be touched! What an embarrassing thing. But it was true. Some nights all Minnie could do was curl herself up around her pillow and imagine the large, warm embrace of a man's body. His smell. His touch as he pulled her closer against his firm chest. She had no idea what that would feel like. She had never been intimate with anybody in that way.

A while later, for some reason, she found herself digging in her purse and pulling out her notepad. REBEL MCCALL. She stared at the letters like they contained a hidden meaning. He wrote like children did, with the pen held between four fingers, as if the page would fly out from under his hand.

It was only because he was so good looking. That was it.

She wondered what would happen if she called his number.

But that would be crazy.

She put away the paper. She might have known a man as attractive like that would be just like the rest of these hill-billies. All their talk about honor and fairness was just smoke. It went right out the window the minute they were asked to play by the same rules as black people. Then they turned slippery as newts.

Yes, Rebel McCall could go to hell.

"MINNIE-MIN-MINS?"

"Chrissie!" Minnie tucked the towel over her breasts and nudged the phone up to her ear.

"Hey girl. Just saw your text. You good?" her best friend asked.

Chrissie's father was a black Rowanville man. Interracial relationships were barely tolerated back then, and to nobody's surprise the man moved back down the mountain in a hurry, alone.

Chrissie grew up on the *po'whitetrash* side of Florin. Down in Chrissie's holler, her uncle sold Pitbull puppies from the back of his trailer, her cousin lived out of an RV and spent all day talking to "aliens", and her other uncle cooked meth in abandoned houses. He went in and out of prison like a candy store.

Chrissie's mother had worked at Florin Drug since she was fourteen years old, which was about the time she'd got pregnant with Chrissie. The holler they lived down was called Dead End. As soon as she graduated, Chrissie went off like a rocket to Rowanville.

Minnie told Chrissie about the rest of the incident, of the Florin Deputy dropping the n-word.

"Didn't I tell you to get away from these hillbillies? When are you gonna MOVE?" Chrissie screamed. "I know you love them ratty little animals, but enough is enough."

"You know, Chrissie, from a nurse I'd expect a little more compassion."

"At least my patients don't have rabies."

"Right."

Chrissie cackled. "So anyway, is Rebel McCall still fine as fuck?"

Of course Chrissie would ask that. "We went to school with him, remember, Minnie? Those tall McCalls. Uh-huh."

"You were older than me. I don't recall 'em."

"Oh that's right. Well, is he still fine? *Rebel*?"

"No," said Minnie, throwing the phone on speaker and toweling off. "He's too...tall. And he's racist."

"Rebel is the big one with the green eyes, right?"

"Yeah," said Minnie. "Kind of a light green. A *racist* green."

"So did *he* say the word?"

"No, his little cop friend did."

"Did he laugh?"

"No. He tried to cover it up, though. Come on, Chrissie, you know these people let that word fly behind closed doors."

"You're right. He probably is racist," Chrissie agreed.

"Even good looking people can be racist."

"But is that dick racist? That's what I want to know."

"You are crazy. I'm getting ready for a date, by the way. A real date with a real man who isn't racist."

"Really? WHO?"

"Lawrence Smith. You know him? We went to church together but he's a little older. Came to Ben's this morning. "

"Very romantic. Did he propose to you with a curly fry?"

"Ha ha. But while he was getting my number some woman apparently keyed his car and he had to leave."

"Baby mama?" Said Chrissie shrewdly.

"No...He'll probably say the lady got the wrong car, he don't know her...and so on and so forth."

But you're still going on a date with him, girl.

"Lawrence Smith...Is his Mama the one with the bad tooth?" Chrissie's encyclopedic knowledge about Florin's people always impressed Minnie. Though Chrissie tried never to set a high heel on the mountain unless she had to, she would have done well for herself simply by knowing everybody.

"I have no idea," said Minnie. "Should I know these things?"

"Well you better get an idea. Because if he's lying, you don't want to fuck him. Does he have a job?"

"He's a lawyer. He lives in Rowanville."

"All lawyers are hoes. Don't fuck him. Or do, I don't know. But use protection! Take it from me, the gonorrhea is crazy right now. Hold up. I think my food is here. HEY! YEAH! YOU CAN LEAVE IT ON THE PORCH! TO THE SIDE OVER THERE. NO, THAT SIDE! THANK YOU. IS THE SAUCE IN IT? Okay Minnie I got to go. I'll call you later, baby. Don't do anything I wouldn't do! Hee hee!"

AFTER CHRISSIE HUNG UP, MINNIE MOVED ON TO THE PROBLEM of The Dress.

The *Date* Dress.

Maybe Mrs. Victor had a point. Nobody covered up anymore. Going out in a church outfit wouldn't impress a man like Lawrence.

Did she *want* to impress him?

No. But did she *want* to remain a virgin for life?

Also no.

Having sex with Lawrence...She shuddered. Something about his staring had unnerved her.

Still, it was better than the way Rebel McCall had stared.

Much better.

Right?

Feeling that she should be prepared for anything, Minnie chose a lacy thong. She shuffled to the mirror and squeezed herself into the dress. It was tight, but comfortable. She risked a peek. Gulping, she tried to suck in her stomach and hunch a little. Did her ass always have to stick out like that? And the cups in front pushed her titties up to show a crazy swoop of cleavage. But the dress covered most of her thighs, and maybe she could wear a little wrap...

She did her hair last. She shook out her low puff and vigorously pumped a spray bottle of water and rosemary oil until the whole fluffy mass was a little softer. Then, after working in leave-in carefully, she did small cornrows in the front and secured them with black clips, leaving the back puffy and pretty. Thank God for the internet, or she never would have learned to do her own hair otherwise. She glanced at the clock. Hastily she made up her face and put in earrings.

Her phone rang. She nearly dropped it in her rush to answer. "Lawrence?"

He sounded like he was driving. "Mindy?" He barked. "Something came up so I can't come get you. You'll have to meet me there."

"I- Oh. Okay." She'd be driving herself to the date. *Good. If it's bad I can leave.* "Um, what restaurant?"

"You know, where we met this morning. Ben's. Cool? I'll be there seven-thirty. See you, baby."

Minnie stared at the black screen.

Mindy?

Well, plenty men were bad with names. It had been crowded at the chicken spot that morning anyway. Maybe he'd misheard her Mama's introduction.

He's taking you to get fried chicken the same place he met you this morning.

Minnie put the phone down, swallowing her disappointment. But then she scolded herself. She didn't need a man to spring for a big fancy dinner at a steakhouse. Ben's Hot Chicken was perfectly fine. Nothing else was open on a Sunday night anyway, and at least now she could drive home quickly...

At seven fifteen Minnie left her trailer, locking the door firmly. Theft was rare on the mountain, but a woman living alone could never be too careful.

Minnie drove slowly over the hills, tensing every time a truck pulled onto the road behind her.

Minnie patted the little car's dashboard in apology.

34

I should have let that bastard fix it.

But she wasn't going to think about him. In all likelihood she'd never see Rebel McCall again. She'd spent the rest of the afternoon post-cleaning trying to file a claim with her insurance while the weak mountain signal kept dropping. If she ever saw him again, she'd wring his neck.

His handsome, muscled neck.

The parking lot was mostly empty. Ben's never stayed open past eight on a Sunday. Minnie scanned the company without getting out of the car. A couple teenagers eating from Styrofoam plates on picnic tables. She couldn't believe Lawrence. Surely there were better places for two grown people to go on a first date?

He was running late when the Escalade pulled into the parking lot and across two spots. He'd already fixed the scratches on the side, Minnie noted..

She got out of the car. Lawrence smiled big and wide and got out too.

"Hi Mindy."

"Hi Lawrence. It's Minnie, by the way."

"Wow. You sure looking good tonight."

His eyes roved over her, lingering on her breasts. Again.

"Thanks," she said.

"I like a woman that can eat." He put an arm around her waist. "Mmm. I'm starving. What do you want?"

Should he be touching her already? *Just give him a chance. He's being nice. He's from the town. Our Mamas know each other.*

"I'll have the hot fries, I think," Minnie said.

"Good. You can take it to go," said Lawrence.

Go? They were going somewhere?

He patted the top of her ass and ducked inside, not bothering to see if she followed him, but holding open the door.

"Two Chicken sandwiches, Junior," he barked to cashier: Ben Simpson's nephew, Junior. "And hurry up. Ain't nobody in here so I know it won't take you long." Junior keyed in the order, looking up as Minnie shuffled awkwardly inside.

"Hi Miss Brown," said Junior, who was a very polite young man. His teak-brown skin was flushed from the heat inside the restaurant. Ben never ran the air conditioning at night to save money.

"Hi Junior."

"How are you doing?"

"Mind your business, boy, " said Lawrence, rapping his card on the counter. The order came to $14.99.

"Shit's getting expensive," Lawrence groused. "What happened to the four dollar meals?"

"We-e-ell, prices rising down the mountain too," Junior replied, looking at him steadily. "We got to make money same as everybody."

Lawrence snorted. "They cost five dollars at the white people's spot."

Junior rolled his eyes as Lawrence turned back to Minnie, remembering he was on a date.

"So. Mindy. You work at the animal shelter?"

"I'm a veterinarian. I bought the practice a year ago from the last man who retired. He only looked after livestock, though."

"I'm surprised," said Lawrence, leaving the remark vague enough to be condescending.

"Yes, we've never had a female vet on the mountain and never a black woman."

"How much money you make? " Lawrence demanded.

"Enough to pay my bills."

"Hey, don't get defensive. You know a lot of country girls want to just sit around and have a man take care of them. I thought you looked like one of those girls."

I'll just get my sandwich and leave.

"Why do you live up here anyway?" Lawrence demanded. "You should move down to Rowanville where they got some civilization. You still living with your Mama too, I bet."

"Actually I have my own place."

"You do? Why didn't you say so? We can just go there tonight instead of parking."

Fuck the sandwich. I'm out.

Minnie might be a virgin, but she knew damn well "parking" was what teens did when their parents thought they were at church group. Nothing her grown ass had any business doing. And she also knew she would not be *parking* with Lawrence Smith. Ever. Clearly he thought this was just a booty call. He had another thing coming.

"Order up!" Junior called.

Oily stains had already smeared the inside of the paper bag with their sandwiches. Minnie mechanically followed her "date" into the parking lot. Disappointment had a smell: cheap hot grease.

Lawrence confidently strode to his car, swinging his keys. He was used to this, she realized. While Minnie had been losing herself to foolish fantasies he'd just seen a sex object.

"Who keyed your car this morning?" She asked.

"Some dumb bitch got the wrong car, that's what."

Lawrence set down the bag of food. She prepared to deliver her goodbye speech, but out of nowhere his hand shot out and pulled her hard against him.

"Come here babygirl," he murmured. Her gasp was lost in his mouth. His lips came down over hers, thick and damp, and his tongue thrust into her. He ground her against the side of his car, cupping her ass with both hands as if he meant to fuck her right there in the parking lot. She choked on his spit, which tasted of tic-tacs. His erection dug into her stomach. One of his big hands worked under her dress and a long finger pressed against her panties. A shudder of revulsion made her whole body spasm, which he mistook for arousal. His fingers skimmed her slit.

She tore her lips away and shoved him back.

"Get the hell off me!"

"What the fuck?" he snapped. She had pushed him a little hard, maybe.

"I'm going home," said Minnie. *How had this happened?*

"You serious, bitch?"

Minnie calmed herself down in a slow breath; her heart was thundering. "I'm not interested in that, Lawrence. I'm sorry."

"You made me drive out here for nothing?"

The nerve. "Goodnight, Lawrence."

As she turned to leave, he snatched her around the waist and wrenched her ass against his still-hard dick.

"Get away from me!" Minnie gasped, but after one humiliating thrust of his hips he released her.

He smirked, as if he'd put her in her place, then climbed into his car muttering about ungrateful country bitches.

She had never felt so degraded in her life. Blinking back tears of rage, she hurried towards the glowing door of Ben's.

Junior saw her coming and gallantly opened the door. As Lawrence rolled out of the parking lot, he tossed the uneaten chicken sandwich out the window. It exploded all over Junior's sneakers.

"What the fuck?" the teenager wailed.

"Aye! Watch your motherfuckin' language, boy!" Ben Simpson roared from the kitchens.

Junior looked down at his shoes again and hissed, "Man what the *fuck*!" But then he remembered himself and pushed the door wider for Minnie, who hurried inside. "Miss Minnie, are you okay?"

"I'm fine," Minnie muttered.

Junior eyed the splattered chicken sandwich on the threshold. "He just throw that shit at you?"

"Let me help clean it," Minnie offered, dabbing at her eyes with the back of her wrist.

"Are you crazy? You didn't throw it." Junior sucked his teeth. "I can't stand that man Lawrence. He's always on some bullshit."

"He's a pig," Minnie agreed.

Junior looked at his shoes with deep sadness. "I just got these today, man!"

"Why are you wearing them in here?" Minnie said, resisting the urge to giggle at the poor boy's face. "You were bound to mess them up in the kitchen. You going somewhere?"

"Uncle said he'd work the fryer if I did the register. I wanted to show them to um, my friend."

"Your friend?"

"Yeah. Katie."

Junior glanced over his shoulder, as if to make sure his uncle wasn't in hearing. He turned back to Minnie and lowered his voice. "Is it true Rebel crashed your car?"

"I- did *he* tell you that?" Minnie's turn to stutter now.

"No, Katie did."

"Who is Katie?"

The red pickup spun into the parking lot, the wail of a blues guitar assaulting them. With a flourish, the truck reversed neatly between two cars, giving Minnie full view of a familiar and most unwelcome sight.

"Katie!" said Junior happily.

I don't believe this.

A pair of flaming red cowboy boots, stitched in silver, hit the gravel. They belonged to a curvy blonde girl who'd been perching in the bed of Rebel McCall's truck. She wore a denim skirt and a tube top that pushed up her breasts. The girl waved happily at Junior.

In slow motion, like a nightmare, Minnie saw the driver's side open and Rebel McCall climb out. He'd cleaned himself up, apparently. Gone were the filthy jeans and raggedy shirt, the crusty fishing hat. The man wore straight blue jeans and a spotless white tee that emphasized his broad shoulders and hugged his biceps as he helped the girl out of the truckbed. For a moment the shirt rode up and exposed a shiny silver belt buckle, a flat, densely muscled stomach, and a patch of thick dark hair knifing towards his groin. Higher up, above his broad chest and neck...His hair was loose, floating about his jaw in rumpled curls.

McCall said something to the blonde girl, who giggled flirtatiously and stood on tiptoe to kiss his cheek. Junior practically shoved Minnie out of the way as he hurried to meet Katie, the chicken salad on his shoes forgotten.

Which left only Minnie and *him*.

Minnie's first impulse was to ignore him. But that would be petty, and she was above that.

"Good evening," she said coolly, walking towards him.

Up close, he was even better looking. Blood rushed to Minnie's cheeks. *He's not just good looking. He's...is there even a word?* The paleness of his eyes took the color of the artificial light, mixed it with the fading rays of the sun, looking nearly transparent to Minnie.

He said, "Wow. I like that dress even better."

"I was just leaving. Excuse me."

He leaned over her– the man was tall as a tree– and sniffed. "Is that chicken salad in your hair?"

She couldn't get to her car fast enough.

In the darkness of the front seat, after she wiped the mess from her hair, she clenched her steering wheel until her knuckles hurt. She just wanted to get home and lie in bed. Maybe she shouldn't even go home. She should just start sleeping at the clinic. Live there with the animals. She was never going out again. No more dates. No more men, period.

She fumbled for her keys. Home wasn't far. At least, she hadn't driven all the way to Rowanville for this mess. Small graces. As soon as she got home, she was going to watch *Preacher Man* and eat enough ice cream to be sick on.

She turned the keys. Her engine rattled like a dry bean in a can.

"No," she gasped, wrenching at the keys. "Oh, you got to be kidding me."

Dead, dead, dead.

Gravel crunched. Minnie screwed her eyes shut and wondered why God had forsaken her. A deep and richly amused voice called, "Need some help?"

"I'm going to call someone," she said, half-opening the car door. Who? She had no idea. "I don't need your help."

"Alright," drawled Rebel McCall.

With a shaking hand and one foot on the gravel she scrambled through the mess inside her purse. Minnie had a habit of forgetting her phone everywhere. She dug through receipts and gum wrappers and baby wipes with a growing sense of doom, realizing she'd left it on the bed.

"You need a jump?" McCall broke in, leaning into the open door. Minnie jumped violently, her indrawn breath giving her a good idea of what he smelled like.

Like sex, her brain thought stupidly. But it was actually just tobacco, pine, and leather.

His eyes *greened* down at her. She choked, "I don't have cables."

"No cables?"

"I must have left them in my other purse in my other car," she snapped.

"Drat. You're out of luck, then, 'cause I ain't got them neither."

"Aren't you a mechanic?"

"My brother stole my spares yesterday. His car's a lemon, like yours."

"My car's not a lemon," Minnie said, at the end of her rope. "Some jackass ran into it this morning and messed it up!"

"But then the jackass offered to fix it because he liked you so much. And he took you on a nice steak dinner afterward, with some champagne and a little dip in the river to cool off."

Something turned over low in Minnie's belly. "Or maybe he thought he could google his green eyes at me and—never mind." She was just entertaining him. "Let me borrow your phone."

"I'm sorry?"

"Please, may I borrow your phone?"

"You can't."

"Why not?"

"It's dead. Dropped it fishing in the creek."

Minnie stormed past him and into Ben's Hot Chicken. Ben Simpson lived above his restaurant, and maybe he could give her a jump. She pulled up short when she saw Junior, now dressed in street clothes, slipping out the back entrance with Cowboy Boots. Clearly the girl had some relation to Rebel. But what business did she have with Junior? Minnie didn't like the saucy look the girl threw over her shoulder, as if daring Minnie to say something.

In the diner, Ben himself stood behind the register with a broom and dustpan, humming along to the slow jazz coming from the speakers.

"Hey baby," he called as Minnie entered. "We're closin' the kitchen down, so you better talk quick if you want something."

What's Junior doing with that white girl? Minnie wanted to ask, but she happened to glance over her shoulder in that moment just like Katie had, and saw Rebel McCall boldly opening the hood of her car. With an outraged shriek she dashed back into the parking lot.

"What the hell do you think you're doing?"

"Just havin' a look-see," Rebel said casually, using a pen light on his keyring to inspect her engine. "I reckon you need a new spark plug. Or three."

"I don't need you to look at my car."

"What you need is a ride home, 'cause this jacked-up box is dead-dead."

Ben stuck his head out of the diner. "What's the matter with it?"

"Spark plug," Rebel informed him over Minnie's head.

Ben shook his head. "You better leave the car for tomorrow, Minnie."

"I'll take her home," gallantly said McCall.

"No," said Minnie. "No way in hell."

THE INSIDE OF REBEL'S TRUCK SMELLED LIKE TOBACCO AND fresh grass. Minnie clutched her purse to her chest. Curiosity compelled her to hunt for concealed confederate flags, discarded dip tins, spit cups, cigarette butts, lottery tickets or stashed fast food containers. All she saw was dried Spanish moss and a turkey feather hanging from the rearview. The truck was shabby, but very clean.

McCall spoke to his niece, who had jumped into the truck bed. Minnie tried not to eavesdrop, so it was completely by accident that she heard every single word.

"He's just a friend, Uncle Reb," said Katie. "We weren't doing anything."

"You sure about that?" Came Rebel's deep voice.

"I swear."

"That boy's not enough for you, Katie. I know you."

Not enough? Minnie thought, outraged. Junior was a sweet, hardworking boy. The Simpson family did well for themselves. She had a notion what part of Junior wasn't "enough" for these McCalls.

"What about that lady you got sitting up there, then?" Katie challenged. "She *enough* for you? Thought you liked 'em loose and trashy. She looks like butter wouldn't melt."

Minnie rolled her eyes.

"I'm just giving her a ride. Relax."

"Okay. Sure," Katie said. "And I'm Loretta Lynn."

"Leave off it, Katie."

"She ain't your type."

"Behave."

"Ha. You wouldn't know a good thing if it smacked you on the ass, Uncle Reb."

Minnie's jaw dropped. She would have been smacked into the sun if she ever spoke to an adult like that.

"Oh, really?" said Rebel. "You reckon so?"

"Whatever. You obviously got a hard-on for her, and— hey!" Katie squealed. "Ow!"

When Rebel returned to the front Minnie wrenched her eyes forward. He folded his big body into the seat. Suddenly the inside of the truck felt very small. She clutched the straps of her purse as he helped adjust her seat.

"You comfortable?"

"I'm fine, thank you."

Instead of instantly driving away, McCall lit a cigarette. Minnie rolled down the window manually. How old was this truck?

His eyes narrowed at her through the semi-darkness. "What's got your dander up?"

"What do you mean?"

"You're all qualmish-like. Is it the car you're worried about?"

"The car...?"

"You know, the car that's sitting dead over there." He pointed with his thumb and the cigarette.

"No. I'm fine."

"The smoking? I can stop." He ashed the cigarette, looking her up and down.

You like 'em loose and trashy. Did Minnie look loose and trashy? Was that why he kept looking at her?

"Is your niece seeing Ben's boy? Junior?" she blurted.

Rebel released the clutch and pulled out of the spot, handling the wheezing old truck with a finesse that surprised her. "Her name's Katie, and they're just friends," he replied.

Minnie bit her tongue. None of her business.

"You don't approve?" said McCall mildly.

"Junior is a very nice boy. *Good enough* for most people, I suppose."

"Katie would be better off with someone who could handle her. She ain't like these country girls— she didn't grow up here, but on the rough side of Tulsa. No offense to Junior, but she could pick her teeth with him."

Oh, please.

"Well, maybe she should find someone from her side of town. Someone who can *handle* her."

48

"You mean somebody white?" Said Rebel bluntly.

Minnie felt annoyed. He made it sound like she was the racist one just for picking up on his own obvious suggestion.

"Do I?"

"Don't give me that. I don't give a damn that he's black, alright? I know a lot of people don't truck with that mixing stuff but I've never had a problem with it."

Oh, really? Was he dropping some kind of hint to her? She couldn't tell. Maybe that was just wishful thinking. *I can't be thirsting this hard after a damn redneck.*

"Don't you think she's just using him to rebel against her parents?"

"She can be friends with him if she wants to, can't she? I tell you, it ain't like what you're thinking."

She sounded like Mama now, sticking her nose in folks' business, dishing out her opinions where they weren't wanted.

Minnie cleared her throat. "I'm guessing Katie's father is *not* the one with the black woman."

"Correct. I have three brothers," Rebel informed her. He frowned. "And look, I'm sorry about our Deputy. Officer Daniel, I mean. The man's dumb as a sack of hammers."

The reminder of their roadside incident that morning embarrassed her. "It's alright. It's not the first time I've heard the word."

"Does it happen a lot?" He sounded genuinely curious.

"Most people prefer to use it behind a closed door."

"I don't use it," said Rebel quickly.

"You don't have to say that to make me feel better, McCall."

"You don't believe me?"

"You want the truth?"

"Always."

"Well the truth is, I think you all use it."

He didn't say anything, in the way of country people pondering some deep internal question, or covering up embarrassment. Really, his silence could mean anything. Minnie wondered if she should have shut her mouth, but she also didn't want to be that black woman that dressed up the truth like a hot beignet so white folks didn't feel guilty.

She glanced at Rebel from the side of her eye. One big hand caressed the gear shift. She stared at it. She imagined those big strong hands circling her waist, thumbs and fingertips touching.

"So, alright. What happened tonight?" Rebel pushed. "I find you dressed like that to get fried chicken at eight-o'clock? But you were there this morning, too. You like chicken that much?" He winked. "Can't be that you're sweet on Ben?"

"For your information, I was on a date."

"A *date*? At *Ben's*?" She was glad at least one of them found it so amusing.

"It didn't go very well," she said stiffly.

"Was it that fella who was leanin' over you this morning? Mister Escalade?" Rebel guessed. "I passed him on the way up."

"It was." How embarrassing.

"Didn't the whole 'woman keying his car' thing scare you off?"

"He said it was an accident."

"An accident. Is his name 'Lawrence'?"

"How do you know?"

"The lady wrote 'Fuck you Lawrence'."

"Oh."

"Yeah."

Minnie covered her eyes. "I got played. It was obvious but...He didn't actually want a date."

"More of a tug-and-suck type of guy, is he?"

"I don't even know what that means."

"Would you like a demonstration?"

She stared at him. "You are crazy."

"That's a no, then."

"An absolute no," confirmed Minnie.

THEY TURNED INTO GRACE HILL, GRAVEL RATTLING THE undercarriage of the truck. She sensed his surprise. He

51

hadn't expected a part of Black Florin to look so nice, she supposed. The trailers were modest, new, and fenced. She wondered what kind of house he lived in.

"Thanks," she said. "It was nice of you to give me a ride."

"Don't mention it." McCall looked at her down his long nose, as if deciding to say something. Minnie quickly opened the door.

"Wait," he said. "What you gonna do about your car?"

"I'll call my mechanic tomorrow," she said, imagining herself flushing money down a great golden toilet.

"Who's your mechanic?"

"Terry."

"*Terry*?" He restrained himself from giving an opinion, saying instead, "Just let me look at it. I'll give you a better rate. You can pay whatever you want."

"Look, McCall," she said, trying not to notice how the single street lamp etched his strong features in red and gold. Her heart began to thump funny rhythms. "I like to support black businesses in town where I can," she explained. "I have a mechanic already. I appreciate the offer, but I don't need your help."

"Minnie? Is that you?"

A woman's sharp voice cut through the night. Rebel craned his neck to look over her shoulder. But Minnie didn't need to turn around to know who it was. Mrs. Mabel, her neighbor. Also known as CNN.

The young woman winced and turned to Rebel. "You should go now. Thank you for the ride."

"Let me have your number," Rebel said.

She smiled at him. "I have yours, remember?"

"Call me, then."

Her heart pounded. "I don't think so, McCall." Minnie shut the door. "Thank you for the ride," she added through the window. *You already said that.*

Katie waved to her as McCall's truck rumbled back down the road. Minnie hesitated, then waved back.

"Who was that just now, baby?" Mrs. Mabel asked, practically falling off her porch to catch sight of McCall leaving. "Was that your boyfriend?"

"Good night Mrs. Mabel!" She hurried up the hill.

CHAPTER 4
MY BROTHER'S KEEPER

The next morning, Rebel was just closing the bonnet of Minnie's car when the Terry's Towing Services truck rumbled into Ben's joint. It was like watching a kitten fall off a chair, watching the small man climb out of the hulking truck.

Terry had even more freckles than Rebel, and his little nose was always twitching like a ferret's, as if sniffing out future marks. Kinky hair curled tightly to the shape of his head. He looked pissed.

"She told me this car needed a tow," Terry snapped.

"The insides look like shit. You sold her that piece of junk?" Rebel demanded. "Only a wish and a prayer is holding that thing together."

"And so what, McCall? This ain't your turf."

"I got a particular interest in this car."

Terry's jaw dropped. "Hold on a minute! Minnie Brown is spoken for!" He bleated.

54

"Spoken for?" said Rebel.

Terry puffed out his chest. "By me."

"Fight me for it."

Rebel hadn't moved an inch for the entire conversation. He smiled to let Terry know he was joking. Mostly.

"I don't believe this. You?" Terry said incredulously. "What you want her for?"

"I guess the usual things we want them for."

"She's shy as hell. You can't get that girl to talk unless the subject is dogs." Terry shook his head. "And honestly, man, you should leave the sisters alone."

"If she wants to take what I'm offering, where's the harm?"

"She ain't for you, man." Now Terry actually looked wounded. "Come on. I seen her first!"

"You had her yet?"

"Hell no. Nobody's been on that girl. Since she moved back everybody want a piece, but she ain't dishing to nobody. Keeps it locked up tight, but I was working on her! You got no right."

Rebel grinned. "That's the game. Dog eat dog."

"You got your own women on your side. Let us have something, man."

"If you wanted her that bad, why'd you sell her a busted car?"

"That was just business," Terry sniffed. "And she was warming up to me."

"So that's the trick? Sell her broken wheels and keep her needing to fix 'em?"

Terry knew he was defeated. The determined look in McCall's eye boded ill. "Fine," he said. "But if I catch you poaching again, we'll have a problem, Rebel."

"Understood."

Ben Simpson had silently listened to the exchange. He frowned at Terry's retreat. "He'll remember that one," the older man said.

A question had been nagging Rebel's mind since he'd first seen Terry. "What makes him one of y'all, exactly?"

Ben played dumb. "What you mean? We ain't related."

"I'm saying, you're Black, right?"

"Last I checked," Ben said dryly.

"Well, Terry don't look Black to me. Where's the line for you people?"

"The 'line'?"

"You know what I mean."

"Terry's mama was my sister's friend. At the end of the day, Terry's just people. I don't fuss with the skin color stuff. I leave that for y'all."

Typical Ben reply to an honest question. Rebel sighed in annoyance. He wanted to get to know that girl, but didn't want to put his foot in his mouth. What was he supposed to do, google that shit?

Ben read his mind. "By the way, McCall. Don't be sniffing after Minnie Brown."

"What do you mean?"

"Terry's right. She's not for you. She's after a nice Black man and if she don't find it, she won't be looking your way for a replacement."

"People ain't checkers, Ben."

"Still. Keep off that woman. She worked her butt off to get to where she is. She don't need any catastrophes."

"Like I'm dirty or something?"

"I ain't saying that. You know what I'm saying. Don't think shit's sweet because you got some height and your nose sits straight on your face. You know yourself. You're bringing trouble."

"Thanks for the vote of confidence," Rebel grumbled.

"Uh huh. Now excuse me— I got to go clean some chicken."

REBEL WATCHED BEN TRUNDLE BACK TO HIS DINER, FEELING provoked.

Every group of people got defensive about their women, he supposed. It was human nature.

But it was a man's nature to go after a woman who made his cock so hard he lost sleep. Last night, Rebel's imagination had turned prim little Minnie Brown into a moaning succubus who rode his dick all night long. He woke up tangled in the sheets with his cock stiff and leaking, his chest full of brambles. He hadn't had a dream like that in years. He got a semi just thinking about it, and he knew come hell or high water he had to see the girl again. His truck still smelled like her, that floral scent with a touch of lemon.

He allowed that he was laying it on thick with the fixing-the-car thing. But should he let her get screwed by a little rat like Terry? Fuck no.

He wanted her. Let the best man win.

McCall tossed his toolkit in the back of his truck, then returned to Minnie's car and popped the hood to start up her engine without the keys. Tricky, with these new-fangled cars, but not impossible. Rebel never backed down from a challenge.

TWENTY MINUTES LATER THE TALL SOUTHERNER PARKED Minnie's car at the top of Grace Hill.

Minnie lived in a tidy white double-wide. Not a dump, but definitely no palace. *Hadn't Grace Hill belonged to the McCalls?* thought Rebel, looking out at the small hillside. The old McCall property had spread out across hundreds of acres, its borders shrinking and changing over time, but not by much.

Rebel's oldest brother Roman knew the land the best. Rebel could ask him about this corner of Florin and probably get an hour-long history lesson. But he wouldn't be asking Roman, because Roman could never know about the Brown girl.

After what felt like hours Minnie finally emerged from her house. Even in scrubs and sneakers she looked pretty as a peach. She'd sensed the coming rainstorm, and prepared for it. Struggling to balance her umbrella, her purse and the house keys, she didn't see him until she was nearly to the gate. She looked up and gave a muffled shriek.

"Who— what are you doing?" Minnie hissed. "What in the name of God—You stole my car!" She nearly dropped everything she was carrying.

"I must be the world's worst thief." Rebel plucked the umbrella from her hands and picked up her purse. She snatched them back.

"I called Terry this morning. He was supposed to tow it to his shop. Did he tell you to bring it over for me?" Minnie demanded.

"I fixed it, and Terry deemed a tow unnecessary." He pressed two fingers under her chin and closed her gaping mouth. "You're welcome."

She jerked away. "How did you start it? I have the keys."

He wiggled his fingers. "Hoodoo."

"Very funny." She blew past him.

He opened the passenger's seat and folded himself inside. Did the woman only know midgets? He cranked the seat back to accommodate his legs as Minnie put her purse in the back seat then slid into the driver's side.

She was clutching something in her hand. Pepper spray.

"Answer me, McCall. You trying something funny here? What is this?"

"Hey, Hey! Whoa!"

"You better talk fast!"

Rebel grabbed her wrist and jerked down. The pepper spray fell from her fingers and he caught it quickly. He tossed it in her lap.

"Take it easy, sweetheart, alright?" He laughed. Why was this funny? She looked adorable, all quivering and mad.

"You came up to my door like some kind of stalker, what am I supposed to think? I don't know you like that."

"No shit. I was trying to be nice."

"You scared me. And I told you to leave my car alone."

"I'm bad with directions. And next time you're gonna pepper spray a man, make sure you're both outside of the vehicle."

"What do you want?"

"A ride to Ben's, where I left my truck."

She tried to start the engine, then realized it was already running. A long pause. "Thanks," she muttered.

"Yeah, don't mention it."

Minnie brought the driver's seat up from where he'd cranked it back. He watched her throw the car in gear and nudge it down the pitted holler road.

"Doesn't somebody fix this?" He commented, eyeing the deep pockets in the road. "You could swim in these holes."

"Public services don't come out here too much," Minnie said testily. "Of course you wouldn't know about that."

"Right."

Suddenly, she slammed on the brakes. Rebel, who hadn't bothered to put on the seatbelt, nearly brained himself on the windshield.

"I forgot!" she gasped, and parked in the middle of the road. She began fumbling for her purse in the back seat, the confining space of the Kia nearly pushing her into his lap.

The smell of freesia wafted from her clothes and hair. Her hair...little tiny curls popped out from her bun and curled against the shell of her ear. He noticed other delicate, feminine things about her. She wore little gold hoop earrings and a gold cross necklace. Her hands were small, with slim, elegant fingers. His own big paws would dwarf them. No nail polish on those nails...nothing artificial about the girl at all, just oozing sex and natural beauty like honey from a wild comb.

She pulled out her cellphone and punched in a number with the desperation of a person in a medical emergency.

"Hello? Mama?"

The phone wasn't on speaker, but Ms. Brown's voice made every word crystal clear.

"Minnie!" The woman said. "I just got off the phone with Mrs. Victor. You need to explain some things to me right quick."

"I got the car fixed," said Minnie quickly. "I'm headed to the clinic now, so you don't have to come get me. Sorry for not calling you before."

"Minnie, what's this I'm hearing about you and Lawrence?" Her mother demanded. "You threw a sandwich at him and you went home with Rebel McCall? Linda Mabel saw you climbing out of his truck in the dead of the night!"

Minnie leveled an accusing stare at Rebel. "I'll talk to you later, Mama."

"Minnie! Don't hang up on me!"

"Sorry, the signal is breaking up." Minnie hung up the phone and put it on silent, tossing it back into her purse.

"We broke a law I don't know about?" Rebel said.

Minnie snorted.

"What does she think I'm gonna do to you?"

Minnie nudged the gas. "Get me pregnant and burn my house down. Lock me in a basement with bread and water for the rest of my life. Or maybe just kill me and drop my body down a mine shaft. She's got a wide imagination, and you're a McCall, which doesn't help."

"Get you pregnant, eh?"

"Shut up. And put on your seatbelt."

. . .

As it turned out, she saved Rebel's life. They hadn't driven a half mile before a supply hauler slammed into Minnie's damaged rear, sending the car hurtling into the mountain.

Distantly Rebel heard the screech of brakes, heard Minnie scream. The impact knocked the breath from his lungs. Black squiggles swam before his vision. After a long moment of ear-buzzing shock, Rebel coughed, and his entire right side went numb. The acrid stink of burned rubber clogged his nose.

Could he move? He raised a hand in front of his face and turned it over. No blood. Dimly he saw the crumpled door he'd been leaning against just moments before. A knot of aluminum dug hard into his thigh, and shards of glass lay scattered across his lap, and in his hair.

Minnie?

His side of the vehicle had absorbed most of the shock. Her hands still clutched the wheel, knuckles almost white. She stared at the smoking engine in petrified horror.

"You alright?" He whispered.

Minnie nodded slowly. "You?" she squeaked.

"Just grazed." Rebel unbuckled his seatbelt quickly, trying not to look at the crumpled aluminum that had been dangerously close to crippling his legs. "You sure you alright?"

Minnie took her hands off the wheel. "My *car*. Oh my God, I just bought this car."

"Let's get out of here. Come on, I got to leave from your side."

"Give me...I need a minute."

"If you're gonna panic, do it outside. Come on."

"What the hell happened? Did somebody hit us? I'm afraid to look."

She was shaking. "Just calm down, okay?" He murmured. He turned and squinted through the cracked back windshield, trying to make out the other car. The driver was coming out of the truck and circling the accident he'd caused. Rain poured down the windshield and pummeled the car, making seeing difficult. But something about the driver's gait...

"What?" Minnie saw his face and began scrabbling for her seatbelt. "Is it gonna explode?"

"I'll be damned," Rebel said grimly. "Get on out, Minnie. Might as well get this over with."

Minnie opened the driver's side and climbed onto the shoulder, and Rebel followed, bringing them face to face with the other driver.

"*Reb?*"

The oldest McCall brother came to a dead stop. Roman. Folks sometimes called him *Gypsy*- but never in his hearing. He was tall, olive-skinned, with full, dark lips.

"What the fuck?" said Roman, his black eyes flicking between his younger brother and Minnie with undisguised shock. "What is this?"

64

Minnie was not in the mood. "We're alright, thank you for asking! You nearly killed us and you wrecked my car!"

"Who the fuck is she, Reb?"

Minnie crossed her arms against the cold. Now soaking wet, her curls popped free from the restraining bun, and her scrubs clung revealingly to her skin, showing the outline of a lacy bra and two hard nipples. Roman's eyes dropped to the thrusting points, then took a slower route over her hips, back up to her face. They moved back to Rebel. The look was chilling.

"She's the vet on Bear Hill. We're neighbors."

"You know each other?" Minnie asked, pointing between the two men."

"He's my brother."

Except for their height, they looked nothing alike. "Give her your insurance and let's get this going, Roman," said Rebel in a *don't fuck with me* voice.

Roman scoffed. "My insurance? Rebel, I ain't paying for your whore."

Minnie gasped as Rebel grabbed a fistful of Roman's windbreaker and slammed the man so hard against the truck it rocked. "Wrong answer."

"Rebel, no!" Minnie grabbed the first thing she could reach—the back of his jeans. She saw the brand of underwear he was wearing and hastily let go.

"I don't see you for weeks, and I find out this is where you been?" Roman growled, shoving Rebel backward with his shoulder. Both men were equally strong.

"Go back to the car, Minnie," said Rebel. She ignored him.

"Does Pa know about her? I'm guessing no." Roman's dark eyes flashed. "He'd kill her."

"You won't tell him," said Rebel grimly.

"Won't I? I could kill you, Reb. While I'm fucking holding the family together with both hands, you're going off to fuck some black bitch over the fence? You selfish bastard."

"You have it all wrong!" Minnie said, shoving herself between the brothers. She looked up at Roman furiously. "And who the hell are you calling a bitch?"

Rebel pulled her behind him and said to his brother, "Apologize."

Roman laughed. "What?"

"Apologize to her."

"Out of your coon-loving mind, Rebel. Kiss my fucking ass," Roman said in disbelief.

Rebel's voice sent a chill up Minnie's neck. "Do it."

Roman watched him, calculating as a wildcat. Then he spat off to the side and nodded to Minnie. "Tell me, girl. He brought my daughter around your way?"

"I have no idea," Minnie said grimly.

"Katie's got a right to be friends with people her own age," said Rebel evenly.

This dark-eyed man was Katie's father?

"Wonder if you'll be saying that when she's pregnant and ruined," Roman said.

"Right from Pa's mouth into yours. I don't truck with that bullshit, Roman."

Roman stared at Minnie, then back to Rebel. "Obviously. You and Ross both, then. Who would've thought."

"I'll take your word you won't tell Pa about her," Rebel said.

"It's nice to see you beg for a change."

It was all Rebel could do not to twine his hands around his brother's throat. "Do it for me, Roman."

"Yeah. Don't worry, Rebel. Your dirty little secret's safe with me."

Roman shoved him away and stalked back to his truck. It vanished into the rainy haze, spitting water off the tires.

"Rebel?" Minnie hurried to his side as soon as Roman cleared off. Rebel stared up the road, frowning. When Minnie came up to him his vision cleared. He took the phone from her shaking hands. "Let me call my buddy. He'll be cheaper than whoever you're dialing."

"But —"

"Get under here," he said, guiding her under an overhang of rock. A trail of moss spilled down like a woman's curly hair. "We can't do nothin' in this rain."

"The police...My insurance..."

"The police won't do shit," said Rebel bluntly. "And your car needs a tow. Come on."

He took some pictures of the crash then ducked back under the overhang next to Minnie.

Deal with Roman later. He punched in Larry's number.

"Yeah?" Came a gruff voice. "Who the hell is this?"

"The IRS."

"Fuck– What? Larry don't live here!"

"It's Rebel."

"Oh. Reb? Hey buddy. Jesus. Scared the shit out of me. What's good?"

"I need a favor."

CHAPTER 5
CHRISSIE'S THEORY

They were soaked. Her scrubs clung to her body, but she was so busy ogling Rebel she forgot to be embarrassed.

Crammed under the overhang, she got another whiff of his amazing smell. It was the kind of drug designed just to trap women, some kind of manly, earthy, aroma that made her common sense evacuate the building and sent her imagination running after it, tumbling straight into the gutter. A nice gutter, though. A gutter full of wild pine and old leather and engine oil, where something powerful and heavy groped all the soft, aching parts of her body...

She could see the outline of his abs through his sodden T-shirt. The muscles of his arms bunched as he moved the towel across his sculpted chest. When he looped it over his neck she forced her eyes back to the rain-slick road. But the treacherous things kept drifting back to Rebel.

He wasn't even that pale, but tanned to a light gold, especially on his face and hands.

"Who is Larry?" She asked.

"Old buddy of mine. He runs the towing place on Muck Hill and fixes up older cars. You know how to drive a manual?"

"I hope you're joking."

"Your daddy never taught you?"

"I didn't really have a daddy."

Green eyes twinkled at her under a mop of wet dark hair. "Do you want one?"

"Stop it, McCall."

He laughed. Not ten minutes ago he'd nearly charged his brother off the mountain. It seemed like they had some personal beef that had nothing to do with her at all. The way Rebel instantly put himself between her and that cold-eyed monster...

"Is that Katie's father?" she asked.

"Yes. His name's Roman."

Roman was exactly what she assumed the McCalls were like: racist, arrogant, mean. If she never crossed paths with that one again it would be too soon.

"You cold?" Rebel murmured.

"I'm fine," she said, hunching under the towel. "Just a little stressed." She blinked quickly. "I can't believe your brother wrecked my car and drove off like that. Does it run in the family?"

"What, meanness? I'm afraid so."

She bit her lip. "I didn't mean you, really."

"It's alright. Where do you work, by the way?"

"The animal hospital."

"You're a vet? You're *that* vet?"

He'd heard of her? She nodded shyly. "Holy moly," Rebel said, looking impressed. "You run that place all by yourself?"

"I have some help– a technician comes by twice a week. I keep expenses low. Not everyone here can afford a vet, so I do what I can. I run partly on donations. " *And my income is tragic.* She looked mournfully at her crumpled vehicle. "I really can't afford to lose my car right now. This is the worst."

"You know, your place is like five minutes from my house," said Rebel. "The clinic, I mean."

"What? Really?"

"Yeah. I live on Flat Hill. My garage is there, too."

He was literally on the hill next door.

"If you want, I can give you a ride to work during the week," Rebel said carefully.

"No," said Minnie, startled. "No, we can't do that." Get a ride from him every morning? Might as well tell Mrs.

Mabel she was entertaining men from the back of her house.

She looked helplessly at the smashed bonnet and the fractured windshield.

I'll have to ride with Mama. God have mercy.

"It's not that I don't appreciate the offer," she rushed. "It's just...You know. People are already talking."

Rebel wanted to scoff at that, but she had a point, as Roman had so blatantly reminded him. If he didn't want word of this woman reaching Pa's ears, offering to ferry her across town in his truck every morning was a dumb idea.

"We might live in the same town, but we're in different worlds, Rebel," she pointed out.

"Maybe I'm just trying to find out where the boundary is," he said, watching drops of rain fall from the trail of moss above them.

He cleared his throat. "Ben sort of suggested...Ah...Your people ain't keen on us mixing either. Is that right?"

She nodded. "For good reason."

"What reason?"

"People like your brother and Deputy Daniel, for a start."

The blast of a horn made them both jump. Through the downpour, twin blurs of headlights. "That'll be Larry," said Rebel. Suddenly a gust of wind and rain slammed the mountainside, dousing them both, though Rebel shielded her from the worst of it with his body. Her breath caught as she looked up and met his eyes. They were green as the moss above them. Raindrops raced down his cheeks, collected on his eyelashes, turned his golden hair into dripping curls.

He tapped her nose. Then he turned and walked straight into the gale, towards the tow truck.

I like him.

Help.

Rebel came back with a thermos of hot sweet coffee fortified with whiskey. It was disgusting. And delicious.

"So here's the plan," he said, combing a hand through his dripping hair. "You'll take a ride with Larry down to your spot. Larry will tow your car and stash it at my garage 'till you decide what you wanna do with it. Sound good?"

"Can it be fixed?"

Rebel shook his head, eyes apologetic. "Sorry, darling. I don't think so."

She bit her lip, steeling herself against a wave of frustrated tears. "Oh. Alright."

"Don't sweat it, alright? You can ride with me until you sort the insurance, and I'll help you get some wheels that won't snap like a pop tart when they get bumped. I promise."

"Okay," Minnie said, taking a deep breath. Her premium would hit the roof. She couldn't afford this. She really, really couldn't. "Just don't screw me over, McCall," She blurted, cringing at how pathetic it sounded.

"Honey, I'd screw you any way but over."

The driver of the tow truck was a younger man with the reddest hair she'd ever seen. Larry. He looked vaguely familiar. His eyes bugged out when Minnie climbed up into the truck and he said, "Where's Rebel been hiding you, darling?"

"We just met yesterday."

"Wait wait wait. I recognize you," said Larry, rubbing his stubbly cheeks. "You went to Florin High. That nerdy girl with all the puppy notebooks."

Minnie's face flamed. "Yeah, that sounds like me."

"She runs that animal hospital, Larry."

"I'll be fucking damned. You married?"

"No, she ain't," said Rebel, giving Larry a look.

"Figures," Larry sighed.

Rebel carried Minnie's belongings through the rain, packing them carefully in Larry's truck. He was soaked to his skin. "Anything in your trunk?" He hollered. "Best we remove it now."

"No," Minnie shouted back. Rain pummeled the mountain, nearly drowning out the words.

"Then we're all set."

The two men got out, leaving the truck still running, and chained the Kia up. When they climbed back in they were laughing about something. They had probably known each other all their lives, Minnie guessed.

"Let's go baby," Rebel cawed, smacking the dashboard. Larry fired the engine and the enormous vehicle began crawling down the mountain. In vain Minnie fumbled for a seatbelt, and found none. She had to brace herself with her bare hands. Oh well. This was part of the adventure. She checked the time. She wouldn't even be late for work.

Next to her Rebel peeled his wet shirt off over his head. For a breathless moment Minnie felt his hot, bare skin against her arm. He was muscled like an athlete, dense and solid and male. Nap of golden hair under his armpits. Golden fur on his chest. Pine, leather... He pulled on a dry T-shirt and the view disappeared.

"Mind if I smoke?" Larry shouted in Minnie's ear.

"Um. N-no."

"She minds," Rebel chuckled. "She's just bein' polite."

She nudged him with her shoulder. And then...

His big, scarred hand came down on her knee and squeezed. Her eyes fluttered shut and she pressed back in the seat, feeling a wave of warm, slow ecstasy spreading from the palm of his hand through her body. Even after he removed his hand, the feeling lingered.

"So was the older brother fine as fuck as well?" Asked Chrissie, sucking down the last of her margarita.

"He was a demon." Minnie gestured with a fried pickle. "He looked like he wanted to shoot me for daring to suggest he ran into my car."

"And Rebel fought him? So sexy. So you gonna take up his offer?"

"No way in hell. I'll work something out with Mama instead."

"With your Mama?" Chrissie hollered. "You want your pussy to dry up like a country ham? Take the damn ride with McCall. What do you have to lose? Except a chance to fuck the hottest white man in five hundred miles?"

"My nosy ass neighbor is going 'round telling everybody that I'm a whore, and now Mama thinks I turned Lawrence Smith down to sleep with Rebel. I don't like my name in everybody's mouths, especially for something I didn't even do. I'm not getting with a white man, Chrissie. Period. And definitely not that white man."

"Is it the pink dick thing? 'Cause let me tell you, it's weird at first but you get used to it."

"Is it pink for real?" Asked Minnie fearfully.

"Why don't you ask Rebel?"

"It ain't happening, Chrissie."

"And why the hell not?"

"Lower your voice. Look, all Rebel McCall sees in me is a piece of ass. Or worse, some charity case he has to help."

Did she actually believe that?

Chrissie looked annoyed. "Why is it so crazy to think he might like you for real?"

"It just is."

Chrissie kissed her teeth. "You better get off that mountain and come to Rowanville, then. Plenty of fine brothers here to go around."

"Don't start with that again. I don't want to leave the mountain, alright?"

"Hmph! Then get used to pink dick. Big, thick, veiny white cock..."

"Ugh!"

The restaurant door swung open. A black man entered, his arm around a round-faced white woman's waist. A little girl with caramel skin and a puffy brown afro toddled behind them.

"You were saying?" Minnie deadpanned.

"Okay, you can't have 'em all," Chrissie amended, raising a finger in the air. "But think. How many eligible black men are left in Florin anyway? If anything, old boy who just walked in? He just proves my point."

"What *point*?"

"While you're over here moanin' about Black Love, the brothers are scooping up all the white girls they can get with both hands. Why shouldn't you let Rebel McCall fuck you seven ways to Sunday, if our men are running behind Becky and Katie and Caroline without a care in the world? I mean, you watched any porn lately? This shit is out of control."

"Chrissie, there's kids in here."

"Girl they can't hear shit. My point is, my sister, we got to elevate. Stop this old-fashioned bullshit. There's a reason

Black men don't be locking us down," Chrissie said sternly. "I figured it out, right? Black men think we won't ever be good enough for them. Either we're broke ghetto birds, or we make too much money. Either we're possessive, and crazy, or we ain't up they ass enough. We're too loud, we ain't loud enough, we're submissive, we ain't submissive enough, we're hoes, we're prudes, we're stuck in church, we don't go to church, we're too black, we sound white…"

"So we got to run out and jump in bed with white man? The *enemy*?"

"They give good head," Chrissie shrugged.

"I really can't with you."

"I mean, when was the last time you got some?" Chrissie demanded. "This decade, I mean."

Minnie blushed and reached for a French fry. She would never in a million years tell Chrissie she was a virgin. It might give her a stroke.

"Poor baby," grinned Chrissie. "Now me, on the other hand…I met up with this light skinned dude from Tinder last week, okay? Fucked the shit out of me. Spit, butt stuff, pulling my hair, right? I'm talking nasty. I swear I fell in love, Minnie. First of all, I nutted like a dozen times."

"Lower your voice!"

"So I go to bed, happy as a bitch, and I let friend-o stay the night. I'm thinking maybe I can get some dick before I go to work. More butt stuff, I don't know. I'm living in the moment. My dumb ass."

"What happened?"

"Middle of the night, I wake up, and what's he doing? *Jacking off into my purse.*"

"Oh hell no!"

"So then I had to get crazy, right? And then he gets crazy. Starts yelling all this shit, says he's got a gun and his "soldiers" are gonna come blow up my spot…Girl. I just started praying. I'm thinking this man is really 'bout to cut me up and wear my face for a durag. But my neighbor Sheila a nosy bitch, and thank God, 'cause she calls the police. Turns out this fool is ducking child support in Alabama. From three baby mamas. They took his ass away so fast I think a dreadlock flew off. And you know what was the worst part was?"

"That he knows where you live?"

"Bruh had the biggest dick I've ever seen. Curved, too." Chrissie sighed. "Pass the hot sauce, baby."

AFTER CHRISSIE DROVE HER HOME, MINNIE SHOWERED, brushed her teeth, and crawled into bed. She lay awake a long time, hugging the pillow to her chest.

Why do you even care? You have a job. Your own place. A vibrator you never use. You don't need a man. You don't need that man.

She didn't know how Chrissie did it. Meeting up with random men, sleeping with them, throwing them away. Minnie squeezed her eyes shut. Two damn years since a man had touched her. No man had ever fucked her.

Spread her legs and lined his thick cock up with her pussy, fed it into her slowly, sucked on her neck, punishing her...

She slowly slid a hand past the waistband of her silky pajama bottoms. Sifted her fingers through her damp curls. She imagined a large man leaning over her, golden hair like a halo in the soft bedroom light. His thick member pressing into her...

She gasped against her other wrist. The faceless man chuckled and leaned down to brush a kiss against her throat. Oh God. How did he know she liked being kissed there?

Don't care what they say, honey, he murmured in his deep gravelly voice. *Open your legs...That's right. So wet...You'll give it to me, won't you? 'Cause you need a real man to fuck you. Fill your tight pussy up with my nut. I'll keep you in my house just getting my babies on you. You're so sweet. So soft. Mine to fuck, when I want. However I want. I'll bend you right over this bed in a minute. You like that huh...You like that, sweetheart?*

Her phone beeped.

Flushed, Minnie rolled over and picked the device up. Her other hand was warm and sticky.

Oh my God. Did I really just do that?

She frowned. She didn't know the number, but it had left a voice note. She pressed play.

"Hi, Minnie."

Minnie froze. Rebel's thick country accent filled her ears, slow and comforting as velvet. "Hi. This is my number, right? You can call me or leave them voice note things. I can't– I mean, I don't really text. I got your car at the garage, so if you need a ride tomorrow let me know. Actually I'll just come get you. I'll bring coffee. Bye. This is Rebel, by the way. Did I say that already? Fuck. Alright, yeah. Bye. See ya."

MINNIE PLAYED THE MESSAGE AGAIN.

And again.

A fourth time.

Then she replied, *Yes please. Tomorrow morning, seven sharp.*

CHAPTER 6
DRIVING STICK

The next morning, just like he promised, Rebel parked outside her trailer. This time in his own truck.

Soft blues music played from the radio. Muddy Waters. He was smoking. The fingers of his other hand drummed on the wheel.

His hair looked nearly brown in the low blue light, and his eyes had two faint rings of blue under them, as if he'd been up since dawn. As she got closer she saw that he'd shaved. She could smell lemon soap under the tobacco.

"Good morning," he said in a voice that matched his eyes.

"Good morning," Minnie said.

"Good morning," called Mrs. Mabel, leaning over her porch railing.

Minnie gave her neighbor a quick wave and swung herself up into Rebel's truck.

They didn't speak much as the truck navigated the potholes. Minnie found herself watching him drive from the corner of her eye. Florin roads were dangerous, twisting along sharp corners and steep curves, but he'd been driving them forever.

They repeated the route of the day before, leaving Grace Hill in a gray cloud of mist. It was still very early.

"One's yours." He gestured to the coffee cups.

"Oh! Thank you." She hesitated, then reached into her bag for the container she'd spent half the morning working to fill. "These are for you," she said, trying to keep her voice as casual as possible. Like she was returning a bag of sugar she had borrowed from a neighbor, and not giving fresh baked cookies to a sexy white man she had no business encouraging.

"What's this?" Rebel said curiously, taking the box from her while his knee expertly guided the steering wheel.

"It's just shortbread." She had racked her brains for something she could give Rebel in payment for helping her. But now the gesture seemed extremely romantic. She hoped he didn't get the wrong idea. But what other idea could a man get when a woman baked him cookies? *I'm no good at this.*

He cracked open a corner of the tupperware lid. "For me?" He said in disbelief.

"As a thank you," Minnie rushed. "For helping with the tow. I baked them last night." A lie. She'd scrambled for an hour in the kitchen to make them, barely awake, timing it perfectly so they'd be still warm when he opened the Tupperware. Doing the most, in other words.

"Last night, huh? Did you warm them up for me?" The teasing look in his eye called her out, but to Minnie's relief he turned immediately to the cookies. He put one whole into his mouth. Chewed. His sleepy eyes lit up like candles. "That's damn good shortbread."

"Don't gas me up for nothing," chided Minnie, secretly pleased.

"Nobody's ever baked me anything."

"I'm just glad they didn't burn."

"I'd eat these burned, no lie." He took another one. "You cook much?"

"I've only ever cooked for myself. But I know my way around the kitchen."

"I can make spaghetti, chicken breasts and uh...that corn-bread from the box," said Rebel, shaking his head. "I just hate all the fiddling around. Hunting is another thing, but I don't do that so much no more."

A smile tugged at Minnie's lips. "Do you use seasoning?"

"On what, the chicken? Sure. Salt and pepper. A little paprika."

"You ever tried following a recipe?"

Rebel laughed out loud.

"You should learn how to cook. You can't expect a woman to cook for you."

She'd never probed him about a girlfriend. This was the closest she dared.

"I could say the same thing about you and fixing cars," he turned it back on her. "When you gonna jump into some overalls and pick up a wrench, smart mouth?"

"Never."

"Good. Wouldn't want you to wreck those pretty hands anyway."

"You don't want to know what my hands are covered in half the time," Minnie laughed.

Rebel shook the container of cookies at her. "Hold on. Should I be concerned?"

"Well, you did put your greasy paws all over my church dress," she teased.

"Fair point," he said, grinning. "And speaking of that dress..."

"No, we won't speak of it."

"Alright, alright."

"Did your Mama cook a lot?" Minnie asked, hoping to stop the flirting, though she was enjoying it.

"Yup. Uhh, illegal things, mostly."

"Oh." *Awkward.*

He shrugged. "I have four brothers. We all got different mothers. None of those ladies could cook. Well- I never met Roman's mama, so I don't know. But kitchen stuff was for the women is what my Pa always said. I'm sorry about Roman, by the way," Rebel said, glancing at her.

"Oh. It's alright..."

"He's like my Pa. Stuck in his ways. Sometimes I think I'd die for him. Other times...I don't really know who he is." He frowned. "I ain't trying to make excuses for what he said. I wanted to hit him, but we been known to go at each other without stopping when our blood's up. It ain't a pretty thing. I didn't want you to see that."

His hands flexed on the wheel. He had the biggest hands she could ever recall seeing on a man. His fingers were scarred and leathered, hard with muscle. Rebel's hands had rummaged through the insides of about every engine on the mountain, leastways his side of Florin, and dipped into a good many other machines. But his hands also told an older story. The more ancient scars came from fights. They were the end results of bitter exchanges settled in blood.

"That's sad," she said softly. "I mean, me and my sisters aren't that close, neither. But I never had to fight them."

"Sometimes going through a hard time together forges a bond," Rebel mused. "That weren't really the case for my brothers and I. Growing up was rough. It was a long time ago, but we hold onto grudges, us McCalls."

"How old are you?"

"Romans's thirty five. I'm thirty three. Rain's a year younger than me, and Ross is the baby."

Minnie knew little about the McCall family outside the standard warnings: they were racist, rich, and mean. And in a way, Roman had cancelled out the positive impression Rebel had made. She wondered what the other two brothers were like, especially the one who apparently had his eyes on a black woman.

She stared out the window at the passing mountainside. Buds were leafing on the trees.

Rebel's eyes moved over her. "Thought I knew everybody in town, But I never saw you before that Sunday. How come?" He tilted his head. "And you don't look older than twenty two, but I know that ain't right. I reckon we would have been in school together, just a few years apart."

"I'm not surprised you don't recognize me. I didn't recognize you, either."

"I never forget a face," said Rebel confidently.

"Maybe you never saw me. You're a little older, so you would have been out of high school when I came in. And I had my head in a book all the time. I was very shy. I had these huge braces and my hair was always a mess. I couldn't keep a pair of shoes clean to save my life. You're getting the cleaned up version."

"I'm sure you were so cute." Rebel grinned. "So where you been since school?"

It was so easy to talk to him. "Out of town for nearly a decade working on my license, certificate, all that."

"And you ain't married yet," he said.

"No..."

"How come?" He demanded baldly.

"Would you prefer it if I was?"

"No, but I bet your Mama would. She's your only family on the mountain?"

Minnie nodded. "My father lives in Rowanville."

"Y'all close?"

"He paid child support, and for part of my school. We don't talk too often." She shrugged. "I'm his outside child, you see."

"Does that bother you?"

"It used to. But not so much anymore. I try not to take things personally. He has his life, I have mine. He did more than a lot of men would for their daughters."

Rebel nodded. "Would he approve of me you think?"

"You're a white man driving a big red truck, Rebel."

"Well you know what they say about big trucks."

"Big egos?"

"You're a mouth," he accused, reaching for another cookie. "Think you could drive something like this?"

"I'm sure it's not that hard," she sniffed.

"Prove it." He took his hands off the wheel.

Minnie screamed and lurched forward in the seat, grabbing the wheel before they plummeted into a ditch.

"Are you crazy?" she cried, nearly sitting in his lap as she guided the truck back to safety. But all along he'd kept partial control by pressing under the wheel with his knee. Rebel laughed and put his hands over hers.

"That wasn't funny!"

"Really? You should see your face. Don't worry darling, I got it. I got it."

She settled back in the seat, heart pounding. "You're insane."

His eyes twinkled. "You like it."

"Oh, please." She did like it.

"And you touched my wheel. I think it's getting pretty serious."

THAT DAY MINNIE'S EYES KEPT DRIFTING TO THE WINDOW, which may or may not have opened in the direction of Flat Hill.

"Lola," she asked. "What's that auto shop up there called?"

"They just call it The Garage," said her assistant, her big dark eyes blinking at Minnie over the operating table. A sedated ginger tabby lay between them. "One of the McCall brothers runs it."

"Oh?" said Minnie innocently. "Which brother?"

"The one you crashed into last Sunday," said Lola, giving her a strange look. "And who drove you into work today."

There was no point concealing anything in Florin.

After the procedure, Minnie washed up and took her lunch break in the tiny private room. As she munched on her rice and beans she picked up her phone and googled Rebel's name.

She scrolled past boring yellow pages about McCall's Supply and Feed, one of the many operations the family maintained on the mountain as a facade for their more illicit businesses. Nothing on Rebel. At least he wasn't a sex offender. But maybe Rebel wasn't his real name? Maybe he went by an alias. Maybe he was a felon. Should she check the County records? Were those online?

You are losing it.

What did she hope to find, anyway? Proof that he was a serial killer? A FetLife profile? Chrissie would love that.

She scrolled, clicked, scrolled, clicked, and inevitably found something. Some person with a lot of time on their hands had been cataloguing the *Florin Herald* online. Through that, Minnie stumbled on a brief profile of Rebel's shop. *NATIVE SON OPENS AUTO SHOP.*

A photo of Rebel accompanied it. A much younger Rebel. He stood in front of his garage, green eyes nearly concealed by an untidy whirlwind of blonde hair. He looked like he wanted to club the photographer with the wrench and get back to work.

He'd opened his shop nine years ago.

I'm just trying to make honest money so I don't have to rely on nobody, he told reporters. *I want to make my own way just like everybody else.*

That was it? Surely there was more...Minnie turned to Facebook. Rebel McCall...McCall...She scanned her contacts list, friends of friends, creeping closer and closer to the dark gates of the Florin Uncensored page.

FLORA MCCALL: CHRIST IS LORD AND MUSLIMS NEED TO go BACK TO AFGHANISTAN!!! Makes me SICK what is happening to this COUNTRY!!

BUB MCCALL: WHOEVER THAT CAT ON PLUM ROAD BELONGS to best take care!!! cause I'm gonna fuckin shoot it and hang it off my mailbox by its tale don't mess with me I hate cats they make my baby girl sneeze

HIPHOPISLIFE MCCALL: WE SHOULD FLY THE CONFEDERATE flag over city hall. What are the n*ggers gonna do about it?

Why did you censor it? Pussy , someone replied under that.

MINNIE'S GAZE TRAILED DOWN THE PAGE, ABSORBING EVERY blast of hatred until she felt thoroughly depressed. But it got worse. Another name jumped out at her.

ROMAN MCCALL: IF ANYBODY'S INTERESTED IN THE MILITIA **group, send me a private message.**

. . .

THE POST HAD SIXTY LIKES.

Militia group? *Oh hell no.* She closed the page in a hurry.

This was surely her sign. Time to stop this little crush from going any further. She'd have to be a fool to put herself in the path of people like that.

Did Rebel know about his brother's "militia"? Maybe he was a member of it himself. Maybe he went cross burning every Tuesday, and had a family album of lynching photographs sitting on his coffee table. How would she know?

Glancing over her shoulder to see if Lola was looking (she wasn't), Minnie pulled up the article on Rebel again.

She stared at the photo for a long time as if she could immunize herself against it. But she kept hearing his laugh and seeing his face when he opened the Tupperware.

Is this real life? Am I falling for a McCall?

No. Nope. Never.

She wasn't.

SHE WORE A LITTLE MORE MAKEUP AROUND HER EYES THAN usual, and dangling citrine earrings. She hoped Rebel noticed. She hoped he didn't.

"Good morning, Minnie," said Mrs. Mabel from her porch. The woman got up annoyingly early every morning. "I see your boyfriend came to get you again? Third day in a row."

Minnie flashed a rigid smile. "He's not my boyfriend, Ma'am."

"Could have fooled me."

Minnie met Rebel's raised eyebrow with a warning look.

"Hi, Rebel. Good morning." He looked incredible, tall and sexy and a little rumpled. Rebel didn't work a suit-and-tie job, and thank God. She was happy to see his jeans a little torn and his boots scuffed, wearing a couple days' worth of golden stubble.

"Wait," he said as she started to open the door. "Go in the driver's side."

She looked up at him, confused.

"You're driving," he explained.

"What?"

"I assure you, this is a privilege few have the honor to experience," Rebel said, boxing her in. He nudged her gently. "Go on. She don't bite."

"I can't drive manual!"

"Giddy up. I'll walk you through it."

"No!"

"Chicken," he accused. "You can snip a dog's nuts off but you can't drive a little old truck?" His eyes twinkled. "Besides, I thought all Black people could drive."

"That's not funny!"

"You took the Rowanville freeway recently? Swear it was the Sprint Cup."

"Maybe they could teach you not to colonize my windpipe with your fender!"

He gave a shout of laughter. "Come on. Show me what you got, sweetheart."

Rolling her eyes, Minnie climbed into the driver's side of his truck. She couldn't keep up the pretense of being annoyed. She'd never driven a truck like this, but she loved the idea of Rebel teaching her. Secretly she was excited. *Sweetheart.*

"Can she even drive that thing?" Mrs. Mabel hollered as Minnie dragged the seat up to the wheel.

"Ignore her," Minnie said.

Rebel leaned out the passenger's window. "She's the best rider I've ever had, Ma'am."

"*Rebel,*" Minnie hissed.

Chuckling, he settled back in the seat. "I like her."

"Show me how to work this thing. It's got three pedals and I'm already confused."

"That's called the clutch," he said. "You push it all the way in and turn the keys. No, not yet. Put your hand on the gearstick and get used to the changes for a minute. Manual puts you in the middle of the action, right? Tethers you to the vehicle. You're in control. You got to learn that."

I'm in control.

She grasped the warm shaft of the gear stick. It still felt warm from Rebel's hands.

"That's it," he murmured, and then he laid his hand over hers, covering it completely. Blood roared in her ears. Rebel's touch was warm, enveloping. She could feel the texture of his palm, the rough callouses, the smooth muscle of his Venus mount. He guided her hand through the gear changes, helping her push it through all six gears. Only the Reverse was marked. She tried to pay attention to Rebel's explanation, but the calm head that carried her through surgery was nowhere to be found. She was going to crash this two-ton monster and kill them both if she didn't pay attention, but all she could think about was how Rebel's hands felt wrapped around hers.

"That third pedal under your foot is the clutch," Rebel explained. "Lower the brake first."

"The brake--"

"It's by your thigh, sweetheart."

Minnie found it. Her palms were slick with sweat. "Okay," she gulped. "Now what?"

"Put your foot on the clutch and turn the keys to start it."

The engine roared to life. Minnie's hands shook as she returned them to the wheel.

"Slowly let go of the clutch and hit the gas-- I said slowly, girl!"

"I can't do this," Minnie gasped in sudden panic.

"Yes you can," Rebel said, unrelenting. "Ease up slow and feel the car underneath you. Don't rush it. It ain't your enemy, just a machine."

By the time they made it to the end of Grace Hill, Minnie was a jiggling mess of nerves, but Rebel's refusal to let her quit pushed her the final stretch onto the main road, and then, just as he said, it became easy.

The manual transmission responded to her every adjustment, like it was a part of her body, and soon she began to enjoy it. The adrenaline pumping through her blood made her feel reckless and free. Rebel was an excellent teacher; none of her mistakes rattled him at all. With the windows rolled down, the pair of them rocketed down the empty roads.

"Take a left here," said Rebel as they approached a crossroads. "We'll go the long way to Bear Hill."

Why not? They had time.

They coasted along the Blue Ridge parkway, where the mountainside fell away and revealed nearly all of Florin hunched inside the hills. The mist was blue. The sun was red. Everything was damp with dew, and quiet. Yellow flowers and hills of pasture blurred into the distance.

"Pull up to the bluff," Rebel said. "Let's show you how to park it."

It was a welcome excuse to stop and enjoy the morning. Rebel guided her through parking, which involved more lowering and raising of gears and clutches, then finally she cut the engine and the lesson ended. She sagged in the seat. "My God. That was crazy."

He laughed, a deep-throated full laugh that twisted her up even more. Suddenly the close air in the front seat became too much. Minnie unbuckled her seatbelt and hurried out of the car, breathing hard.

Rebel handed her the coffee cup she'd forgotten in her haste to escape him. He'd brought coffee, too, just like the other time.

She took the warm drink carefully, making sure to keep at least a foot between them. He leaned against the hood of his truck and fumbled in his Carhartt jacket for a cigarette and lighter.

"See?" he said, his green eyes warm. "We're in one piece. You did great."

She smiled back. "I actually enjoyed that."

"You're a natural. I wanted to teach you stick 'cause there's a car Larry's working on I think you might like. It's old but I think you'll like it."

She nodded. "We'll see. I just got to figure things out. I wasn't planning to buy another vehicle so recently."

"That's alright. No rush."

Bluish light played across Rebel's face, showing the veins under his eyes, the strong lines of his cheekbones... As she stared, his eyes flicked up, green and slanted, studying her. He could play up the dumb redneck act-- he'd be happy to do it, just to entertain himself-- but underneath was a cool intelligence. He shifted his attention to the view, ears turning pink.

Crows swooped and danced against the nearby mountaintop. "If we could be so free," he murmured.

"Did you know they remember faces? They're smart animals."

"More than people, I'm sure." Rebel frowned. "I got something on my hands?"

"No," Minnie said, gaze flicking away hurriedly. "You're just a little ashy right here."

She tapped one of his knuckles. He laughed, spreading his fingers all the way open so he could examine them. "Ashy?"

"I recommend cocoa butter."

"Is that like chocolate?"

"It doesn't taste like it, speaking from experience."

"It's like a lotion, right?"

"Uh huh."

"Katie has some. I think Junior gave it to her."

She took a hasty sip of coffee.

"So is it true black women don't like white men?"

"What?" She sputtered.

"That's what Ben said."

What the hell was Ben Simpson doing saying that stuff to Rebel McCall? "I guess Black women just have preferences, is all. Everybody does."

"I reckon they would," Rebel said. "What's yours?"

"Kind, responsible, thoughtful–"

"I mean physically."

"Short and ugly," said Minnie, taking another sip.

Rebel chuckled. "Really? Me too."

His lion-colored hair tumbled backward in the wind and his eyes drifted shut. He leaned his weight against the bonnet. She watched the powerful corded muscle of his throat above the collar of his flannel, moving as he inhaled the cigarette.

Minnie gripped the coffee cup against the urge to thread her fingers through his hair.

"Don't these taste bad?" She wondered.

"It ain't the taste I'm after. It's the feeling."

"What feeling?"

He shrugged. "Warmth. Just doing something. I can't really explain it."

"Let me try it," Minnie said impulsively.

His eyebrows lifted. "You never smoked? Are you a country girl or what?"

"I don't know what country girls you know, but lots of women don't smoke."

"Want to try it?"

"I don't think...Okay," she said. And quickly added, "But if I try it, you can't have one tomorrow."

"Now how is that fair?" But he agreed, and held the little cylinder out to her, the end still glowing.

Minnie carefully put her lips around the end. Rebel didn't move his fingers at first, and her lips brushed against them briefly. Her eyes fluttered shut. Did she taste anything? Salt and coffee...fresh bread. The moment became strange and intimate. He fed it to her, that little piece of poison. A moment later she jerked back, coughing.

"Ugh! That is nasty!"

He gave a shout of laughter and went into the truck to conjure a bottle of water.

"How's a woman get to your age and never try a cigarette?"

"You make it sound like I'm ancient. I haven't tried a lot of things, for your information."

"Oh really?" His eyes hooded. "Like what?"

Minnie's heart began to pound.

"Like what, Minnie?"

"Like nothing."

"Chicken."

"I'm not a chicken."

"I wanna deep fry you right now, that's how chicken you look."

She should stop this game. Quickly. She drifted closer to Rebel and his arm came out and twined about her waist. He tinkled her earring with a finger. "These are pretty. You wear 'em for me?"

"Maybe," she whispered.

From the road, no one would see them standing in front of the truck. Ahead was a steep drop off the mountainside, looking out on an impossible view that rendered them small and insignificant specks on a mighty landscape.

Rebel's hand slid right under the hem of her shirt, fondling her bare skin.

"You smell like flowers."

He cupped her waist with long, strong fingers. Stroked her very slowly, up and down the curve. She could count the callouses on his fingertips. He took the coffee cup from her and set it on the hood of the truck. He didn't say anything. He just petted her under her scrubs, getting her used to his touch. The thick pad of his thumb stroked lightly near her navel. And then dipped into her navel.

She gasped softly. They were nearly face to face. A thread of desire tugged sharply on the knot under her belly.

"Don't be scared," he murmured. "Come here."

He kissed and then sucked the tender skin on her neck.

She whimpered as his tongue pressed on the pulsing area, soothing it.

"You like that?"

"Uh huh," she gasped.

His knuckles brushed the top of her ass. Her arms twined around his neck and now she had an excuse to comb her fingers through his thick wavy hair.

His knee worked between her legs, pressing his own long thigh into her sex. He was hard against her stomach.

"Rebel..."

His lips were warm. Soft. He rocked her against the solid wall of his body, moving her up and down his knee. She pressed forward, gasping at the rush of sensation deep between her legs. He teased and sucked her tongue. She could feel the grill of his truck digging into her ass, and her calves ached from standing on tiptoe. He was so tall...

Minnie found her common sense flying away like the blackbirds. Rebel found the band of her scrubs and tugged it down, shielding her from the mountain wind with his body.

His eyes were hooded, such a pale green she felt like she'd been caught by a wicked god of the forest.

"Somebody will see--"

"Ain't nobody up here but the two of us," he said, voice husky.

He turned her around and rolled her panties down to her knees. She moved slowly, blinking as if drugged. Surely he didn't mean to...

Rebel bent her over the hood of his truck with a firm, commanding touch. Grabbed her ass with both hands.

Knelt.

Even as the first deep pass of his tongue stroked her trembling inner thighs, Minnie couldn't believe it. Even when he parted her with both hands and delved his thumbs inside her, spreading her open to lick and tease, she thought she must be dreaming. Hidden from the road only by his truck, anyone pulling onto the shoulder might have seen Minnie Brown bent over Rebel's truck.

But it was hard to care. Hard to care when Rebel was screwing his hard thumb deep inside her. Hard to care when he was sucking the cream right out of her pussy like he couldn't get enough...

Minutes later, panting, delirious, she met his eyes. Holding her gaze, he sucked her juices from his fingers then began to slowly rub her clit. She cried out at the new, dizzying sensation.

"Chocolate," he murmured in wonder. "Cherries. Cream. I don't even know."

"It feels so good," she whimpered.

"You got a pretty pussy." His shoulder muscles flexed as he drove his fingers deep inside her sex, through the mess she was making, against the soft inner part where all her desire was building...

Her insides clenched around his digit, begging for another orgasm. She was begging him too, out loud. "Rebel, please...Please..."

Over her own moans she heard the clink of his belt buckle. A warning bell sounded in her head.

Minnie grabbed the first part of his body she could reach--his wrist--and squeezed.

"W-wait," she gasped.

"Get in the truck then," he rasped, but before she could move he pulled her up and kissed her again, this time soft and slow, his hands moving chastely to her waist. He stroked her there again, smooth calming touches that made her hungry for the rough fucking of his fingers.

Feeling herself slipping back into the delirium, Minnie tore her lips away. "Rebel, wait."

She pushed him off and turned around, hauling her scrubs up, covering herself completely. She was still so wet...Her thighs rubbed against each other slickly. It would barely hurt if he took his big dick out and...

He reached for her. She pushed his hand away.

"No," she said, shaking her head, heart hammering wildly. "We got to stop."

"The hell we do. Get your ass in my truck. I ain't done with you."

"Rebel!" She grabbed his other wrist. "Rebel, no."

He blinked down at her, confusion and lust swirling in his eyes. He was breathing hard. "Okay," he said.

"Don't you think..." She could barely breathe. "We're grown. We're standing on the side of a road! Anyone could see us." She jerked away. "And we haven't been tested. We could catch a disease," she babbled.

His face darkened. "I was tested last month, and I ain't had a woman in over a year."

And I'm a virgin.

"We can't do this, Rebel." Shame fell on her like a sack of sugar. What the hell was she thinking? Anyone could drive past and see...

"You got a man I don't know about?"

"No! It's not that."

"You got kids?"

"No, but — "

"So what's the problem? Look, we can go somewhere else..." He frowned. "Or never mind all this. We can go somewhere off the mountain. I want to take you out. Like a real date."

"No," she cut him off, suddenly panicking. "No. I think this is over. I can't do this with you. Not...Ever."

He let go of her hand. His eyes cut away to the view, narrowed and disturbed. When they returned to hers, she could read absolutely nothing in them.

"Alright," he said. "Okay then."

She climbed back into the truck, this time into the passenger's seat.

Rebel got in the driver's side. He took a deep breath. "I'm sorry. I thought... you wanted it."

"It's alright. It's my fault." And it was her fault. *And I did want it.*

"We just can't do this," she said. "I thought...I don't know what the hell I was thinking."

"Don't I get to know the reason?" he said in a tight voice.

"It's complicated."

"So is everything."

She pressed her lips together, not trusting herself not to blurt the truth. Rebel looked like he wanted to say something, but didn't. They drove to Bear Hill in silence.

"I'll get you Roman's insurance," he said quietly as he idled in the parking lot of the Brown Veterinary Clinic.

"Thank you," said Minnie meekly.

"I can pick you up tomorrow morning if you want. Until you get a new car." His voice was carefully neutral. "Like we agreed. I ain't trying to be pushy, but I did promise."

"That won't be necessary," Minnie said. Better make a clean break of it. She felt sick. "But thank you, Rebel."

His eyes narrowed. "Suit yourself."

He was angry. Her pussy throbbed, and her heart ached. But it was for the best.

"Goodbye," she said.

They stared at each other for another heartbeat. The corners of his eyes tensed. He looked...Oh, never mind.

Minnie hastily shut the door.

REBEL MCCALL WAS CRAZY. ONLY A CRAZY MAN WOULD PULL A woman's clothes off on top a scenic bluff at seven in the morning, then eat her pussy like a birthday cake.

What if you'd been in his bed? A nasty little voice whispered. *What if no one could see you? Don't say you would have stopped him. You know you wanted that big thick dick inside you...Where no man's ever touched...Imagine if he knew you were a virgin.*

Why did her inner voice sound so much like Chrissie?

Minnie changed into her spare pair of scrubs and rubbed her hands viciously under hot, steaming water. Just forget it ever happened. Deal with your insurance. You thanked him already for his help. You baked him cookies, for God's sake! Don't think about the rest.

Anyway, she had other priorities. Before noon she had given eyedrops to a cat with cataracts, plucked porcupine quills from a terrier's nose, euthanized a family's beloved farm hound, which was devastating, and expressed an abscess on a bearded dragon that caused her to abandon the unfortunate lunch she'd brought with her: pea soup.

During her free hour she called Mama. Then she called the car insurance. A migraine later, she was wishing all McCalls a hot ride to hell. The snide voice on the other end informed Minnie that crashing twice in twenty-four hours into two different members of the same family at the same stop sign "raised red flags". Their agent would be in touch.

By five, Minnie was eager to be home with her hot water bottle and sleeping pills. She was in the middle of a writeup to the bearded dragon's owner when the clinic's front door burst open. A harried-looking woman in overalls thrust a box through the door with a booted foot, then leapt into her truck and sped away.

"Another runner?" Lola complained.

"Shoot!" Minnie cried, hurrying from the other room. "Did she give a--"

"Nope. She's gone."

Minnie braced herself and strode over to the box. Five puppies squirmed against each other. Pink, rashy skin showed under patches of dirty fur. The box was crawling with fleas.

The puppies looked old enough to be weaned, clearing the biggest hurdle to saving their lives. But the mange was terrible and would need intensive treatment. Starting now. Shutting off her sadness and anger— a routine, at this point— she hurried the poor babies into the back room. By the time she weighed, washed, medicated and gave them the the first de-worming treatment, it was already six o' clock. She coaxed the puppies to eat a little more shredded chicken, then tucked them into one of the quarantine cages with a warming pad. One of them looked sicker than the rest.

"Sorry, little guy," she whispered, removing him from his brothers to a separate cage with an extra heating pad, and lots of water. In the beginning she had cried over things like this, but six months of daily horrors put some iron in her heart. If the puppy didn't survive the night, at least she'd made him comfortable. She made sure he had his warming pad, water, and a fresh pee mat. Closing the cage, she hesitated as her gaze fell on the little block of whiteboard fixed to the top of the cage. She took out a dry-erase and wrote NEMO.

. . .

As she drove her daughter to Grace Hill, Ms. Brown finally was able to speak her mind.

"So," said Ms. Brown. "You and that white man."

"What white man?"

"Don't play dumb with me, Minnie." Her mother pressed her lips together in disgust. "Did he stay the night?"

"No."

Now Minnie regretted pushing Rebel away. If she was going to be accused for it anyway, what was the point in denying herself the pleasure of letting him take her?

"I'm warning you, those McCalls are trouble."

"I know that."

"Do you? 'Cause I'm hearing different," snapped Ms. Brown. "I'm hearing all types of stuff from all types of people. Stay away from him, Minnie, do you hear me?"

Minnie dug her nails into her palm. "You can't be believing what everybody says."

"Oh really?" Ms. Brown said, her voice rising. "So Eleanora Mabel was lying, then? She saw him drive right up to your house! Twice! After I went through all this trouble to raise you decent...Nobody will want anything to do with you. Is that what you want? You care more about some dirty animals than what people think?"

"Times are changing, Mama. People are more tolerant. And from what I seen, Rebel McCall is a nice man. He's got a job—" Minnie had never imagined herself making this argument, and she had to admit it wasn't a very good one. She barely knew Rebel, at the end of the day. Some laughs and stolen kisses didn't make up for the fact that his family was crazy, which meant he was probably crazy too.

But her mother didn't know anything about men. That fact had been obvious to Minnie from an early age. Her mother was a selfish, vain woman. Minnie could remember the boyfriends that came and left, those creepy, shuffling men who had stared and even groped her, while Mama batted her eyes and laughed it off...In truth, the woman had never forgiven her daughter for driving a wedge between her and Minnie's father. She made Minnie pay for it every single day in subtle, cruel ways. Desperation to leave her mother's negativity had motivated Minnie to spend the past decade of her life in school.

But in the end, her stupid soft heart brought her right back. Her mother had no other children, no family. She could barely hold down a job. Who else would look after her?

"Listen to yourself, girl!" Ms. Brown said in disgust. "Is that what you want? To play the whore? You think Rebel McCall's gonna put a ring on your finger? Think again. You'll be nothing but gutter slut if you keep sniffing after him. And I'll tell you something else. No man is gonna want you with that nasty attitude you got. You gonna work work work all your life and get absolutely nothing."

"And then I'd be just like you, wouldn't I?" Minnie said before she could stop herself.

Her mother inflated. "What the hell did you just say?"

"You let your friends dogpile me about never getting a man, as if the only thing I'm good for is between my legs!" Minnie said angrily. "I wonder why! I'll tell *you* something, Mama. Rebel McCall is a hundred times better than that nasty bastard you set me up with last Sunday. He was a pig!"

"Don't you dare cuss at me, Minnie!"

The fight went on for hours.

CHAPTER 7

THE VISITOR

Lola cleared level 400 of Fruit Crush with ease, then yawned and looked up from her phone, blinking blearily at the clock. Noon. Doctor Brown had run out to get a package, taking Lola's car since her own was still a pile of scrap at The Garage. Lola wasn't sure how Doctor Brown managed to wreck her car twice in a week, but she was impressed.

So for the time being the clinic was empty except for Lola and about a half dozen furry patients. The air conditioning had been acting up, so Minnie allotted the cool air to the animals, leaving Lola in the muggy haze of the waiting room. Lola yawned again...So sleepy...

When she picked her head up from the desk, a man's shadow had darkened the doorway. Lola frowned, flicking her eyes over the appointment book. They were supposed to have the afternoon free. The man was tall, wearing jeans and a button down, and he had paused with his hand on the door handle. He seemed to be reading the signs Minnie had plastered to the glass.

. . .

EVERYONE IS WELCOME!

DO YOU HAVE AN APPOINTMENT?

PLEASE DO NOT DROP LIVE ANIMALS AT THE DOOR. CALL FIRST!

LOLA TENSED. ANOTHER RUNNER? THESE ASSHOLES JUST wouldn't quit! But no; she couldn't see a box in his hands. The man walked in a moment later.

He had menacing dark eyes and a shaved head. Without thinking, Lola immediately hid her phone under her desk. Who was this creep?

"Hello," he said in a rasping voice.

"Hi," said Lola. "Uhh...Can I help you?"

"I'm looking for the vet. The Brown woman."

"She's not here."

"When's she coming back?"

Lola looked him in the eye. "I have no idea. You'd better just leave a message."

Instead of replying, the man began to pace the waiting room. "She bought this place, did she?"

"Do you have an appointment with Dr. Brown, sir?"

The stranger stared at Minnie's certificates and diplomas hanging on the wall. "She bought this place. Where'd she get the money?"

"We had some donors, and some loans. Her daddy works at a bank. He helped her secure it."

"Her daddy," the man repeated. "And who might that be?"

"He lives in the valley."

"And works at a bank, you say. They let him handle the money?"

Lola wasn't sure what to say to that. She thought the man was being offensive, but couldn't be sure. "Are you...Rebel McCall?" Lola wondered. as the thought occurred to her. But wasn't Rebel blonde?

The man narrowed his eyes, looking even more terrifying. "No, sweetheart, I ain't Rebel McCall."

"Oh," Lola laughed awkwardly. "Sorry, I just thought—"

"He come around here often? Rebel?"

"Um— no." *He's got to get the fuck out of here. This is weird as fuck.*

The man snorted and his eyes shifted to a framed picture of Minnie and Lola hugging Champion, a Golden Retriever that belonged to Hannah Queensbury, the principal of Florin High. Champion was the unofficial mascot of the clinic.

"That's the Queensbury's dog," said the stranger, gesturing to the picture. "Ain't it?"

"Yes. One of our first patients."

"I thought the Queensburys didn't like coloreds." The man folded his arms and looked down his nose at Lola. "What are you? Mexican?"

Lola glanced down at her phone. Should she call the police? The man hadn't done anything yet.

"I asked you a question."

"And I chose not to answer it, because it's none of your business, Mister."

The sudden whine of the puppies made the man turn his head. "People actually bring their dogs here?" Lola was used to the noise, but it grated on some people.

"It's an animal hospital. What do you think? Now you need to go, alright?"

He glared at her and she almost wet herself. Could the man look any more demonic? But his eyes lingered on the photograph of Minnie one more time, and suddenly they didn't look so evil. "Alright," he said slowly. "But...Tell her I came by. Tell her I want to talk."

"And who the hell are you?"

"She'll figure it out."

Lola gritted her teeth. "Message received. Now please leave, *sir*."

No way was she going to tell Dr. Brown some nutcase had come looking for her. The woman had enough to worry about. But Lola might suggest putting a shotgun under the receptionist's desk...

The man picked up Minnie's picture as if he wanted to take it with him. He caught Lola's stare then set it down hard, turning red. He practically slammed out the door.

CHAPTER 8
THE NIGHTIE

"Rebel's gone to the dark side," Larry confided to Chick Wilson. He neatly caught the can of Bud Light Rebel threw at his head. He opened it with his teeth, sending a volcanic malty spray nearly a foot in the air.

"Got himself a woman," Larry continued cheerfully, mopping up with a filthy corner of his shirt. "And you'll never guess who."

"Tell me it ain't Speedy Stacy?" Chick looked concerned. "Rebel, that girl's got more disease than a fruit bat."

Larry shook his head. "Unless Stacy changed race, she ain't the one. Rebel's got himself a black woman."

"Bull," Chick said, eyes wide.

"Her name is Minnie Brown."

"Minnie? As in the *mouse*?" Chick demanded.

"She's the vet with the place on Bear Hill," Rebel finally broke in, glaring at Larry. "And we're just friends. Not even that. I helped tow her car."

"You fondled her knee," Larry jeered.

Rebel's ears turned red and he turned the chicken over in the flames. "First of all, I don't *fondle*, second of all, you can kindly go to hell."

"What she look like?" Chick demanded, impressed. "She light or dark?"

"Medium, I'd say," said Larry swiftly.

"Wait," Chick said, holding up a hand. "Rebel, didn't you have some black girl you was after? Back in high school?"

"Oh yeah," Larry nodded. "That dark girl with the long legs? What was her name?"

Rebel knew who they were talking about. "Rita," he nodded. "But that wasn't me. That was my cousin had her."

"Rita!" Chick said, slapping his knee. "That's right. Tall dark girl. Looked like Naomi Campbell."

What happened to her?" Larry asked.

Rebel shrugged. "She wasn't my girl, like I said." He too wondered what had happened to Sam McCall, one of the few cousins who didn't have a chip of flint where his heart should be. Sam and Rita had flaunted their relationship in high school, but it had ended tragically. They both left the mountain not long after.

Chick frowned. "Okay, black females, right? Is the pussy pink or brown on the inside, or is it like both? Like that ice cream. What the fuck is it called? Napoleon?"

"Will you two chimps shut the fuck up? I don't want my niece hearing that shit," Rebel snapped. He turned the sizzling chicken over again. "And it's *Neopolitan*."

Larry set his beer down. "I got to piss."

Chick patted his pockets. "I got smokes. You coming, Reb?"

Minnie leaning down to try his cigarette...

"I'm good," he said. "And the chicken's ready, when you're done jacking each other off."

Right as Chick and Larry shuffled to the garden, Katie opened the screen door and stuck her head out. Curly blonde hair tumbled into her eyes. She glanced at the grill and wrinkled her nose. "You burned it."

Rebel poked one of the stiff chicken breasts. "It ain't burned, it's charred."

"Next time let me do it, Bobby Flay."

"Hmph. You finished the tea?" He grunted.

"Yeah." Katie strolled out onto the porch, barefoot and slender. She was getting taller, nearly to his shoulder now. With her fair hair, freckled skin and straight nose, Katie looked like Rebel's own daughter. Legally, of course, she belonged to Roman. Yet the girl had nothing of his older brother's exotic looks or winning personality, a fact that didn't escape the gossips any more than it did Roman.

And this fact, among others, was one reason the brothers barely got along.

Rebel watched Katie from the tail of his eye as she brought out the tea and laid a couple places on the wide picnic table. The resemblance uncle and niece shared had only grown stronger with time.

"You talked to your daddy lately?" He asked mildly. Sometimes the only news he received about Roman came through Katie.

Katie's face scrunched in disgust. "Talk? He don't talk to me, Uncle Reb. He keeps fishin' through everything I tell him, like he knows about Junior but he ain't got the balls to just ask me." Her sharp little face got blotchy with anger, like Rebel's sometimes did. "I told him once I turn eighteen I'm away back to Tulsa and he can't do diddly. So he told me if I tried it he'd drag me back and tan my hide, so then I told him to go to hell and suck the devil's dick."

Rebel stared at his niece. It still caught him off guard to hear her sound just like her mother.

"Tell me you didn't actually say that?"

"I did," she said proudly. "You know I can't stand the man. Why the hell did he have to be my Daddy? I don't even know why Momma got with him. People say he's good lookin' and all, but I don't see it."

Rebel bit his tongue, and Katie continued breezily, "I used to pray and ask God if He made a mistake. If maybe you were my Pa for real. Everybody says we look alike."

Her eyes darted to his, hopeful.

He avoided her gaze. "Come on, Katie."

Liar.

Months ago he'd asked Ross about one of those DNA tests, a time when he and Ross had still been speaking. His younger brother arranged the kit, told him about "samples", which involved q-tips, vials, hair, the post office, getting a smug Larry to read everything aloud to him, and two weeks of poor sleep. But when the results arrived, Rebel turned craven and never opened them. He was ashamed to admit they were still sitting in his drawer.

He'd decided he wouldn't open them without telling Roman first. Of course, the opportunity to tell Roman mysteriously never appeared. In his heart, Rebel feared that the truth laid bare would be the final straw between him and his older brother.

The boys were near in age, but Roman had grown up his early years in some other part of Florin. Rebel wasn't too clear on the details, since Roman never spoke about his childhood. In fact, Roman didn't say a word until he was eight years old. Long after that he still preferred to talk with his fists.

They'd gotten along sometimes. Rebel had a couple fond memories. More than anything, those memories kept him strangely defensive of his brother even as the years and resentments stacked up, one after the other.

"Katie. Don't say that stuff to Roman, alright?"

"Whatever."

Rebel raised a knowing eyebrow at his niece. "Don't act like you ain't scared of him."

"I ain't!"

Rebel didn't believe Roman would ever physically hurt Katie. But the man was mortally old-fashioned and controlling, and had a nasty temper best not provoked.

Only Rebel's intervention stopped Katie from running back to Tulsa. He convinced his brother that Katie didn't need to wear floor-length skirts and stay inside until she was thirty. Instead of laying all the chores on the girl, maybe Roman should get off his ass and wash a dish once in a while. And maybe forcing Katie to go to church with those frenzied bible-thumpers might just turn her into a devil worshiper. Maybe Roman should get the girl a damned cellphone like every other kid her age.

Sometimes Rebel's suggestions didn't go over too well. So Rebel had stopped "suggesting" and took some matters into his own hands. Like the thing with Junior. No reason why he couldn't help Katie see her friend once in a while, if he was going over to that side of Florin anyway. Or so he'd thought. He was beginning to regret bringing those two together, as a matter of fact.

"How did Daddy find out about that lady you're seeing?" Katie asked, nudging a fallen cherry blossom off the porch with a toe.

"Excuse me?"

"He asked me if you were seeing a you-know-what." She mouthed the word.

"I ran into him while I was with her. And I'm not seeing that lady, Katie. She called it quits."

"Daddy was looking her up online."

"She's online?"

"Yeah. Everybody's online but you, Uncle Reb. No offense."

"So what did he say?"

"That she was pretty for a you-know-what."

"And so you said...?"

"That he's a racist turd."

Just then Katie leaned over the grill and some of her hair fell back over her shoulder. "Ugh. You definitely burned it, Uncle Reb."

"Hey," said Rebel sharply. "What the hell is that?"

Katie straightened, a hand flying guiltily to the vivid purple blotch under her ear. "What? Um. Nothing."

"It don't look like nothing. It looks like I need to hang Junior by the toes over Buffalo Mountain and send you to boarding school, that's what it looks like. What the hell, Katie?"

Katie winced, pressing the hickey with a fingertip. "I got it from softball."

"Yeah, and I'm a monkey's uncle."

"It's true!"

"I thought you and Junior were *just friends*. That's what you told me."

"Me and Junior can still be friends and fool around," she explained, as if he was stupid.

"So you been 'fooling around' with Junior this whole time? And telling me it was all innocent? You think your Pa won't notice that thing on your neck?"

Katie raised her chin and looked just like her mother. "That's why we have concealer."

"You got an answer for everything, don't you?" Rebel had the feeling that Ben Simpson's hunch was right. The man thought Katie McCall was only using Junior to act out— to *rebel*— against her father. Did Katie understand the consequences of that? *Friendship, my ass.* Minnie had been right all along.

Rebel felt sick at himself. He had allowed this. Encouraged it.

Selfishly putting a young boy, his friend's nephew, in danger.

"You promised you'd be careful, Katie. This ain't careful. If Roman finds out you're canoodling with that boy on my watch, that's a whole new storm of shit."

Katie sulked. "I'll cover it up. Come on, Uncle Reb. We didn't do nothing."

"I'll have a nice little talk with Junior to confirm that."

"You wouldn't!"

"I would," said Rebel grimly. "And it had better be 'nothing' or it'll be something. Right? Are y'all using protection?"

"Oh my God," said Katie, her face flaming red.

Just then Rebel's cell buzzed in his pocket. "CALL FROM MINT GREEN DRESS," it declared in a cheery utterance, clear as a bell. There was a drawback to that text-to-speech business Katie had put on there.

"Oh my God, it's her," Katie squealed, eyes wide as dollars. "You gonna answer it? Answer it!"

"Stay out here and watch the chicken," Rebel grunted.

He swiped the green button and ducked through the sliding glass door.

Now what the hell did she want? She'd made her point. Message received. But immediately his heart began to pound, and he flashed back to her writhing and panting on his fingers, whispering hotly in his ear.

"Rebel?" Her country drawl had been flattened off by education and travel, but the way she said his name sent a tingle up his neck.

"Hi, Minnie."

"Um...This is kind of stupid. I'm sorry to bother you..."

"You good?" He said gruffly.

"Um. Yeah. I'm alright."

"Okay then," he said. Rebel heard a clinking noise, like ice swirling against a glass.

"Oh shit," Minnie mumbled. "Why did I do this?"

"Hold on," said Rebel. "You *drunk*, church girl?"

"Oh no. Can you tell?"

Rebel glanced out the window, towards the garden where Chick and Larry had disappeared. A trail of smoke rose up from the magnolia tree. Katie sat on the porch, texting furiously. No doubt "spilling tea" to Junior.

Just hang up. He rubbed the back of his neck, feeling a flush already spreading up his chest.

"What you drinking?" He asked.

Minnie Brown cleared her throat. "Bourbon."

Rebel choked back a laugh. "It's like that, huh?"

"I had a stressful day. And I wanted to...apologize."

"Apologize for what?"

"I led you on," she said. "I flirted with you. I encouraged you to flirt with me."

"So you didn't mean it?"

"No, I did." She sounded agitated. "But I shouldn't have let it get so far."

His voice lowered. "But did you like it, honey?"

Silence. Then she whispered, "Yes. I liked it."

"I guess I came on a little strong." Rebel raked a hand through his hair. "Maybe I got carried away."

"I feel the same," Minnie said. She took another drink and said in a shaky voice, "It's wrong, isn't it?"

Rebel thought of Roman's disgust. His father's threat to Ross. *Is it true your brother's seeing a nigger?*

Black and white in Florin. Living together, but separate. Always separate. Some lines didn't get crossed. Some rules never broken.

"It would never work out," Minnie continued. "Nobody would like it."

"That don't make it wrong."

"Rebel..."

"You scared?" He asked quietly.

"I feel ashamed to be scared. It's the twenty-first century, right? If we want to mess around why should anybody stop us?"

"I don't want you to be scared." He clenched his fists. Life had made him tough as dirt. He'd could take punches and keep moving. He didn't fear anybody, or anything. But he couldn't protect the woman he wanted from his family. The thought enraged him. Had he been living a lie all this time? He thought he'd escaped. Found his independence as a grown man with his own property and business separate from the McCalls. All along, he was still under their control.

Protect her.

He began pacing his room. "I wouldn't let anything happen to you, Minnie."

"You'd hurt me?"

"Never."

"You mean your family?"

"You don't have to worry about them," he said quietly. He'd make sure of it. "And I don't care what label we put on it, Minnie, as long as it's what you want."

Ice clinked against her glass. "Just sex? Is that what you want?"

Rebel closed the window, sealing off his view of the porch. He sat on the edge of his bed.

"You alone?"

"Yes, Rebel."

"Describe it for me."

"I'm in my bedroom. It's not that big. I have blue curtains. The wall is blue. Blue is my favorite color. I have a lamp next to my bed...This isn't very sexy, is it?"

"What color are your clothes?"

"Well..."

"What?"

"I'm not really wearing clothes," she whispered.

Holy fuck. "You're bare, then." He fumbled for the zipper on his jeans.

She laughed. "I got on a nightie."

"We talking lace and ribbons, or those sack things your Mama wears to bed?"

"Oh Lord. I hope you got no idea what my Mama wears to bed." Her voice lowered. "Uh, it's a nightie. It's got frills on the bottom."

"Does it open over your stomach?" He cupped himself.

"Not this one. I'd have to roll it off me." Sweet Lord.

"Why aren't you wearing panties? You been talking to me this whole time with your kitty out?"

"It's the Bourbon," she confided in a sneaky whisper.

"What color is it? That getup you're wearing?"

"White."

He could just picture it. Minnie's thick curves cupped by lace and ribbon, waiting for him to unwrap her. Minnie lying back on a mountain of pillows, knees up, black hair loose...eyes lidded from the Bourbon...And God, how would that white satin look against her cinnamon skin?

"Tell me more."

"Caveman."

"I saw your pussy already, honey. Why you acting shy?" He stroked his dick.

"We shouldn't have done that."

"Really? You came all over my tongue and begged me for more."

"Keep talking," she gasped.

Gladly. "Next time I'm gonna sit you naked on my lap and take that nightie off real slow until you're naked. I want you bare for me, touching those pretty tits...Holding them up for me to suck on until the tips are hard and you're putting cream all over my jeans. I won't get undressed until you're coming all over me."

"Maybe there won't be a next time," she teased.

He laughed softly. "Shut up and touch yourself."

"You're so mean," she whispered.

He put the phone on speaker, falling backwards on his bed and closing his eyes. For days now he'd called up the memory of Minnie bent over his truck, legs parted, her pussy juicy and tight and tasting, as he'd predicted, just like wildflower honey. He'd had no idea why he'd done something so reckless, after just swearing to himself to keep her a secret. But in the moment her sweetness and prettiness and all that just overcame him, and he had to have her.

"I never done this before."

"Done what?" Rebel cupped his balls, squeezing lightly. "Fucked yourself over the phone?"

"Yes. No."

"Say it for me."

"I never f-fucked myself over the phone."

He cursed. "You got a toy?"

"The battery died," she groaned. "I tried...I tried but I couldn't."

"Good." He lazily stroked himself, imagining her spread out on the bed, her knees up, pussy plump and needy. A bead of silver pre-cum spilled over the head of his cock.

He groaned and spread it with his fist, up and down, up and down.

"Why is it good?"

"I want you to use your hands," he said.

He remembered exactly how she tasted. He could almost taste it now, a riot of sweetness, cherries and wildflowers, cream and honey.

He loved it. He loved how her pussy lips were darker than her skin. He loved that, when he opened her up to the first stroke of his tongue, it was actually a soft pink like the inside of a rose. He wanted to be inside her. When she climaxed while riding his face he could feel her clenched around his fingers, so tight...He'd lost his mind and tried to fuck her right then and there. Big mistake. Women like Minnie needed a tender hand...Was he the man to give it to her?

Minnie moaned. "This is so wrong."

"You're just horny, baby, ain't nothing wrong about it."

"I wish you were here."

He wished it too. He wished he could get off this bed and drive up the road this instant. He'd be buck naked as soon as he got to the door. He wished he could take Minnie in her bed, rip off white teddy thing she was wearing, and give her a seein'-to to end them all. God, he wished it. But there was Chick, there was Larry, there was Katie. The whole damn mountain lay between them.

The thought made him harder. It was better to wait. It would be all the sweeter when he took Minnie. "I got to have you. Naked...Bare. Your pretty brown skin..."

She gasped. "Are you t-touching yourself?"

"What you think?"

"I never sucked a dick, Rebel. I want yours," she blurted.

"Fuck, baby." His rough hand worked up and down himself faster. He imagined Minnie kneeling at the foot of the bed, obediently opening her plump, pretty lips to take his shaft. Spilling that first drop of cum on her tongue. *She's never done it before?* Every woman Rebel knew had sucked a dick. At least once.

"So you're like a blowjob virgin."

"Is that bad?"

"I ain't complaining." The opposite. He could teach her exactly how he liked it. *God.*

"Is it pink?" Minnie said suddenly.

"What?" he panted.

"Your dick. I never seen a white man's..."

He glanced down. "I'd say more of a dusky rose."

"How big?"

"You'll find out when we fuck."

"Do women...Do women have a problem with it? Will it fit?"

She was gonna kill him. "Sometimes," he said honestly. "But I think you could handle it. I got to get you slick first...And then I give you just a little bit. Just a little bit to stretch you. We'd take it slow..."

"I'm wet," said Minnie.

"You are right now?" he bit out. "You wet for me?"

"I am...It's getting everywhere."

He ruthlessly fucked his fist. "Stick two fingers inside and work it. Use the other hand to play with your nipples."

"What are you doing?" She moaned deliciously. "Oh... That feels so good..."

He turned his head into the sheets, imagining her beautiful brown body sliding over him. "Minnie, my God..."

"I don't believe this...Rebel...It feels so so good..."

"Keep fucking yourself," He said, voice raw. "You're so tight, darling. Gotta get you nice and wet before you take me."

"I want it," she whimpered.

She wanted it. Sweet, pretty Minnie with her infectious laugh. He'd give it to her on her hands and knees. He'd spill his seed down her throat. Minnie on top, her full brown breasts swinging in his face as she rode him. Fucking her...His long white cock sinking into her, claiming her, owning her inch by inch...

Cum charged up his shaft. With a cry he spunked all over his fist and stomach, ropes and ropes of thick seed, in time with the soft moans coming from the other end of the phone.

"Minnie," he said, jerking the sweet hot shudder up and down, up and down.

"Oh my God...Oh my God."

"Listen, Minnie--"

"I can't believe we just did that." Her voice went crackly again.

"I know," he grunted. "That was...incredible."

"Oh no," she said. "Oh no. No, no."

Uh oh. "Baby, calm down. It's fine."

"I got to go," she whispered. "Rebel, I'm sorry. I wasn't thinking. I can't— Oh my God..."

The line went dead.

Rebel stared at the black screen of his phone in disbelief. What the fuck? What had just happened?

He looked down his long torso at the drying trails of his desire and his somehow-still-hard cock, feeling...

Completely gutted.

She fucking led me into that one. Led me by the dick. Jesus. I'm done. I'm done with that shit.

A few minutes later, Rebel emerged from the house, fully dressed, his hair dripping wet, his temper bubbling like a volcano. For some reason, Chick and Larry made themselves scarce after trying a few bites of the blackened chicken. Katie sat in the same place he'd left her, texting rapidly on the phone.

"Go watch TV or something," Rebel said, piling up the dishes.

She looked at the stack in his hand. "You don't want me to do 'em?"

"No." The girl did all the chores at Roman's house, and all the cooking. Rebel didn't have these rules.

"You alright, Uncle Reb?" She asked slowly, like he was a dangerous lunatic. "You're like...twitchy."

"I'm fine," he said gruffly.

"She blue-ball you? That lady?"

One look sent her fleeing into the house.

CHAPTER 9
VISIONS IN CHURCH

That Sunday in church, Minnie hoped to purge her mind of Rebel McCall once and for all. Heat crept up her neck steadily as the service went on, heat that had nothing to do with the broken air conditioning.

Pastor Gabriel's sermon focused on Dinah, daughter of Jacob, who betrayed the Israelites by sleeping with Canaan. That was how the pastor said it. "With Canaan". As if Dinah opened her legs to let the entire tribe fuck her.

Minnie stared ahead at the tabernacle until her vision blurred. A drop of sweat rolled down her spine. Her eyes drifted shut. She saw a tall blonde man leaning over her, felt the firm pressure of his lips, tasted tobacco and mint and orange blossom honey. She felt his hands circle her waist, his long arms wrapping around her to tug her close to his chest...working a thigh in between her legs.

"Sit on it," he murmured. "Take what you need."

She rocked her hips, thrusting her clit slowly against his hard muscle. One giant hand palmed her breast. *I'm so sensitive there...Will it hurt?*

"No," he whispered. "Play with it while I fuck you."

She gasped softly and opened her eyes, heart slamming in her ears. Ignoring her mother's look, Minnie quietly left the pew, her fan pressed tightly to her mouth.

The congregation of Faith Baptist Church was elderly, mostly female. Minnie avoided curious glances as she slipped through the side door, shutting it firmly on Pastor Gabriel's droning voice.

Outside she tucked herself against the back wall, breathing deeply of the sweet mountain wind. The choir started up. Bricks vibrated against her shoulders with each rising note of the organ. She shut her eyes, pushing her ass against the brick unconsciously.

Spring. Magnolia scent on the wind. Birds chirping. Yellow pollen dusted the parking lot and collected in the gutters. The air smelled of life, love, and new beginnings. Also of car exhaust and burning coal.

She used to like church. It was a time to let her mind wander, to meditate on the higher power that guided her life, and to come together with the community. But somewhere along the way it had become a kind of pointless ritual, an obligation meant to quiet one among Mama's long list of criticisms.

Now, she found it had become, like most of her attempts to please Mama, a thankless ordeal. Pastor Gabriel sure had a lot to say about Dinah. As if he was so innocent!

Everybody knew about that woman in Danville. And so what if Dinah went out and slept with a whole football team of Canaanites? Maybe Dinah had her reasons.

Over a week had passed since Minnie's disastrous phone call with Rebel. She still had no car, and she was going insane.

She could remember every word he said to her. Every single dirty promise. So forbidden, so thrilling... She daydreamed about his mane of golden hair, the hard muscles of his chest that shifted under his shirt. The way he dwarfed her, his big work-hardened body tucking her close... *I wouldn't let anything happen to you, Minnie.* Her attraction to him had spiraled out of control. Just like it had that morning, when he bent her over the hood of his truck and ate her pussy, tried to fuck her.

She wished...

Nevermind.

Masturbation was a sin, they said. Now she understood.

The more she denied herself the more depraved her fantasies became, until, in one knee-trembling vision, she'd pictured Rebel tying her naked to his bed and leaving her there for a whole day while he went about his business. Stopping every once in a while to stroke his dick over her, never putting it inside her...Keeping her needy and begging.

A white man tying me to his bed. There's something wrong with me.

Minnie pulled her phone out. She could hear the organ music swelling again, and the church filling with voices.

Her thumb hovered over his name. *Block, delete.* Why hadn't she done it yet? After all, she'd blown her last chance with him. No man stuck around after two rejections.

"Minnie?"

Minnie jumped, startled to find herself in company. "Mr. Simpson?"

Ben rarely left his restaurant on Sundays, his busiest day. Today he was dressed for the service in a brown suit, shiny brown shoes, with a bright blue kerchief in the front pocket. He must have slipped in through the back all quiet, and no one had recognized him.

"You mind if I join you?"

"Not at all." She moved aside so he could share the narrow patch of shade. "It's hot as blazes in there."

"Uh huh. Makes my kitchen look like a refrigerator. Reminds me why I never come to church."

Mr. Simpson was a dry-humored but very kind man. His younger brother, Junior's father, had been a junkie. Ben took in the boy and raised him very well. He was a generous character in the community, always loaning money out, never asking for it back. Even Mama didn't have a bad word to say about Ben.

Neither Ben nor Minnie were the kind of people to pointlessly ruin a good silence by talking. They looked at the road. A red truck came up at a slow crawl. Minnie's heart leapt, but it wasn't Rebel's.

"How is Junior?" she asked, shoving down her disappointment.

"Running the kitchen. I got to keep him busy or he'll get up to trouble with that girl."

The downward twist of Mr. Simpson's mouth was a warning. She fanned herself nervously, reminded of what linked her to Ben and his nephew's romantic life.

"I got to talk to you about Rebel McCall," said Ben.

Oh, please don't.

"I wanted to do it after church, but when I saw you jump outside I figured this is better. More private." Ben looked awkward but determined. Minnie knew for certain there would be no putting him off from the subject. But she had to try.

"Thank you, Mr. Simpson," she said hurriedly. The prepared answer leapt easily to her lips. "But there's nothing to talk about. Rebel and I are just friends. Not even that. We have an entanglement. I mean, we *were entangled* over some insurance issue, and he was generous enough to drive me to work for a couple days until it gets taken care of. There is absolutely nothing going on romantically with me and Rebel McCall."

She thought she had pulled the thing off, but Mr. Simpson's mouth twisted again, this time in the opposite direction. Now he was smirking. "I see," he said.

He knows! He knows everything!

Ben folded his hands behind his back. "How much do you know about the McCalls, Minnie?"

"Well, what everybody knows, I guess. They got money and land."

"What you heard about them lately?"

"Nothing. Rebel and I didn't talk much about his family. While he was riding me. While he was giving me a ride. In his truck. While he was driving me to work," she babbled. *Kill me.*

"Okay," said Ben, giving her a strange look. "Well, I've known Rebel McCall for years," said Ben Simpson. "Ever since he opened that shop on Flat Hill, he's been coming to my place. To be honest, I never had a problem with him. He's an honest brother. Of course, he ain't exactly a *brother...*"

"Yes," said Minnie faintly.

Ben rasped a hand over his stubble. "Look. I don't like Junior seeing that Katie girl. She's too fast. And she's a McCall, and we folks stay away from those people for a reason."

"Are they all that bad?" Minnie wondered.

"Let me tell you a story about a girl named Ruthie," said Ben. "When I was growing up she used to live on Plum Hill. One leg was shorter than the other, and she had a stammer, so some folks thought she was simple. But really she was a smart girl. Just like you, she loved them animals. Always saving squirrels and raccoons, keeping them flea ridden things in shoeboxes until she could let 'em go. We used to call her Zookeeper." Ben chuckled, his eyes growing distant. " Ruthie would go on across the hills looking for some cat or dog or pigeon that needed rescuing, dragging that leg behind her. But it never slowed her down. She knew them hills better than anybody. She went everywhere, that girl, and even the white folks never bothered her about it. Or so we thought. One night she didn't come home. Next morning her Mama is running up and down Plum Hill like she lost her mind, screaming if anybody seen her baby."

Minnie swallowed. She had never heard this story, but knew the ending.

"Finally Ruthie's mama went to the police. My father and some other menfolk went with her. The Sheriff – Earl Jackson was his name- just laughed in their faces. 'You want me to get off my ass for some nigger?' He said. So the men got a group together and went to look for Ruthie. Nobody believed a girl like that would just run off on her own."

"Did they find her?"

"No," Ben said. "But there was witnesses. The Burley boys were coming back from fishing, and they saw Duke McCall and his posse pick a black girl up on Red Hill. Burleys said they heard her calling out, but nothing came of it. Duke McCall is Rebel's father, Minnie."

She reached out for the reassuring warmth of the brick wall. *Does Rebel know about this?*

"My father and the men went to the spot the Burley boys said they'd seen Ruthie. They only found a bloody pair of drawers. Ruthie's mama ain't been right since."

"And nobody got punished," Minnie said, a statement of fact.

"Are you surprised?"

How could she be? It was an open secret that McCalls bribed the Sheriff to turn a blind eye to their many nefarious business schemes. Why not rape and murder?

"You know Mrs. Dimple?" Ben asked quietly.

Of course. Julette Dimple never missed a service. The old woman was about four feet tall and had sugar-white hair. Her eyes were unique and slanted, a feature once common among the Plum Hill folk. If she had a husband he was long dead but everybody called her Mrs. Dimple. The woman never exulted out loud. She just sat in place and swayed along with the music, eyes closed as if in dreamland.

For all her strangeness, nobody ever said a bad word about Julette Dimple. Now Minnie knew why.

"Ruthie's Mama?" Minnie guessed.

Ben nodded. "She never had other children."

"How terrible. I never knew..."

"Nobody likes to tell that story," Ben said. "Black folks be too proud sometimes— we bury things deep. I get it. The truth hurts. But I don't want the younger generation forgetting what we went through. There were other Ruthies, you know. There was a lot of pain back then. That's why so many left." He frowned. "Folks say your man's the spitting image of his father. You ever seen Duke McCall in person?"

Minnie shook her head.

"Pray you never do."

"Rebel is different, Ben. You said so yourself."

"Maybe not," said Ben thoughtfully. "Blood is blood." He looked Minnie in the eye. "I'll tell you what I told Junior, Miss Brown: there are some lines we don't cross in Florin. Some rules we got to follow. Don't mess with that McCall family, no matter what you do. Arm's length. No closer than that."

CHAPTER 10
GETTING SOBER FROM MINNIE

The Bear Claw, Saturday night. A Hank song playing off the crackly speakers. The smell of cigarettes and bourbon was tough as the steak on his plate. Rebel drank a dark stout while his younger brother Rain sipped lemon water and pretended to enjoy it.

Out of his three brothers, Rebel got along best with Rain. Unfortunately it seemed like these days Rain preferred bottles over brothers. One or two months clean, and then a wild bender to start it all over again; that was how the third McCall brother had been living for the past two years. Tonight marked his first sober night out in a long time. But the night was still young...plenty of time for mistakes.

"You been seen," Rain said casually. "Redhead at the bar's got a bead on you."

Rebel glanced over his shoulder. A curvy woman about the size of a pool cue cut in half was giving him the eye. The black corset she wore left little to the imagination.

Her pale belly was exposed, and a thick leather belt cinched her jeans above her snatch. Heart-shaped buckle. Cowboy boots. *Hillbilly bait.*

"You know her?" Rebel grunted. The woman hooked a thumb in her belt, and her fingers fanned over her pussy.

"Nope," said Rain.

"Maybe it's you she's looking at."

"I doubt it."

Rebel eyed the woman again. *Minnie's prettier.*

"She's all yours," he said, losing interest.

His little brother waved a hand. "I'm good. It's part of the whole detox. Celibacy, sobriety, prayer."

Rebel snorted. "You can't have sex? What the fuck kind of rehab is that?"

"Methodist," Rain replied grimly. "You really ain't biting? She's exactly your type. Bullshit."

"I didn't come out for that."

Truth was, he hadn't been able to think about another woman for weeks. Just Minnie.

They hadn't spoken since she hung up on him. Rebel's masculine embarrassment had thrown him into a brooding temper; despite his every urge, he didn't call her back. In the end he decided Minnie Brown just wasn't worth it.

It would be easier if he wasn't certain about Minnie's feelings. The girl had melted for him. He'd burned hotter than hell for her. It was real, he knew it. She knew it. She was kidding herself...

He peeled the sticker off the stout bottle. Rain's eyes looked nearly vacant as he stared at the baseball game on the bar TV. Rebel's thumbnail scraped across the sticker. He watched the short stop faceplant into third base, but he was picturing Minnie laughing as she maneuvered the stick shift. He felt her hands stroking his shoulders. Her lips between his, soft and tender. Shortbread cookies.

Like Rain with his drinking, he needed to get sober from Minnie.

He eyed the redhead again. He'd spent his twenties sleeping through hordes of women like that. Easy, cheap lays. Could he still do it? He tried to see it for the redhead. He imagined putting a pale breast in his mouth, feeling her sharp claws on his scalp.

"I thought you liked the spur-chasers," said Rain.

"It's like heroin. Just 'cause it feel good don't make it good for you."

"I get it." Rain grinned. "Katie says you're all hung up on that Black girl who dumped you."

"The fuck does it matter if she's Black?" Rebel said testily.

"'Course it matters. You and Ross should start a club."

Rebel snorted. He had the least in common with Ross, who liked tailored suits, caviar, and pretending he wasn't a hillbilly in front of his hoity-toity friends. But now it seemed the brothers had something to share after all.

Rebel wondered what Ross's woman was like.

"You heard anything about that?" Rebel asked his brother. "You talked to Ross?"

Rain shook his head, his chestnut hair falling over his gray eyes. "Talk to Ross? While I was getting my head shrunk by a preacher? I couldn't do that shit and stay sober."

"You live in Rowanville. You ain't seen him around?"

"No. And I'd sooner keep it that way. If Pa knows I know something, he'll crack my head. Ross was always his favorite, next to you."

"You can't live in fear of Pa, Rain."

Rain shook his head. "Watch me. He ain't dead yet, Rebel. Until I see him buried, I'm shitting-piss-scared of him."

"It would help if you stayed sober for longer than a month."

Rain winced.

"Look, I'm sorry." Rebel was. He had to be careful with Rain. "I'm glad you're doing better, brother. I still feel like maybe a bar ain't the best place to kick off your sobriety, but I'm glad all the same."

Rain raised an ironic eyebrow. "I can resist all temptation through the power of prayer."

"Yeah, maybe I ought to take a vow of celibacy," muttered Rebel.

"You'd be wasting a fine piece of ass. That redhead's still got her eye on you." Rain squinted. "She just blew you a kiss."

"Really?"

"Go knock one off," said Rain sagely. "Get it out of your system."

Rebel shook his head. "I ain't leaving you alone in here."

"I swear I won't move from this table. You got to trust me, Reb. Besides, I like the Dodgers. By that I mean I like watching 'em lose." Rain leaned back in the chair and turned his gaze back to the TV. "Shoo."

Rain was right. The girl was still eyeing him like a juicy steak. He finished his drink. Why not? Easy. Simple. No games, no fuss, no attachments...No pretty brown eyes.

He took his time walking over.

"Hi," the redhead said. She had a husky voice, the kind that would sound good moaning facedown in bed. Freckles covered her arms and the tops of her large breasts, and makeup covered the freckles on her face in a chalky mask.

"Aren't you just the best looking fella in here?" She purred, looking up at him with piercing blue eyes. Her pupils were pinpoints. Her drawl was thick and sweet. "It's gonna cost you to keep staring at my titties, though."

"Oh yeah?" He rumbled. "Why, when everyone else is doing it for free?"

"You're mean." She looked him up and down. "Yummy."

You're so mean...

Don't.

He hooked the redhead's belt loop with his finger.

"Let me buy you a drink."

She giggled. "Alright."

He forgot her name as soon as she told it to him. Something about her seemed familiar. Had they screwed before? No, probably not... Jesus, was she his cousin? No; Rebel wasn't good with names, but he remembered faces.

Rebel ordered another stout. Amber— or was it Amy?— pummeled back a vodka cran and tapped the glass on the bar for a refill. The bartender gave her a considering look and topped her off with more cranberry, less vodka.

"So was I right?" she asked, swinging back to Rebel. Some of the drink sloshed on the floor.

"About what?"

"Your cock," she whispered. "I'm thinking it's got to be huge. Or is your brother's bigger?" She jerked her head towards Rain, who was sitting in the booth, absorbed by the TV.

"That ain't my brother, that's my boyfriend," said Rebel.

The woman jerked back, eyes wide. "What?"

"I'm just playing."

"Aw, you asshole." She bit her lip and lowered her lashes. "I'd fuck the two of you at once if you asked me. Or you can fuck me first. You the older one, right? 'S only fair."

Rebel was amazed. "You're kind of a whore, Amy."

"It's *Amber*." She didn't seem offended at all. "And if I'm a whore, then what are you?"

"Thirsty."

Amber cupped his cock through his jeans. "Me too."

She let him go and strode out of the bar. He followed her. But as soon as they stepped into the trash-littered street Rebel's flaring arousal died.

"We can fuck right here," she panted. "You want me to suck on it first?"

"Jesus, honey, take it easy." She nearly gouged his balls with her nails.

"I don't care. I'm so sick of my fucking husband." Her mouth opened wide over his, and she nearly swallowed his tongue. She scrabbled at his back, jerking at his fly.

"Hold on. Wait."

"We can still do it. I don't fucking care," Amber slurred, jerking her corset's zipper down. Her tits spilled out, creamy and pale and enormous, with dark red nipples. "I'm pregnant anyway," she giggled. "Shh...Don't tell." She began to unzip her jeans.

"Hey!" He hissed. "You're in public, lady."

"I don't fucking care! You gonna fuck me or not?"

Jesus, what a turnoff. Rebel clamped the corset together with one hand and roughly zipped it up with the other.

"What the fuck is your problem?" she shouted, slurring.

"I think you're too drunk and I ain't drunk enough."

"Can't get it up?" she said spitefully.

"I'll call you a ride."

"Fuck off," she said. She swayed on her feet and muttered, "I need a fucking cigarette."

"Ain't you pregnant?"

"Yeah? So? Mind your business, cowboy."

A mud-splattered F-150 screeched up to the curb. *Oh shit.*

The driver leaned out of the window. Rebel tensed, but the man pointed a finger, not a gun. "Amber! Get your *ass* in here you fucking *slut!*" He roared. He had a blond goatee and wore a fishing cap.

"Go to hell, Bonky!" Amber screeched. "You can't tell me what to do!"

"Bonky" pointed a thick finger at Rebel. "Who the fuck is that? That who you been screwing behind my back? One of them dirty McCalls?"

"Hey," said Rebel.

Amber turned to Rebel with sudden glee. "Wait a minute. You're a McCall?"

"Yeah. Who's he callin' dirty?"

"Ooh, I'm gonna make his ass so jealous," Amber hissed.

"Get in the car, bitch!"

"Kiss my ass, Bonky!" Amber took Rebel's arm in a forceful grip. "Bet you didn't think I could get a McCall, huh? Well I DID! And he fucks me EVERY NIGHT!"

"You like that don't you? WHORE!"

"Fuck you!" Amber sang delightedly. "This big 'un's gonna knock your teeth in if you keep talking to me like that!"

"Now hold on a minute," Rebel said.

Bonky roared, "Oh yeah? Well I'm gonna go fuck your sister. How do you like that? She sucks dick better'n you anyway!"

Amber dropped Rebel like a live coal and turned nearly as red. "You fuckin' pig ! Go ahead! See if I care!" People were starting to come out of the bar. "And don't think I'll let you put it up my ass neither! You and me are finished!" Amber screeched.

Bonky's face crumpled. "Amber, baby, come on."

Amber faltered, but only for a moment. "You ain't never getting my cookie again," she declared. "Never!"

"Baby, don't be like that." Bonky turned off the engine.

"And I'm pregnant," Amber added in a watery voice. "So fuck you."

Bonky got out of the car, tears streaming down his face. His head barely reached Rebel's elbows. "Babygirl, Amber...You for real?"

"Yeah! And I'm keepin' it, so there!"

"Really? That's my young in there?"

"Yeah! I think." She sniffed.

"Oh my God." Bonky wiped his eyes. "We're gonna be a family...I lied, sugar. I never fucked your sister."

"You fucked Jennifer!"

"She's your half sister," Bonky soothed.

Rebel had turned to go back into the bar and order himself a very strong drink when a musical laugh from across the street caught his attention.

Nah. No way.

Fate, or God, or just an insane coincidence? Apparently someone else had decided to throw away a Saturday night in Rowanville.

Two black women got out of a silver car he didn't recognize. One of them was tall and busty, the other's head would barely touch Rebel's chest. He stared at the second woman, the sounds of Bonky and Amber fading away with the passing rumble of cars.

He went inside to talk to Rain.

•

"Look who it is," the light skinned girl hissed in a not-so-quiet voice, clamping hard on Minnie's wrist. Minnie turned halfway in her chair, and their eyes locked.

She'd dressed up for a Saturday night down the mountain. She wore some flowy, silky blue thing that would slide through his hands like smoke. Her hair was loose, curling right around her heart-shaped face. She wore a little dash of black around her eyes, and the beauty mark was still there, a tiny fairy button.

"Hi, my name is Chrissie," said the light skinned girl in a friendly voice, ignoring Minnie's deer-in-headlights look. "You must be Rebel."

Rebel frowned, recognizing the girl. "You went to Florin High, didn't you?"

"Uh huh. I was a cheerleader. Go Buffaloes." She pumped her fist, then tilted her head. "Weren't you the tight end for a year?"

"Yeah."

Rebel remembered Chrissie now. One of the more popular girls, always laughing. Minnie was her friend?

"Minnie says you didn't remember her from school," said Chrissie. "But now you know each other, don't you?" Chrissie jumped suddenly in her chair. "Ow, Minnie!" She glared at the smaller woman, who looked ready to bolt. "So anyways, what are you doing here, Rebel?"

Rain finally appeared, striding through the swinging bar doors. "Rebel, what the...Oh, hello." His eyes fell on Chrissie and Minnie. Chrissie suddenly looked like a child eyeing a piece of forbidden candy. "Oh my goodness. Is that his *brother*?" She said to Minnie in a loud whisper.

"Yes."

"Is that the one who—"

"No," said Minnie. "Shut up."

Rebel introduced his brother to the ladies.

"How come I don't know you?" Chrissie said, doing the math in her head. "I know Rebel from school, but not Rain."

"I dropped out even before Rebel did," said Rain.

"You dropped out of school? Both of you?" Minnie said,

"I got my GED," Rebel was quick to say. He was embarrassed to admit how much he struggled at completing that thing with no Katie around to read the questions out loud. Minnie probably thought he was dumb as a box of nails.

"I'll be damned," said Rain, staring at Chrissie. "You got the biggest eyes I ever seen. That color real?"

"Real as life," said Chrissie, smiling flirtatiously. She was pretty, Rebel thought, but he preferred Minnie's doll-like features to the sharp lines of Chrissie, who was probably mixed race. "Why don't you boys sit down?" Chrissie said sweetly. "Since Rebel took all that effort to come say hi."

"Let us treat you," said Rebel automatically. "Get whatever you want."

Rain fell into the seat next to Chrissie. Rebel had no choice but to take the seat next to Minnie, who began nervously folding her napkin.

"Hi," he said.

Minnie replied in a strained voice, "How are you, Rebel?"

"Better than I was ten minutes ago." He watched her. She couldn't have looked more uncomfortable if she was sitting on tacks. His fist clenched against his thigh.

Maybe he'd been wrong about her feelings for him. But nothing felt wrong about this. Just sitting next to her. Everything about her was all soft and subtle, from the brown hues of her skin, hair and eyes to the smell of her soap. His mouth went dry. *It's her I want.*

"I guess you kind of look alike," Chrissie was saying, looking between the two McCalls. "Maybe if your nose went in a little bit." She pointed at Rain. "You're younger, right?"

"By two years," said Rain. His eyes flicked over Chrissie warmly. Rebel supposed the Methodists wouldn't approve, but in fairness, a no-sex rule for rehab was the dumbest thing he ever heard. And maybe Rain could distract the friend while Rebel worked on getting Minnie to stop looking like a prisoner bound for the chair.

The waitress materialized. "What are y'all having, folks?"

"Bourbon," said Rebel, nudging Minnie's foot under the table.

Minnie gave him a sidelong look. "I'll have a gin and tonic," she told the waitress. "Thank you."

"A Margarita for me," Chrissie added.

"Sir?" the waitress prompted, turning to Rain.

"I'll have...Uh, I'll have a water," Rain said. "Thanks."

"Your glass is full," the waitress pointed out. "Do you want another one?"

"Another what? I...Um. I'm fine," he said. "I'm good."

"Okay," the waitress said. "We got a cocktail list--"

"He's fine," Rebel broke in sharply. "Thank you, Ma'am."

The waitress blushed. "Okay. Um, let me know if you need anything else." She fled.

"You're straight edge?" Chrissie said tactlessly, rounding on Rain. "How is that?"

"Blows." Rain draped an arm around Chrissie's end of the booth and said in his sleek voice, "So what are you ladies up to tonight?"

"We were just gonna grab a drink here then go to the Barnhouse," replied Chrissie. A sharp jerk under the table suggested she'd dodged another kick from Minnie.

"The Barnhouse?" Rain's eyes lit up, as they always did when music was involved. "Y'all are going *dancing*?"

"Yep. My Mama taught us the country dances. Do you boys dance?"

Rain laughed. "Yeah. Sure we can dance. Right, Rebel?"

"Stop," Rebel warned him. Dancing hadn't been on the agenda. He'd meant to get hammered, get over Minnie Brown, and spend the night at Rain's. Rain was DD, being forcibly sober. It was all supposed to go to plan. Absolutely no dancing.

"You dance?" said Minnie, turning away from her origami napkin to stare at Rebel with her big, beautiful eyes. He was halfway tempted to ignore her.

He shrugged.

"Well that's easy, then," said Chrissie, looking pleased. "You boys come with us tonight and be our partners."

"I'm with it," said Rain immediately. He was already Chrissie's slave. "What do you say, Rebel?"

"Excuse me," Minnie said, rising from the table. She picked up her purse then hurried to the bathroom.

A vein pulsed in Rebel's jaw.

Chrissie looked at him. "You gonna sit there and stew, or go after her?" she said pointedly.

"She ain't interested."

"As her best friend, I'm telling you that's bullshit."

Rebel went after her. The little minx was actually trying to slip out the back door near the bathrooms.

"Don't run off, Minnie, damn it!"

"Let go of me!"

"Why? So you can hide in there like a goddamned gopher instead of talking to me?"

He bent his head, enjoying the closeness he had forced between them, enjoying her smell and the way little shivers raced up her back. "Minnie. Come on."

"Let go of me, Rebel, or I'll scream."

He didn't let go, and she didn't scream, but she still refused to look at him. "You're driving me crazy, you know that?" He said furiously. "You kiss me, you fuck me over the phone, and that's it, we're done. But it don't feel done, Minnie. It feels like I ain't had enough of you yet, and I know you feel the same."

She covered her eyes. "Rebel, please."

"Tell me I'm lying, then. Look me in the eyes and tell me you haven't thought about it. Tell me you didn't picture what we'd be like..."

"I have..."

His hands skimmed her waist, unable to stop. "It ain't just the sex," he murmured. "We both know that."

"We can't."

"Why not?"

"You're a McCall." She swallowed. "People been telling me things, Rebel. Things I don't like."

"I ain't denying anything, Minnie."

"I'm afraid you'll hurt me."

"Darling. Baby. Look at me, alright? Why won't you look at me?"

Her eyes were blurry with tears. "I don't want to."

"You got to understand. I'd never hurt you, Minnie. I'd sooner bleed."

"How will I know you ain't like them, Rebel?"

Like his family. Minnie must have heard some hair-curling story that raised every doubt in her mind.

But how to prove himself now, beyond making promises she'd never believe?

"You can't know just yet," he said, touching her chin with his thumb. "You ain't known me long enough. But let me show you. I'll show you every day until you see it." He pulled at a loose curl. "Christ, you look so pretty tonight."

Suddenly she jerked him forward by the lapels of his shirt and, shooting to tiptoes, pressed a hot hard kiss against his lips.

He reacted instantly, cupping her against his body. The silky material of the dress felt like heaven sliding between his palms and the swell of her juicy ass. His mind went blank with pleasure. He passed over her lips with his tongue, tasting wine and cinnamon. She gasped and sank into him, her nails digging into his arms, pulling him close.

Her fingers dug through his hair and raked his scalp, driving him wild. His tongue dipped into the flowery wet heat of her mouth, and she actually whimpered and clung to him so hard he knew he'd guessed rightly; she had imagined this moment a hundred times since the last time he'd put hands on her. Just like he had.

She made a sulky noise and drew him in for another kiss. Her hands fumbled at his wrists and she clumsily put his palms over her breasts.

Rebel jerked open the bathroom stall with one hand and pushed her in. He had her back up against the door in under three seconds.

Her lips grew swollen from his harsh kisses, and his hands focused on getting under the skirt, which was actually a dress, and freeing the clasp of her bra. He undressed her under her clothes, tugging her panties off and gliding his thumbs through the moisture there.

"You were gonna find another man tonight, Minnie?" He said, not recognizing his own voice.

"I wanted you," she gasped, a small hand tunneling under his shirt to stroke his muscles. "But everybody says...I shouldn't...I can't..."

"Why do they say that, Minnie?"

She moaned an unintelligible reply. He screwed a long finger slowly inside her and she moaned, arching her back against the door.

"Lift up that dress."

She did, slowly, baring her pussy for him. Clear wetness streaked the insides of her thighs. Lying little Minnie, acting like she wasn't hotter than a pepper bush for him. He smeared her cream over the fleshy button of her clit, and she clamped down hard on her lower lip to keep from screaming.

"You're so *wet*. God."

She moaned deliciously as he added a second finger. She staggered a little, dropping her head back. "Oh my God."

She reached for his belt, her hands shaking as she undid the buckle and tore at his buttons. He crowded her against the door, fingers pumping inside her as she cupped him through his boxers.

"If you start that, darling, you got to finish it," he warned her.

"Let me do it for you," she begged. "The way you did for me. On the bluff."

"You want to suck my cock?"

She nodded. Shit. He hadn't meant for it to go this far. He didn't want Minnie kneeling on a bathroom floor. He hiked her leg over his arm and skimmed his thumb over her slit.

"Not here," he grunted, fighting every filthy urge in his brain. "We'll get a real bed."

"I can't..." She groaned as he deepened the thrusting of his fingers. "I can't...Oh my God, Rebel," she whimpered.

He fought for control. "You're gonna come real hard for me right now, and I'll give you the rest later, baby, when we got all the time in the world."

He leaned into her, letting her twist the fabric of his shirt and scream her orgasm into his shoulder. His own arousal throbbed and strained against the dry tightness of his jeans. *Sorry, bud.*

As she started to come he pushed up the dress and lowered his head, taking a thick nipple in his mouth. She gasped, her hands thrusting in his hair and digging hard against his scalp. He fucking loved when she did that. She had the best nipples, fat and dark as blackberries. Using tongue and lips and teeth, he suckled her...Using his fingers, he fucked her, delirious with his own arousal, his cock edging towards a painful but explosive release.

The bathroom door vibrated. " Y'all better not be fucking in there!" a deep voice bellowed.

Minnie gasped in horror, then pleasure as Rebel kept the rhythm of his fingers going, building faster, losing himself in her tightness, the wet splatting sounds mingling with Minnie's (now muffled) cries like a symphony as she completely fell apart.

"Don't go," he said into her mouth, keeping her close. "Tonight, Minnie. It's got to be tonight. We finish this."

"Alright," she whispered, slack and heavy-eyed. She kissed him with her soft, sweet lips.

A minute later he buttoned himself and tidied her dress. She looked even more beautiful when her neat appearance got mussed up a little, like it was now. Rebel felt a flare of wild, possessive jealousy. He pushed her up against the door again, holding her off the floor, straddling him.

"Rebel?"

"Hold still," he gritted. He hiked up her dress again with one hand, bundling it around her waist. He ground himself into her thigh slowly.

"Ohh..." Her head fell back, eyes slitted. She swallowed. "I want it," she panted softly. "I want you."

"Not now." He kissed her neck. One more thrust...One more...

"Fuck." Had to stop. Had to let go. *Don't want to.* He cursed, setting her down. She straightened her dress, then, hesitating, pushed a curl off his cheek. He took her hand, kissed it, then put it on his painfully hard cock. She squeezed him gently. Way too gently. "We should go back."

Rebel opened the door and confronted the waiter: a black man as tall as Rebel with a done-with-this-shit expression.

"Just get out," the man said tiredly.

"You got it, partner." Rebel took Minnie's hand and led her out. He could feel the waiter eyeing her. Casually Rebel pulled her close and placed his hand on her ass.

At the table, Rain and Chrissie wore identical smug expressions.

"So," said Chrissie. "How about that dancing?"

CHAPTER II
THE BARNHOUSE

"Chrissie Harper! Nobody asked you to play matchmaker!" Minnie hissed to her friend once Rebel and Rain had moved to a safe distance.

"He's looking at you like a chicken wing just missing the hot sauce," Chrissie said. "You really gonna waste a man like that?"

Minnie wanted to strangle her friend with both hands, and at the same time wrap her in a hug.

"You were still out of line," Minnie said, sipping her drink nervously and scanning the crowd for Rebel. He wasn't hard to find, standing head and shoulders above most people, but she'd lost sight of him.

"I think what you mean to say is, 'thank you so much, Chrissie, for making sure I didn't sabotage my sex friendship with a fine piece of McCall booty.'"

"It's not a *sex friendship*."

"Didn't he just eat your pussy in the bathroom?"

"Chrissie, really—"

"Hey," Rebel's deep voice cut through the music and made both women jump. Minnie wiped sweat off her forehead with the back of her hand. The Barnhouse was roasting hot, thanks to all the people packed inside the wooden frame, and the humid summer night outside.

Rebel looked edible tonight. A light sheen of sweat on his collarbone and cheeks, his white T laying flat on his broad, hard stomach. It drew attention to his crazy bicep muscles. Rebel had to be one of the strongest men in the room right now. Minnie couldn't stop staring at him as he crossed the straw-strewn floor, not-so-subtly keeping tabs on Rain.

The younger McCall brother was being good. Rain talked to musicians and friends and avoided the bar. Some minutes later he came up to the little group, his eyes shining, but clear and sober.

"There's a competition tonight," he said. "Y'all in?"

They were.

"It's a couple's dance," said Rain helpfully.

The MC's voice cut over the music. "Dance contest in fifteen minutes, folks! Make sure you got your numbers!"

Chrissie cringed. "We have to wear *numbers*?"

Excitement went through her in a shiver. The Barnhouse air pressed around her like thousands of little shoving hands, and Rebel was looking so sexy in his white T-shirt and jeans, catching the eyes of every woman in the building. Minnie even saw some hussies sidling up to him, and watched with growing embarrassment and jealousy, but Rebel always put them off and returned to her side. *He likes me.* His eyes feasted on her when he thought she wasn't looking. It was so forbidden to feel a man's stare sliding up her back, to know she would be going home with him tonight. She felt electric. The music was loud and the McCall brothers were paying for everything. When was the last time she'd done something like this? Had she ever done something like this?

Rebel had been staring into the crowd. Suddenly his eyes narrowed. "Oh hell naw," he said, and pushed his way into the throng after Rain. He reappeared a minute later, looking grim and annoyed.

"What is it?"

"See that man over there? Red hat? That's one of Rain's dealers."

"Oh!" Minnie understood. The thin-faced man Rebel had indicated made swift tracks for the door, looking back over his shoulder at Rebel every few feet as if the tall McCall would pounce across the room at him.

"That's right, skedaddle," Rebel muttered. "Rain ain't seen him yet. He's clean tonight, and gonna stay that way." He shook his head. "Believe it or not, that waste of air is one of our cousins."

"How many cousins do you have?"

"Many."

"Will he tell someone he saw us?"

"I got the jump on him. He never noticed you, I think."

Minnie swallowed. "Will we always have to hide?"

Rebel looked down at her. "No, darling. Not for long. I just got to get a few things straight with some people first." He pulled her close. "Don't worry, alright?"

Chrissie didn't hear this exchange, being engaged in conversation with a woman in shiny pink cowboy boots. Rebel's eyes flickered down to Minnie, bright and teasing. "Nervous for the contest? "

"Just don't make us lose, white boy," she taunted. "I hope you got some rhythm in them boots."

Very soon the DJ gave a last call for dancers. It was a kind of square dance she didn't know very well, but they allowed a warmup. Instead of practicing with Rebel, Minnie found herself being swept off by Rain while Chrissie and Rebel partnered up in the other direction.

Rebel's brother was slimmer, shorter. He whirled Minnie across the floor with surprising grace. "So you like him, then?" He said in her ear.

She looked up into a sweeter, softer version of Rebel's face. Minnie could see what Chrissie saw in him. The boy looked like DiCaprio. "I do," she said shyly.

They whirled around some more, Rain stepping light and quick in his scuffed cowboy boots. But then he pulled her off to the edge of the dancers, halting. "Just be careful about it," he said.

"What do you mean?"

"You'll want to keep it a secret in Florin."

"I know that," Minnie said. "I know your family won't approve. Neither would mine."

Rain nodded, but his eyes were disturbed. "My family... You just don't want to cross 'em. I hope Rebel knows what he's doing. You seem like a sweet girl."

"Find your partners, folks!"

Rebel appeared and Rain shut up quickly and went to find Chrissie.

The dancers faced each other, and the strange conversation with Rain left Minnie's mind. She had eyes only for Rebel. *Does he really know how to dance?* She couldn't imagine his big self spinning on the floor like some kind of redneck Channing Tatum. *Don't laugh.* Next to them, Rain was making Chrissie giggle hopelessly into his shoulder.

The music changed, a loose and strummy Brace Sheland song, and people started clapping along. It was just like church, being under the roof of an old barn catching a rhythm with a whole bunch of people. The Barn House was a honky-tonk that had once attracted a certain kind of crowd, but new ownership and changing times removed the possibility that a black patron would get dragged outside and roughed up just for being there.

Now, people from the farming towns nearby, black and white, mingled on the straw-strewn floor. It was an uneasy truce. Mostly, black folks only came to this place to have a party that wouldn't get shut down in thirty minutes.

"Partners!" called the DJ again, and then it began, and a white T-shirt suddenly filled her vision and large male hands went right to her waist in a confident grip that made her look up in surprise.

Later, she would try to recall every detail of it in her mind, but all she could remember was Rebel's green eyes squinting with laughter, looking down at her. As the music reeled and spun around them, they spun inside it, even faster, until her skirt became a blue blur and her calves burned. He was a capable and creative dancer, and he had rhythm. Oh yes, he did.

The music raced to its climax, and as it descended Rebel drew Minnie against his broad chest, her cheek separated from his heart by thin layers of cotton and skin and muscle. The heat of his body and the slight dampness of his T-shirt were intoxicating. When she looked up, breathing hard, she found him looking down at her with the same breathless wonder she felt. Then his thick golden eyelashes shuttered his gaze. Sweat shimmered on his skin. She pressed her soft body against his unbending hardness, reveling in the heat they made together.

It became one of those nights that somehow never ended and yet ended too soon. A stone sober Rain drove them up the mountain in Rebel's truck. Chrissie, who was somehow still sober, sat up front. A slow country tune crackled on the radio and Rain sang along. The third McCall brother had an incredible voice, powerful and loud, and his impression of *Always on My Mind* made them all laugh. Minnie's legs were over Rebel's knees. His scarred palm laid across her thighs, stroking up and down. She leaned back against his chest, watching the glow of passing headlights scroll up the pale skin on his arms, turning the golden hair a frosty blue and highlighting, in shadows, the masculine structure of his anatomy. Leaning against the door, his long legs stretched out on the seat, he took up most of the space, and she fit just right against him. He might have been asleep, but the back of his thumb slowly stroked up her leg, a reminder that the night wasn't over yet.

SOMETHING KNOCKED AGAINST THE WALL IN A SLOW, THUMPING rhythm. Minnie's senses brought things to her one at a time: a King-sized plush mattress...white cotton sheets...Rebel's tongue in her mouth...salty sweet...hard thighs pinning her hips to the bed...A hot hand cupping her sex over her dress, squeezing softly.

Dreaming again, she thought sadly. But she wasn't dreaming. No, this was real. Her eyes widened. Rebel McCall was dry-fucking her into his bed, and her drunk ass had blacked out underneath him.

"Mmm...Oh my God," she whimpered as he stroked the inside of her lips, sucked them, while his enormous hands slid up her body to squeeze and plump her breasts. Coming back to life, Minnie kissed him back with a feverish hunger, her arms wrapped around his neck, her knees clenched tight around his pelvis.

"I'm dead gone on you," he murmured. "I'm gone, I'm gone...I got to touch you. Let me touch you..."

Her dress rode up to her waist, exposing her panties to the rough stitching on his jeans. She rolled her hips, rocking her clothed clit against his hardness, sending veins of hot sweet pleasure coursing through her body.

He dragged down the strap of her dress and bra at the same time. He kissed the side of her breasts , grabbed one fully in his enormous hand, plumping it. He bent his head. Oh God...Her nipple thickened in his mouth, his stubble chafed against her smooth skin. She arched off the sheets.

Rebel wrenched at the buttons on his Wranglers. "Take your panties off. It's time."

Oh my God. Black spots danced in her eyes. No! She had to stay awake. *I'm so drunk.*

He pulled away suddenly, and his voice came from far away. "Woah."

"I'm alright," she assured him, taking care not to slur the words.

He drew up the strap of her dress. "You got a cup too full, darling."

"I ain't drunk. I swear."

"You sound more country when you're drunk."

Rebel kissed her again, balancing his weight on his arms so his body made a protective cradle around her. He smelled incredible. Her body cried out, wanting more of him, wanting him inside her. "We'll stop. You feel the room spinning?" He murmured.

Instead of replying, she locked her legs around his waist and stroked his big muscled arms. *There. See? Just hold on to Rebel and you won't pass out!*

"It's alright," he rumbled. He detached her gently from his neck, then heaved himself off the bed. "Give me a minute." With a sigh he ducked into a rectangle of light that must have been the door to the bathroom.

I don't know where the hell I am.

You're in Rebel's bedroom, bitch.

Oh my God. YES!!!

Get it together!

Sex! Sex! I want to have sex with him!

You don't have a condom.

So? I'm gonna have SEX with him!

You're too damn drunk!!!

Shut up, brain!

She shimmied out of her dress, tossing the silky fabric down the bed. She flung away her bra. Now she only wore her panties.

Rebel came out of the bathroom, shirtless, hair dripping, wiping his face with a towel. He froze. Giggling, Minnie cupped her breasts.

"You think it's funny?" he said softly.

"Yeah," she taunted. He liked when she sassed him back, and just as she predicted his eyes went small.

"You think it's funny?" he repeated.

She pinched her nipples so hard her eyes watered, and nodded.

He swallowed. "You're drunk," he said, but she could see the outline of his hard dick straining through his jeans. "Fuck. Minnie, we can't."

"You're drunk too."

"I can still walk," he said. "I ain't sauced."

"You could do anything you wanted to me right now," Minnie whispered.

"Really?" he said quietly. He moved towards the bed. "That's nice."

"Anything."

"So if I told you to suck my cock, you'd do it?"

Her hand slid under her panties and found a flood. "Yeah," she whimpered.

He sat on the edge of the bed and leaned over her. He was so enormous he blocked out all the light.

"If I told you to swallow every drop of my nut, you'd do it?" he murmured. "If I told you, starting right now, you had to learn how to deepthroat a ten inch cock, you're telling me, Minnie, you'd get on your knees and open your mouth and let me fuck it long as I wanted?"

"Rebel," she choked, stroking herself. "Baby..."

"Yeah?" he said, fisting the sheets next to her head. "You can come now, honey, but the next one is for me."

Minnie buried a hand in his thick yellow curls, desperate to feel more of him. She dragged his head down, but he resisted, his lips hovering just an inch from hers. But his rugged face was rigid with lust. This would be the last time he let her escape him.

Throwing back her head, Minnie came in a sticky torrent all over the clean cotton sheets. For a starry-bright moment, the orgasm took her out of reach of the alcohol's grasp. It was different from other times she'd made herself come to Rebel McCall in the lonely darkness of her room, since now Rebel hovered over her, his physical presence making great contributions to the fantasies her drunk brain was weaving. But it still wasn't close to the pleasure she'd feel if Rebel put his hands on her for real, hands that looked strong enough to bend iron but were gentle on her skin.

Fingers slick, pussy pulsing, Minnie gasped and fell back on the sheets. "Good girl," Rebel murmured. He took her wrist and raised her wet fingers to his mouth, tracing them over his lips. He kissed the inside of her wrists and carefully set her hand back down on her stomach.

"I just want it so bad," she whispered, tears in her eyes.

"Me too," he said. "But I want you to remember it. I can't fuck you drunk."

"The night's over. I don't want it to be."

"It ain't over until you leave my bed." He kissed her while her eyes drifted shut. In minutes Minnie was asleep.

CHAPTER 12
THE LOCKED DOOR

"Minnie?" Rebel murmured, waving a hand over the young woman's eyes. But she was out cold, her expression soft, her features looking so exotic and beautiful, from her slanted eyes to the lush unbelievable fullness of her lips, to her flawless brown skin. Her hair was loose and puffy around her face, each curl tempting his finger to wrap around it and tug hard just to watch it spring back again. And her body...Christ Almighty. He stared at the deep curves of her hips until his cock stiffened again. His balls ached, needing release. It seemed like he'd had a month-long case of blue balls.

Rebel turned into his bathroom, cranked the dial on the shower. Under the steaming water he was able to orgasm, but it felt nothing like it would if he was inside his woman. In a blink the water spraying across his belly and thighs washed his seed away. He took deep, heavy breaths. In his mind's eye he saw Minnie under him, begging him for a release, her legs wrapped around his waist, heels digging into his back, taking his dick deep inside her. He leaned against the hot tiles, idly stroking and cupping his sore balls, his whiskey-soaked brain arguing with itself in a low, lazy murmur.

She's asleep in your bed. She was all but gonna let you rape her. She got no sense at all? She do this stuff with other guys? Naw... She ain't the type. She's all but a damned virgin. You got no business messing around with her...Sick bastard...You like that she's all innocent... Don't hurt that she looks like a fucking queen...

What if he finds out?

The thought had been waiting to pounce on him all night. Rebel turned the water to glacier-cold. After a minute, teeth clenched, he reached for the soap.

He got out feeling clear-headed, but uneasy. Still dripping, he walked past the sleeping Minnie, stopping to admire how cute she looked. How vulnerable. *You can do anything you want to me.* He flicked a blanket over her, as much to give her warmth as to hide her body from him. He had to think. Not with his dick, but with his brain, if that was even possible.

He opened the sliding door to his porch and stepped into the darkness.

It was three in the morning. A coyote howled somewhere on the mountain, and Rebel was tempted to howl back, one wild thing to another.

That woman...Every little thing about her just did it for him.

The old fear rose up in Rebel swiftly. Women could be dangerous. He knew that. They could wreck a man's whole life. He thought of the woman he'd nearly fucked just before he saw Minnie and felt sick, angry at himself for even taking it that far. He was tempted to tell Minnie about her, but how would she react? He'd known right away that Amber wasn't the woman he wanted.

The powerful attraction he felt towards the woman in his bed couldn't be explained. He wanted to own her, to possess her, to claim her and leave his seed deep inside her.

He looked over his shoulder at the dark brown shape tangled in his sheets, backlit by the nightlight. A protective male instinct swelled inside him. He walked back to the bed, lowering himself next to Minnie.

I want her. I got to have her. I'll kill to have her.

He hauled her into his arms, cupping her sex and breasts, and fell asleep.

A NAP OF GOLDEN HAIR TICKLED HER NOSE. SHE WAS SLEEPING on Rebel's chest. "Where are we?" she mumbled.

He looked at her through gold-tipped lashes. "My place."

"Where's Chrissie?"

"With my brother down the hall. They're still going at it."

"Oh my Lord." She blushed. "Did we—?"

"No, sadly." He swatted her ass. "Get off me real quick. You want water?"

"Oh...you don't have to..." But he was already out of the room. He came back with water and aspirin. After she

179

drank them down he climbed in bed with her. They stretched out side by side. Rebel ran his knuckles up the incline of her waist. "It's four in the morning."

"Mm," Minnie murmured sleepily.

Her smooth legs tangled with his hairy ones under the sheets. Birdsong filtered in through the screen windows. Rebel's house smelled incredible, like a woodsy-scented candle was burning in every room. She smiled and snuggled closer to him. Oh, he smelled so good. So beautiful and big and warm...*Mine.*

"Rebel."

"Yeah?"

"You really been thinking about me like that?"

"Of course. You don't believe it?"

"I've been thinking about you, too."

"Thought I'd scared you off."

"I'm sorry." She paused. "I was afraid. People tell me all this stuff about the McCalls, I start to believe it."

"A lot of what you hear is true."

She swallowed hard. "I was hoping you'd say the opposite."

"I'm sorry."

"How much do you know?"

"Some of it, I was there for."

"Rebel..."

"That's why I left."

"Is there any leaving a family like that?"

"Not really," he admitted, voice low. "I come from violent blood." His arm cinched around her. "I wouldn't let anything happen to you. I'd protect you from them. Not all of them would approve of this, right?"

"I see."

"I can't lie, some might try to make trouble for us. For you. But Minnie, I want to get to know you... I know it's selfish but how can I help it? You've got my heart in your hands, you know."

"You'd protect me?"

He nodded.

She snuggled closer. "Tell me something about yourself."

"I'm left-handed."

"I figured that one out."

"You never seen me write."

"You drive and pick up drinks with your left hand. Can you write, Rebel?"

"No." He sounded embarrassed. "I just never cottoned to it. Reading— it's all mixed up when I look at it. I can do figures and write my name, but that's about it."

"You're probably dyslexic."

"Katie says that."

Another hesitation from Minnie. He sensed the unspoken question.

"Go on, ask it." He said quietly.

"Well...The girl really looks like you, Rebel. She doesn't look like Roman," said Minnie carefully.

"Yes," Rebel admitted bluntly. "I might be her father."

Minnie felt the breath leave her lungs. "You slept with your brother's girlfriend?"

He nodded, eyes vacant. "It was years ago, and only once, but I did it. Probably the worst thing I ever did to Roman. I was just trying to screw him over. I wasn't thinking."

"How old were you?"

"Seventeen. Roman was nineteen. But we never knew about Katie until a few years ago, when her mama passed. Katie came out from Tulsa to live here."

"Why didn't you claim Katie?"

"Roman was over the moon about her at first. And Eileen claimed she was his, not mine." Rebel shrugged. "She'd wrote a letter. 'Course, Roman knew I'd slept with Eileen around then. But he was so damned happy about Katie... He asked me not to look into it. He wanted Katie so bad. And I didn't mind sharing her— I mean, she belonged to both of us. That's how I saw it."

"Didn't people notice you looked alike?"

"Not right away."

"So why did you do it with Katie's mother?"

Rebel looped his long arm around her naked waist. His callused thumb caressed the edge of her breast. "Years back, I used to run with a fella named Scudder lived down the mountain. That man taught me everything I know about engines. He looked after me, just this angry crazy kid. Treated me like a human being.

We used to talk about going into business, opening up our own shop. 'Course I couldn't wait to get out of Pa's house. I was always running off, which pissed off Duke bad. We were always fighting, and sometimes those fights got...bad. Scuds offered to hide me out at his place until I turned eighteen. I went and opened my trap to Roman about it. Big mistake."

"He told your father?"

Rebel nodded. "Yeah, he ratted on me. Pa never liked Scuds. And he didn't like me leaving the family. He's used to everybody doing what he says. Being scared of him."

And he's a murderer.

"He jumped me while I was sleeping. He told me he'd run Scuds off the mountain. I'd never see him again."

"Oh my God, Rebel."

"I got up and fought. I went at Pa like I was gonna kill him. And I really meant to, but he was so strong back then, and I weren't grown like I am now." Rebel shook his head. "Ross got involved—we shared a room— and then Roman came in. Shit, we all just started going at each other. We tore up the goddamned house, us four big boys and Pa. It was Rain who stopped it. He went into Pa's room and fired the old man's gun. It startled Pa away from me. Once the bastard let me loose, I ran. I ran all the way down the mountain with not a stitch on me. Blood in my eyes, my hands all tore up, buck ass naked...and the first person I see is Eileen."

"Katie's mother?"

Rebel nodded. "She picked me up and tended to me, took me to her cousin's trailer. We got drunk. I slept with her a couple times. I just wanted to hurt Roman. He'd betrayed me. So I got even by getting his girl."

"Did he fight you when he found out?"

"No." Rebel's voice went lower still. "He just cried."

"And Eileen..."

"She skipped town after Roman confronted her. Ghosted. Eleven years later, Katie turns up at Roman's door. State says Eileen is dead, and she put Roman on the birth certificate so he's Katie's Pa, and Eileen had written a note basically saying the same."

"Were you disappointed she wasn't yours?"

Rebel shifted uneasily. "Do you really want to hear this?"

Minnie nodded.

"I got a DNA test done, but I never opened it. I'm scared. Like if she's mine, it will make Roman hate me forever. But if she ain't, then I feel like I'll have lost her in some way. Maybe it's better not knowing."

"You love her very much, Rebel. I'm sure it's like having two fathers for her."

"I ain't the best at it. I'm too soft on her."

"She probably doesn't see it that way," Minnie grinned.

"No, probably not. What about you, darling? You want any children?"

"Mmm. Of course. Family is...the most important thing."

"I agree," he murmured.

Minnie shivered as his thumb touched her nipple. "Maybe that's why I chose to work with animals. They love unconditionally. I never had that love from my parents."

"Neither did I," said Rebel. "It's a bitch, ain't it?"

Minnie made a dark confession. "I'm scared if I ever had children, maybe I couldn't love them."

"You're kidding."

She nibbled her lower lip. "I never told anybody that."

"I think you'd be a great mother, Minnie."

"I didn't have the best example, I'm afraid." She smiled sadly. "I'm afraid I won't even have the chance to have children. Working all the time like I do." She rubbed her thumb against Rebel's gold-furred abs.

His eyes slowly heated as he stared at her. "If you were my woman, I'd work my fingers to the bone for you."

"That sounds nice," she whispered.

"Be my woman, then."

Her head swam. His eyes were green, somber.

"Okay," she said.

A fist hammered on the door.

"Rebel, I got your phone. Katie's calling you," came Rain's sleepy voice through the door.

Rebel pulled Minnie against him and kissed her neck. His cock thickened against her thigh. "Fuck," he muttered. "I got to take this."

"Mmm..." She stroked his shaft through his boxers. *It's huge.*

"I'm glad you're in my bed." He kissed her lips. "Be back in one minute." He adjusted his erection before he wrenched open the door. Rain whistled suggestively while Minnie scrambled to cover herself with the bedsheet. Rebel cuffed his brother on the head, took the phone, and shut the door.

"Katie? What's going-- Woah. Woah. Where are you?"

His tone brought Minnie wide awake, and he wasn't gone very long. When he came back his demeanor had changed completely. He looked grim and wide awake.

"What happened?" Minnie exclaimed, rubbing sleep from her eyes.

"I got to leave," he said shortly. He began pulling on clothes before she could even say a word. She had never seen Rebel rush over anything, but he was practically sprinting around the room, hunting for his boots and keys and hat before Minnie had left the bed. "Get dressed, I'll take you home," he said brusquely.

"Is everything okay with Katie?"

"I don't know," he said. "Could barely get a word out of her." Expressionless, he opened the top drawer and took out...a *gun*. Her eyes nearly popped out of her head. Rebel casually took out a box from the drawer, removed five real life bullets, then dropped them in his Wrangler pockets. The gun he stuffed in his waistband.

"What's happening?" said Minnie, frightened.

"It's alright. Can you get dressed?"

The edge to his voice unmistakable, Minnie got up and self-consciously fumbled on the floor for her dress, shoes...Shoot, what else had she been carrying last night?

"Chrissie!" she exclaimed, remembering.

"Rain's gonna drive her down the mountain later," said Rebel, as if it had all been decided. He recovered Minnie's dress and shoes from somewhere on the floor and handed them to her.

In the bathroom, Minnie pulled on her dress and swished water in her mouth, avoiding her reflection. This hard-eyed Rebel was a stranger to her. Her heart pounded. What had happened to Katie? Was Junior involved?

Rebel handed Minnie her purse as she left the bathroom.

"I want to talk to Chrissie," she insisted.

"Alright. Hurry."

She found the guest room easily. Chrissie and Rain were both sprawled out on the Queen bed, completely nude. Minnie nearly tripped over an open box of condoms. The room smelled of sex and Chrissie's perfume. She gently shook her friend's arm.

"Chris! Wake up."

A green eye cracked open. "Mmph? Oh, Minnie. Hey girl," Chrissie croaked.

"Just making sure you're alive."

Chrissie sighed. "I don't know. That white boy's got a horse dick. I think my pussy is broken."

"Ha," said Rain, muffled by the pillows. Thankfully he was lying facedown. Minnie didn't need to see a horse dick at this particular moment. Rain's curly dark hair reminded Minnie of Rebel's unruly mane. One of his broad hands snaked down and groped Chrissie's ass. Yep, that was Rebel too.

"She's good, honey. I'll take care of her," the younger McCall brother mumbled to Minnie. "Now get on out before Rebel shits himself."

"Do you know what happened?"

"Katie on her bullshit again. Spare me. Girl's a brat. She got Rebel...little finger." He fell asleep.

Minnie turned back to Chrissie, tugging one of her curls to keep her awake. "How are you getting home?"

"Big boy right here is taking me. Go on, baby." Chrissie waved her towards the door, yawning like a well-satisfied lioness. "I'll text you when I can move again."

Minnie returned to Rebel, who was all but pacing the room.

"You done?" he demanded.

"Yes."

"Good. We got to go."

They left at once through the veranda connected to Rebel's bedroom, down a flight of wooden stairs that met a path to the driveway where his truck was parked. It was freezing cold. Rebel said nothing more to her, but he did give her a blanket to put over her legs. Her thin dress offered no protection against the icy mountain air.

Rebel jerked the car into gear and whipped his foot off the clutch, reversing down the entire driveway rapidly. Then back again into first, and they tore out of the gap onto the main road, flying down the mountain.

"Who are you gonna shoot with that gun?"

"Not sure yet."

Minnie pressed her lips together.

"Sorry," he said gruffly. "I'm just worried about Katie."

"What did she say?"

"I couldn't really tell. She was crying a lot." Rebel's hands gripped the wheel hard.

"Shouldn't you call the police?"

"Who, Deputy Daniel?"

She saw his point. Minnie touched his knee. "Just be careful."

He shook his head. "I'm sorry. This isn't how I wanted the morning to go. Can we do this again?"

"Of course. Just don't shoot anyone."

He made no promises.

They reached Minnie's holler in record speed. Rebel idled at the bottom of Grace Hill.

"You don't mind walking up?" he asked, impatient to be gone. "I'd drop you at the top but--"

"No, it's fine. You're in a hurry, and it's not far at all."

The corners of his mouth turned down. "I'm sorry, Minnie. I just got to take care of this. I'll make it up to you."

"You can make it up to me by not going to jail."

He didn't laugh at the joke; his eyes were straying back to the road already. "I just got to make sure she's okay."

Minnie nodded. Rebel's priority was his niece; she understood that. She clumsily gathered her things and slid out of the truck.

She hadn't gone ten feet up the hill when Rebel's voice rang out suddenly. "Minnie?"

She turned. Had she forgotten something?

Rebel frowned, his eyes shifting from her to the top of the road, invisible through the heavy white mist. "I'll walk you up," he said decidedly, unbuckling his seatbelt.

"No need," she assured him. There really wasn't; Grace Hill was a very safe neighborhood. "It's alright. You better look for your niece."

He hesitated, torn. Then he nodded. "Alright. See you soon."

She blew him a kiss, which put some light back in his eyes. He tipped his hat to her and she waved. The truck rumbled off towards the main road, vanishing back into the gloom.

EVEN MRS. MABEL WASN'T AWAKE SO EARLY, BUT AN unfamiliar truck was outside her house. *Maybe her sneaky link,* thought Minnie, smiling to herself.

Birds chattered in the trees. A sweetgrass-scented breeze caressed her face. She planned to take a long shower, then get to the clinic and tackle the mile-long to-do list. Yawning, Minnie opened her gate and walked up the path. A rabbit darted away from her into an iris bush. She liked her house. She liked her yard. It was quiet and tidy. Pretty. The cherry tree had bloomed last night, and she plucked a sprig of blossoms before she went to the door.

A gust of wind blew round her legs as she fished in her purse for her house keys. *Cold...*Would summer come soon? She hoped so...

The door creaked open. Minnie froze.

I locked it, she thought. *I always lock it.*

But the lock hung off the door, broken.

Call the police.

She never made it to her purse in time, but it would have been a wasted effort, since her phone was sitting in between the cushions of Rebel's passenger seat.

Her door opened from the inside. And then the barrel of a pistol appeared, pointing right between her breasts. A man so tall his features disappeared in the darkness of her doorway leaned down into the light. A scream locked in Minnie's throat.

"Hush," said the man, taking another step.

The hair at this man's temples was white as snow, brushed back to a thick knot behind his head. He wore a dark flannel shirt and worn jeans. Like every man over fifty. She must memorize everything. Everything that happened from this moment was evidence.

But she knew who the man was. No evidence in the world would help her.

"Miss Brown," said Duke McCall, pushing the pistol into her breasts. "Nice to finally meet you."

"I- I-"

"Let's talk," said McCall. His eyes were horribly like Rebel's, the same shape and color exactly. Except colder. Crazed. "Get in here."

"I d-don't want any t-trouble."

"Me neither," said Duke McCall, taking another step and putting an arm around her shoulder. "So why don't you just come on inside. Double-quick, girl. I don't have the time."

"No!" She tried to step back, but he moved faster than she ever would have expected. He jerked her by the arm, impossibly strong, and sent her sprawling through her own doorway. He shut the door firmly, sealing them inside her trailer.

CHAPTER 13
KATIE'S TROUBLES

"Just calm down and tell me what happened," said Rebel for the dozenth time. "Start from the beginning."

"I already told you!"

"You got to take a deep breath and calm down for me, alright?"

"That nasty man said I can never see Junior again."

"Alright, alright."

"I'm heartbroken!"

Good grief. Rebel pulled into Doobie's Gas, the only place open at this ungodly hour, and bought Katie an Italian Ice. She ate it in between sniffles as he turned the truck back towards Flat Hill.

"Look," Rebel explained, "Junior's just a kid. Boys at that age go through a lot. He's probably just confused."

"He ain't confused!" Katie snapped. "All the black folks in Florin are scared of McCalls. That's why Junior can't see me no more! *He* didn't want to break up with me, it was his uncle made him. Because of Grandpa, and Daddy, and you! It's not fair! I wish I was never part of this family." She added, "I wish I was Black!"

Rebel forced back a laugh with difficulty. "Come on, Katie. And anyway, how can you break up with a *friend*?"

"We were dating, Uncle Reb."

"So you been lying to me this whole time, Katie?"

"So what, I stretched the truth—"

"Otherwise known as lying."

"You'd only tell me to quit him if I told you the truth!" Katie snapped.

"For damn good reason!" Rebel angrily replied. He was annoyed with Katie for making him think she'd been on the verge of death, making him drive all the way out here with his gun, for nothing. He was starting to notice a pattern with his niece, and it was a pattern he didn't like. He tried to see the bright-eyed little girl who had showed up on Roman's doorstep those years ago, but she was gone. He wasn't sure he knew this girl at all.

Katie slouched in the passenger's seat. "I reckon if you hadn't run around town with that whore so much, nobody would even care about me and Junior!"

Rebel's ears went pink. He pulled the car over at the first opportunity and killed the engine. "Outside. Right now."

They climbed out of the truck. Katie looked pale, realizing she'd crossed a line.

Rebel hunted for his cigarettes, remembered they were at the house, because he was quitting, and cursed.

"Let's get a few things straight," Rebel said, turning to his wide-eyed niece. "Don't ever in your life use that word about a woman who ain't done you nothing. You get me? Minnie is not a part of this discussion. From now on you put respect on her name when you talk about her. You got that?"

Katie bit her lip and looked away.

"I drove hell-for-leather out here to get you, thinking you were in real danger. For fuck's sake, Katie! I thought you'd been raped! You were screaming!"

"I was upset!"

"No, you pitched a fit to rush me out the door. You know damn well what you were doing."

"How can you see that woman but I can't see Junior? It ain't fair!" Katie burst out.

"I can protect Minnie. You can't protect that boy from nothing. And if you're running around lying to everybody about where you're at, and what you're doing, then you can't handle the responsibility of a relationship." As the words left his mouth, Rebel saw the irony of them straightaway. He was a hypocrite.

"You're running around and lying about *her*!" Katie threw in his face. "I'm not a kid anymore, Uncle Reb! I'm grown too."

"So what happened last night? Tell the truth."

"We weren't even doing anything. We fell asleep...then this morning, his uncle caught us and got real mad. So Junior broke up with me, and then I ran down the hill and called you."

Rebel suspected there was more to the story. He'd get the truth from Ben, if the old man could stand to talk to him. What the hell had Katie been doing in Junior's room? He could only guess. Ben must have been furious— and scared. Ben didn't want the McCalls to find out about Katie's liaisons with Junior. Rebel was convinced if they never took it past a friendship the kids would be alright, but he saw now he'd been deluding himself.

You promised Ben it wouldn't get this far. While you were running off getting drunk and dancing with Minnie, Katie needed you.

Rebel rubbed his temples. "I dropped you at Emily's. How did you get to Junior's house?"

"Walked," she muttered.

"That's like seven miles, Katie."

"I know." Her cheeks were blotchy from crying. "His uncle is so mean!"

"Ben's doing what he thinks is right for Junior. I know it's hard to understand, darling. When you're older--"

He bit his tongue. He'd hated hearing that shit when he was Katie's age. But what to say? He stared down at his sniffling niece, feeling out of his depth. She was right. It didn't make sense why she couldn't keep seeing Junior if he was seeing Minnie. But that meant it would fall to him to keep his family off their backs. Rebel saw the bitter war ahead of him, and felt very tired.

But he didn't show it. He put his arm round Katie's shoulder and kissed the top of her fluffy blonde head. "It's gonna be alright," he said gruffly. "But don't scare me like that again."

She let him embrace her, but her voice grew dull. "I'm tired of this stupid town. It's the same thing every day. Nothin' changes and everybody's all hung up on what don't matter at all. I wish I could just go back to Tulsa."

At Katie's age he had wanted the same thing. Only the excuse to run, for as long as he could, as far as the wind would carry him.

But he'd stayed in Florin. Off the mountain, a barely-literate grease monkey didn't get doors opened for him just because he was a McCall.

For Katie, he wanted different. She could leave. She ought to go to college and make something of herself. Minnie had studied nearly a decade to become a Vet. Maybe Katie could do the same: keep her nose to the books and out of boys and drama.

Too late, though. Rebel looked down at his niece's unhappy face and an ugly thought struck him. Katie didn't care about school. She didn't care about studying. She never had. Being raised in Eileen's chaos left Katie with no ambition. Not the right kind of ambition, least-ways. Katie liked her thrills. All she did was run around with her friends, sneak into cars with boys. Lie.

Bad cop Roman, Good cop Rebel. Helping her sneak around behind Roman's back with her "friends". Swallowing every duck tale she told him. Making up a few of his own to cover her tracks. Whatever Katie wanted, he got it for her. Rebel's gut twisted. Roman's accusations were right: Rebel had spoiled her. To prove some stupid point to Roman?

Katie hadn't needed an enabler. She hadn't needed a friend. She needed a father.

He hugged her tighter.

"It's alright, darling. You'll be fine."

"I'm just so sad."

"I know."

"We were in love, Uncle Reb."

Rebel sighed. "I'll talk to Ben," he said. "Maybe it will help, some."

Katie looked up at him, eyes shining. "Really?"

"Yeah. But you got to promise me you'll focus on school."

"I will," she said, lying prettily, like Eileen used to.

"I think your phone's ringing, Uncle Reb."

The unfamiliar electronic chime came from his truck. He found the device buried in the passenger's seat and realized it was Minnie's. She must have forgotten it. Chrissie's name flashed across the screen.

"Hi. I think Minnie left her phone in my truck."

"Rebel." Chrissie's voice was clear as a bell. "Rebel, is Minnie still with you?"

"I just dropped her off twenty minutes ago."

"I just- I just had a feeling." Chrissie sounded panicked. "A really bad feeling."

"Yeah, a hangover?"

"Minnie and I have been friends a long time, and spirit's telling me she's in danger. Spirit don't lie, Rebel!"

At that point Rain took the phone from her. "Rebel. Is Katie okay?"

"She's dandy. What's the matter with you two?" Rebel demanded, uneasy.

"Um." Rain lowered his voice. "She's going crazy, Reb. She says its some kind of psychic thing."

"It's not a 'psychic thing'!" Rebel heard Chrissie snap. "It's real!"

"Tell your girl to calm down, alright? I'll head to Minnie's now." He dropped the phone in his pocket.

"What's happening?" Katie asked, her green eyes wide with interest as he pulled up behind the wheel.

"Just checking on something, sweetheart."

As Rebel drove back to Grace Hill, Katie sat silently in the passenger's seat. His calm act wasn't fooling her. He hit seventy miles an hour.

Chrissie was right. He'd felt it. That black tickle of dread as he watched Minnie walk into the gloom of Grace Hill half an hour ago. But he'd attributed it to his worry for Katie, and Minnie herself told him to get his shift on...No excuse, if Chrissie was right and he'd let his woman walk into a trap.

A trap laid by the McCalls.

You were careless.

He slammed the steering wheel. "*Fuck!*"

Get to her. Get to her.

"Uncle Reb?" Said Katie.

"What?" Grace Hill flashed into view for a moment, and Rebel saw all the trailers laid out in a row like candy, Minnie's perched on top. Then a turn in the mountain covered it.

"Why do you have a gun in here?"

"Close that," he snapped, slamming the glove compartment shut.

"Need it loaded?"

"No," he said. But Katie did anyway.

CHAPTER 14
BIG BROTHER

"Take that dress off."

"Please-- don't do this."

"Take it off," said Duke McCall in a tone that brooked no argument. He sat on Minnie's sofa, and Minnie sat on the chair opposite, staring down the barrel of his gun. The closest thing she had to a weapon was her pepper spray, and the moment she reached into her purse Duke McCall would shoot her dead.

"My mother's coming soon," Minnie bluffed. "She's coming to take me to church. Please-- I won't tell anybody. Just don't hurt me."

She could see a mote of pleasure in those cold green eyes, eyes that reminded her so horribly of Rebel. Her begging excited him.

"Take her dress off, Bubba," Duke McCall told his crony.

McCall had come with backup: a stooping, heavy-browed man Minnie didn't recognize. He wore a raggedy flannel and spat tobacco on her floor. His hands were hard and his nails were dirty.

"No!" Minnie choked, skin crawling. God, let her keep her dignity for a little longer! "I'll do it." Hands trembling, she reached for the straps of her dress.

Her eyes darted around her tiny living room, searching for an impossible escape. There was none. Her trailer was her haven. Nowhere else in the world did she feel safer. Now this sanctuary would become the place of her complete violation. It had become her cage. But to stay alive, she would submit. She didn't have a choice. Sickened, she slowly drew the dress down over her shoulders, thankful she was wearing a bra, any excuse to delay exposing her body to these monsters.

"Why are you doing this?" she whispered. "Maybe if we just talked—"

"Shut the fuck up," McCall said. She shut up.

"Go on, take it all the way off. Or Bubba can help you."

Shuddering, Minnie slid the dress over her hips. She let it pool at her feet. Now she sat in her bra and panties. McCall's eyes traveled over her with a passing interest. As for the other one...

The dirty man's eyes were bright and hungry. Like a rabid animal's.

"See this fella here?" McCall told Minnie, gesturing with the gun. "He's a nephew of mine. Not technically a McCall, but close enough. You like McCalls, don't you, girl? So you should like Bubba. He likes you."

Bubba said nothing, but his eyes latched hungrily on Minnie's breasts, still covered by her bra. His heavy gut nearly concealed the thick bulge of his erection. Nearly.

"Take the rest off," said Duke McCall. "All of it."

"Please--"

"Do it."

Minnie's hands trembled violently on the clasp of her bra. Unclipped it slowly. Her nipples stiffened as she peeled the bra away from her cold skin.

They're going to rape me.

The material came away, exposing her brown breasts, the nipples dark and upthrust. Bubba made a soft, ugly noise deep in his throat. McCall did not react at all.

"Rebel is your son," said Minnie, her mind latching on to the desperate idea that if she kept him talking she might change his mind, or invite some miraculous intervention from God to save her. "You'd only be hurting your son."

"Hurting him?" Said McCall. When he talked, the muscles on his left side barely moved, as if he'd had a stroke. "I ain't hurting him. This is called making a point."

"Rebel doesn't deserve this. He's a good man, and a good son."

"You keep my son's name out of your whore mouth, do you understand?"

"Are...are you going to kill me?"

"Yes," said Duke McCall. He gestured to Bubba. "But first, he's going to fuck you." McCall leaned back in the chair. "Kneel."

Minnie swallowed.

"I said, kneel. Kneel, or Bubba will make you."

Minnie knelt.

McCall settled back in the chair, looking at her down his nose in a way that was all Rebel. "When the first white man set foot on this here mountain, he claimed it for the McCall clan. My ancestor Sean took every hill the eye can see, from the top of the Buffalo in all directions...Touch your breasts," he ordered.

Skin crawling, Minnie cupped her breasts. *It's just nudity. It could be worse...*She struggled not to give in to begging and pleading, knowing it would make no difference. They would only enjoy it. Duke watched her fingers moving, but his eyes looked almost vacant. "Sean McCall took every hill and valley...For the sustenance of the white Christian men and women who followed him. We been keeping the lineage alive ever since...uncorrupted, untainted..."

He's insane.

Someone slammed on the front door. A scream startled from Minnie's lips, the noise snapping the tension that had been coiling inside her. McCall sat bolt upright in the chair. "If it's the mother, bring her inside," he ordered. His reptilian eyes bored into Minnie's. "Even better. She can see you get fucked to death."

"No!" Minnie choked, tears rolling down her cheeks. "Please—"

"Hello?" A deep male voice hollered from the porch.

Rebel!

Relief pounded through her. She snatched her dress back up with shaking hands, but didn't dare scream again. Fury moved across Duke McCall's face, and the hand holding the gun shook.

"Open it," ordered McCall, pointing the gun at Minnie. Bubba left the room and turned into the hallway. The pounding of his boots shook her floorboards. Minnie head her door open, and gave a silent prayer.

"You?" Bubba growled.

Roman McCall pushed his way into Minnie's tiny sitting room. His black eyes widened in utter shock. Minnie knew in that instant she was going to die. But first, they would torture her. They would rape her over and over. The corners of her vision filled with black spots. No; she wouldn't faint. She must stay awake. No matter what, she would survive this. Somehow.

"What the fuck?" Roman McCall said after an excruciating silence. His eyes darted between Minnie, his father, and Bubba. "What the fuck is going on?" He growled.

Duke McCall sneered at his eldest son. "This is the nigger your brother's been screwing. Pretty thing, ain't she?"

"What are you doing?"

"I'm teaching her what happens when she opens her legs for my kin on *my* mountain. I got eyes everywhere, girlie. I got eyes. I know everything that happens to my boys."

"Pa," said Roman.

"I'm thinking this one just needs a stiff fucking to learn. Maybe I won't kill her yet. Eh, sweetheart? Close the damn door, boy."

"Close the door," Roman ordered his cousin. His eyes never left his father's gun.

"She's just one of Rebel's side pieces," Roman said "Is this really worth it?"

"Worth it?" McCall got up strode over to Minnie, who scrambled backward onto the couch, recoiling away from him with a scream. McCall dragged her off the couch, his crushing grip bruising her wrist. She tried to keep her dress up with both hands, but it slipped down over her shoulders, exposing her bare flesh.

"You want to be a whore, don't you? You want to whore your filthy body to my son..." McCall hissed, his breath smelling strongly of mash liquor. Minnie squeezed her eyes shut. "Time was you niggers knew your place...Last thing I need is more halfbreed bastards running around my mountain. Eh, Roman?"

"Let her go, Pa," said Roman, more forcefully. His father looked up, green eyes going vacant for a moment, then back to Minnie, and narrowed with hate.

He's mad. Crazy.

"You can start your little businesses...fuck, breed, and kill each other for all I care. But you do it on. Your. Side." He shook her. "You won't dirty my blood. Now lay down and take what you've been asking for. Don't worry- I won't kill you. And I'll get rid of any brats he seeds in you. Maybe, if I'm generous."

Bubba advanced on Minnie, but Roman shoved the man so hard he stumbled against Minnie's coffee table, sending a vase Mrs. Victor had given her smashing to the ground.

"Enough," Rebel's brother said, palming Minnie by the back of the neck. "Pa, it's enough."

McCall's eyes sparked. "This isn't your concern, Roman."

Roman McCall's fingers fanned out and dug through Minnie's hair, sliding against her scalp. She shuddered.

"I'll take care of it," said Roman curtly.

"Excuse me?"

Roman didn't stay to argue. He hauled Minnie out of the room, hand still buried in her hair.

"Roman!" Duke barked.

"Where's your bedroom?" Roman said gruffly in Minnie's ear.

"Leave me alone," she gasped. "Please don't do this..."

He found the scruff of her neck again. His lip curled. "You really want that dirty bastard to fuck you? Either you deal with me, or both of them."

It would never end. "Well?" Rebel's brother grated in her ear.

"Roman! Bring her back in here!" McCall roared from the other room.

"Where's your room, girl?"

Minnie pointed. Roman shoved her inside and shut the door, throwing the lock. He was so tall his head nearly knocked against the ceiling.

"Will he shoot through the door?" She gasped.

"Not if I'm in here."

Minnie put as much distance between them as she could, scanning their new surroundings frantically for a weapon she could use. Unfortunately, she kept her bedroom neat by stuffing everything in the closet, which was firmly shut. Unless she planned to beat him to death with a pillow, options were few. Her bedroom window was latched, locked.

And Rebel's brother was built like an NBA player. She would never be fast enough to run.

But maybe she could reason with him.

"Don't let them hurt me. Please."

Roman gave her a look of pure disgust and hatred.

"I should let them do it," he said. His voice was like Rebel's, but hoarser, grittier. He rubbed his jaw in utter frustration, acting like she'd greatly inconvenienced him with her problems.

"You brought me in this room, didn't you?" Minnie whispered, wondering to heaven what she'd ever done to deserve the man's ire. "You don't want to hurt me, right? Your father--"

"He's a psychopath," said Roman bluntly.

"Rebel said he's the reason your brothers don't get along."

"It ain't the only reason."

"Is Katie the other reason?" Minnie pressed.

It was the wrong thing to say. Roman snapped, "Katie ain't your goddamned concern. I don't need to talk to some fucking whore about my daughter." He pointed at the bed. "Sit your ass down," he snarled. "And shut the fuck up."

She had to remain calm and take deep breaths. Provoking Roman would not help the situation. "Get them to leave, please. I won't call the police or tell anybody what happened," she pleaded.

Bubba's fists pounded on her bedroom door, causing pieces of plaster to rain from the ceiling. "Bring her out, Roman!" the man shouted. "What the fuck are you doing?"

"Get away from that door you sister-fucking bastard, or I'll blow a hole through your fucking throat!" Roman roared so loud the entire trailer vibrated. The tendons in McCall's neck stood out and his face went a dull red.

Minnie's guts turned to water. Rebel's brother was terrifying. She tried to pull on her dress, struggling with the zipper in the back. Suddenly Roman was there, pulling it up with a gentleness she never would have expected. She spun around and found herself face to face with him, heart pounding hard.

The corners of his eyes tensed. A bell of recognition rang distantly in the corner of Minnie's brain. Where had she seen eyes shaped like that before? They looked nothing like Rebel's. In fact, Minnie could see no resemblance between the two brothers but the shape of their ears and their height, the timbre of their voices.

Roman's gaze drifted from the bed, then back to Minnie. "Let's talk about Rebel," he said.

"Okay. We can talk about Rebel when your father and that man get out of here."

"No. Now." Roman's jaw worked. He kept looking at her like he expected her to say something. Finally he said, "You been seeing him? Tell the truth."

"I...Yes." Somehow she suspected lying to Roman McCall would be a huge mistake. But he didn't seem to like her answer. He snarled, "Why?"

"Um...why? I don't know." Minnie had reached her breaking point, and an uncontrollable anger began to rise. She backed away from him. "Why would two grown people attracted to each other want to see each other? Maybe it's because a little thing like skin color only matters to stupid, ignorant people stuck in a time where people lived in shit and bathed once a year!"

"I see people living in shit on this mountain all the time," Roman sneered. "Bringing all their violence and disease. This is about our way of life. About blood."

"There are no proven, scientific genetic differences between you and any black person on this mountain. Or in the world. Our blood is all the same— we're human beings. Rebel can see that. Why can't you?"

"There's weakness in any lineage," Roman replied with a quickness. "Every member of a species differs from another in small ways, and some differences make each individual better, stronger, faster. Thin blood is culled. The strong survive. That's nature. That's science."

Minnie countered, "Our species only survived because the strong help the weak. Mothers with babies. Men with women, young with old…How do you think we survived this long? By senselessly killing each other? That dog-eat-dog theory makes no sense if you know anything about animal behavior. And like I said, there's no proven genetic difference— oh, never mind! Why bother? You've probably never read a book in your life—"

"Has Rebel?" Roman snapped.

"He has honor, unlike you!" Minnie cried.

"Some mouthy bitch, aren't you?"

Minnie shrank, cursing herself for becoming a sassy know-it-all when the situation least required it. How far could she push Roman before he snapped?

She reversed tactics. "Think of Rebel. He's a good person. He doesn't deserve this. He's your little brother."

"I'll be the judge what Rebel McCall *deserves*."

She didn't like the look in his eyes. "Nothing of mine was ever safe from Rebel," Roman. "So why should you be safe from me?" He stepped towards her again. Minnie could feel waves of rage radiating from his body, and his words came out in bursts, as if he hauled them from some black and sticky place inside himself. But in his eyes...lust. She felt naked and exposed.

"You're going to hurt me?" She whispered.

"No." His hand twitched at his side, as if he wanted to touch her, but restrained himself. "Of course not."

"But you were willing to let your father do it just to get back at Rebel? Do you hate him that much?" She cried.

Guilt— was it guilt?— flashed through Roman's eyes. "I didn't know Pa would be here."

"What do you mean?"

"I came up here on my own," said Roman. His tone was bitter. "I came to see you."

Minnie wondered if she'd lost her mind. Or maybe in her panic she was hearing things. "Me? Why?"

"To talk."

"To *talk*?"

"If I knew he was going to hurt you, I would have stopped him before he ever came up the hill. I didn't want this...I just wanted to talk." Roman looked agitated. "I came by your hospital weeks ago."

"You *did*?"

"Your receptionist sent me off. I told her to tell you I'd come by."

Minnie racked her brains. Lola hadn't said a peep about Roman McCall. But come to think of it, the assistant had suddenly began insisting Minnie replace the security cameras and install an alarm. She even asked about buying a shotgun, which Minnie obviously did not take seriously. Roman must have sent the girl into a panic.

"Well," said Minnie, remembering it was better to keep him talking, "We can talk now. Say what you have to say to me."

"It's too late."

"It's not too late. Let's talk, Roman," she said desperately. She remembered an episode of *Preacher Man* when Father Noah had to talk a crazy kidnapper into releasing hostages. *Use his name often, keep him talking.*

Instead of talking, Roman paced her room, lifting up things on her dresser. He stopped in front of her bureau and slowly slid open her top drawer. Frothy lace spilled out. Roman raised one of her skimpy white panties on the hook of his finger.

Minnie splurged on nice underwear, and this was one of her favorites. Roman rubbed the material between his first two fingers, then let the panties fall back into the drawer in a silken heap. "You wore these for Rebel yet?" He rasped.

"N-no."

Minnie's eyes darted to her bedside lamp. The one Mama had given her. Old-fashioned, brass, and nearly fifteen pounds. A last resort. But how to reach it in time?

"You should call Rebel," she whispered, trying to sound brave.

"You like being his fuck toy? When he's done, he'll throw you out."

Minnie didn't believe that for a second. "You'll talk about your brother like that?"

"I know him better than you."

"Let me go."

Black eyes flickered. "Beg me."

Just like his father, her humiliation aroused him. "I have an elderly mother. I help animals every day. If you kill me, you'd only be hurting innocent creatures."

He stepped closer. She froze. His thumb came up and stroked her lower lip. "You count yourself among the innocent?"

"The only thing I'm guilty of is loving your brother. If you let me go...I'll do whatever you want. I promise." She fought back nausea. Was this what it had come to? Bartering with her body?

Roman hesitated.

"Roman. Please." She was close to tears, out of options. She just couldn't die with freedom so close. She had to try to save herself. When an animal was trapped, sometimes it chewed its leg off to get free.

Her gambit seemed to work. Roman released her and reached behind his back. He pulled a pistol from his waistband and laid it carefully on the dresser. Minnie nearly fainted at the sight; she'd had no idea he was carrying one. Of course, a man that size could force her to suck and fuck him even without a gun. He could snap her neck with his bare hands.

He sat, drawing her down next to him on the bed. She could read nothing in his eyes but a nervous eagerness, a hunger that, in spite of her devotion to Rebel, and her terror, made her heart beat with a familiar, sickening rhythm. She scooted down the bed, closer to the brass lamp.

"You're shaking," he said.

"I'm afraid."

"I ain't gonna hurt you." He sounded exactly like Rebel when he said that. "I can't fucking get you out of my head. That's all. I just want you out of there, girl."

This had better work, or I'm dead. "Then let me go. Let me out through that window, Roman, and I swear I won't tell nobody." Her voice broke. "Just let me go. Please. I'm so scared."

Rebel would have done it without hesitation. But she wasn't dealing with Rebel.

Roman stared at the door, which held back the worse threat, for now. "I won't let Duke hurt you. You have my word."

She nodded.

"One kiss," said Roman McCall, turning back to her. "That's all. One kiss and you can go."

"You said you wouldn't hurt me. You promised."

"A kiss don't hurt."

"It hurts in here." Minnie pressed her chest. "It hurts me that you would hurt Rebel. He loves you, Roman."

"If you bring him up again, you go back out there," Roman snarled.

"Alright," she whispered.

Minnie still couldn't place where she'd seen his features before. Rebel claimed his brothers were all half brothers, so Roman's mother must have been a woman with dark hair and an olive skin tone. But something about the freckles, the moles on the older McCall brother's smooth throat, the bristly stubble on his head, was not giving...*white*.

The hair on his head looked as if it would erupt into tight curls if he let it grow. His eyes were black and slanted. Full, dark lips and a nose like Mrs. Victor's, only smaller... Was he...*mixed*?

The wild thought flashed into her head, the truth coming to Minnie like a bolt from the blue. The olive skin was no farmer's tan, but a natural feature just like his freckles. His nose was a little too broad at the end, his lips too full... *A drop's all it takes*, folks always said. But how could it be true? She must be wrong.

One of Roman's enormous hands cupped her chin.

I'm sorry, Rebel. As the older McCall leaned in and touched his lips to hers, Minnie shut her eyes and wrapped her fingers around the stem of the brass lamp. To her surprise, Roman's mouth was warm and soft. He tasted of mint toothpaste. The scrape of his stubble against her cheek reminded her of Rebel. Her fingers loosened around the lamp for a dizzying moment. His tongue entered her mouth. His hands cupped her waist.

"My god," he gasped. "You taste like candy... so soft."

She shuddered as he cupped her waist, her ass. "Kiss me, darling..."

Minnie steeled herself, then jerked her wrist down hard. She ripped the lamp from the socket. At the sudden motion Roman tore his lips away from hers, expression dazed. "What—"

Moving faster than she'd have ever thought possible, she whipped the base of the lamp down with all her strength.

The room exploded into motion. Roman roared in pain and crumpled to the bed, clutching his head. Minnie sprang away from him and snatched his gun where it rested on her dresser. Though she'd walloped him good, Roman was already getting to his feet. He reached out and got a handful of her dress, started dragging her backward. Minnie jerked away, and a huge piece of the dress ended up in Roman's hands. Half-clad, she hefted the gun and backed up to the door, unlocked it, and darted into the hallway.

Roman roared, bursting out of the room behind her. Blood was everywhere, spilling between his fingers down his temple. His father and cousin jumped up from the sitting room, their surprise playing to Minnie's advantage.

"Stay back or I'll shoot!" She screamed.

She never remembered her feet touching the floor. Barefoot and nearly naked, she shot past the men to her back door. Was it that easy? The lock sprang apart in her hands. Pure adrenaline charged through her blood as she jerked the door open and stumbled into the sweet, free air.

Stumbled into Rebel.

"Minnie?"

"Rebel!" She shrieked.

He opened his arms; she threw herself into them. She was practically naked. He clasped her tightly as she utterly fell apart. "Rebel," she sobbed. "Oh my God."

"It's okay, baby. It's alright." He cupped her head. "Where are the sons of bitches?"

He didn't have to wait long to find out. Bubba came sprinting out of the house. At the sight of Rebel he froze. "Oh, fuck—"

Rebel thrust Minnie aside and raised the gun she hadn't even realized he'd been holding. The gunshot was like a cannon blast. Rebel's aim was true, and the big man tumbled to the porch, two hundred and fifty pounds of dead weight splintering the plywood.

"Go to my truck," Rebel said, turning back to a shell-shocked Minnie. His face was pale, determined.

"They got guns, Rebel!"

"Go, Minnie!"

Getting to his truck required her to parade past her entire neighborhood in her underwear. Dumbly she watched Rebel step right over Bubba's body and slam into her house.

Mrs. Mabel burst onto the porch. "Minnie! What the hell is going on?" She quacked, halfway ducking into her house in case more bullets started flying. Up and down the hill people began to pour into the street to see the commotion.

An animal roar of fury came from inside Minnie's trailer.

"Lord have mercy!" Cried Mrs. Mabel. Minnie's front door exploded off its hinges. Rebel and Roman tumbled to the ground like two fighting dogs.

"Somebody call the police! They killing each other at the Brown girl's house!" Mrs. Mabel shrieked, taking her chances with the bullets and racing down the hill.

The brothers battered each other with their fists, evenly matched in strength and size. Just when Rebel's bright head cleared from the grip of Roman's arms, the older brother would drag him back to the grass. But Rebel overpowered his brother. Screaming in berserk rage, he wrapped his hands around Roman's throat and bore him down to the ground. He pinned Roman in a wrestler's hold, and began scrambling for something in the grass— for his gun, Minnie realized.

Rebel was going to kill his brother.

At that moment Duke McCall limped out of the house, trying uselessly to call the boys off each other. Too late. With the last of his strength Roman shoved Rebel off him. He scrambled to his feet, his face a mask of dirt and blood, the flesh around his eyes swollen beyond recognition. And somehow, Rebel's gun was in his hands.

"No!" Minnie screamed, but Roman aimed.

Rebel froze.

Roman fired.

Missed.

"Daddy!" Katie screamed, leaping over Minnie's fence. "Daddy, stop!"

"Katie?"

Rebel seized the distraction and tackled his brother, sending the gun spiraling out of his hands dangerously to land in the grass with another small explosion. Duke made his way towards Minnie, but even in his shock Rebel's protective instinct alerted him, and he threw Roman off him and altered course in the blink of an eye. Before Duke could take another step Rebel had him by the collar, and his fist arced through the air to crack hard against his father's temple. Duke fell to the ground and did not get up.

Roman was hurt bad. Blood coursed down his temple, and he seemed dazed. He sank to his knees. Katie had wrapped her arms around her father's neck, sobbing. It seemed her presence had ripped Roman from the killing fury. He looked horrified; he'd nearly killed his brother. "Reb. Oh my God, Rebel."

"You dirty bastard!" Rebel's voice broke with rage. He strode up to Roman but Katie's screams made him halt. "Not man enough to come for me first?" Every vein in his head was standing out, but he looked pale as a sheet. "I ought to bury you under this mountain! What did you do to her?"

Minnie ran to him. Rebel pressed her close, protectively, and by an extreme effort lowered his voice. "Did they hurt you, baby?"

"Nobody laid a hand on her," Roman snarled.

Liar!

"Is that true, Minnie?" Rebel demanded, his arm crushing her so tightly she could barely breathe. "Tell me right now. Say something."

Oh, God. *What if he knows Roman kissed me?* Rebel would kill his brother. He'd go to jail. Her eyes fell on the still bodies of Bubba and Duke McCall. In the distance she heard sirens. *He's already going to jail.*

She sobbed and wrapped her arms around Rebel, burying her face in his shirt, shutting out everything else. His heart slammed against her ears. "N-no," she lied. "No, he didn't hurt me."

"Why are you in your panties, then?" Rebel thrust her away from him, eyes wild. "Minnie. Did they rape you?"

"No," she whispered, relieved that it was the truth.

"Did they lay hands on you? Any of them?"

"I— no. They just made me strip."

Liar.

"Alright." He patted her head, suddenly calmer. "Get in my truck, sweetheart. I got to take care of this. Get in the car and wait for me."

"Uncle Reb, no. No, no! Daddy, stop. Please stop, all of you," Katie howled.

"I'm not your daddy, Katie," Roman said through a mouthful of blood. His voice rose, full of so much pain tears filled Minnie's eyes, though she had no reason whatsoever to feel sorry for Roman. "He's your father, Katie. Aren't you, Reb? You fucked my girl, you low down bastard...Acting like a fucking saint...I could never have nothing. You were always there to take it away. Could never have nothing."

"So you and Pa go after my girl?" Rebel roared, apoplectic at Roman's justification. "That's it, then? Some bullshit revenge over that whore?"

"Stop!" Katie screamed. She no longer needed Roman to pull her off him; she did it on her own. "Stop it, the both of you!"

"I did a paternity test," Rebel said, glaring at Roman. "I got the proof if you want to know. I never even looked at it. You know why? Because when Katie turned up here I knew you would love her unconditionally. I would never try to take your daughter away from you. And I don't need a goddamned piece of paper to tell me what I already know— Katie is like my own blood. She's as much my daughter as yours. I've always said that!"

"And I'm supposed to thank you for that," Roman spat. "I ought to be grateful, huh? Saint Rebel!"

"I don't care what you think." Rebel strode up to him and. "You took it too far. Come near my woman again, I'll kill you with my bare hands."

"Fuck you. And fuck your whore."

It took six men from Grace Hill to pull the brothers off each other.

BUBBA AND DUKE MCCALL REMAINED WHERE THEY'D FALLEN. A carpenter bee took its rest on Bubba's chest, then crawled to the edge of the spreading bloodstain on his shirt. It remained there until the sirens circled the hill, and then the creature looped off in the other direction towards the sanctuary of the forest.

CHAPTER 15

SHOW ME HOW YOU LIKE IT

"You're asking about inmate 32?"

"Yes. I'd like to pay his bail," Minnie said, glancing over her shoulder to make sure no one was coming into the kitchen. Mama was still talking to Mrs. Victor and Ms. Greaves, her loud tone never breaking stride.

"I'm sorry?" said the operator. "His what?"

"His bond," Minnie said, feeling stupid. She'd never had to bail someone out of jail before. "His bail. Whatever you call it. How much is it? I want to pay it, please."

"He hasn't seen the judge yet," the voice said, bored.

"When does he–"

"I have no idea. He hasn't seen the judge yet."

"But–"

"*Yes?*"

"Minnie! What in the hell are you doing?"

224

Minnie jumped, nearly dropping the receiver. Shoot! She hurriedly put the phone to her ear again, but the operator had hung up.

"What are you doing?" Ms. Brown repeated. "You lost your damn mind? Were you calling the jailhouse?"

Minnie caught the lie on her tongue. No; she wasn't a child. She also wasn't going to lie about Rebel any more. "Yes, I was calling the jail," she said, setting down the receiver. "I'm going to get Rebel out today if I can."

"Don't you have any sense at all?" Her mother snatched the receiver up and slammed it down again.

"A man is locked up for protecting me. For saving my life. I'm trying to do something about it."

"You haven't shamed yourself enough?"

"Shamed myself?" Minnie said, not bothering to lower her voice. She was past caring now; Mrs. Victor could go spread the story all over town if she wanted to. "Do you think I asked to be attacked in my own home?"

"If that's even what happened!" Ms. Brown snapped.

"What the hell does that mean?"

"I told you running around with those McCalls would only bring trouble, but you went on ahead and passed yourself around those men like a bag of chips. You have any idea what people are saying? I can't even repeat it."

"I don't care what people are saying. Let them say whatever they want." She was shouting now. She never shouted. "Minnie Brown, the town whore! Talk about it! I don't give a damn, Mama!"

The slap flung her against the counter. She put a hand to her stinging flesh, utterly stunned. She couldn't remember the last time Mama had actually hit her.

"Keep talking!" Ms. Brown threatened, her shoulders tucked, ready to strike again. "Keep running your mouth! How dare you speak to me like that?"

"Betty!" Mrs. Victor burst into the kitchen so speedily it was obvious she'd been listening in the doorway. "Betty, you took it too far."

Ms. Brown hesitated. She said in a plaintive voice, "What did I do to deserve a girl like that?"

"Come on now," Mrs. Victor said, holding up her gnarled hands. "Minnie, apologize to your Mama and stop this nonsense."

"I don't want her apology," said Ms. Brown.

Minnie looked grim. "You'll never be happy with me, Mama, because you ain't happy with yourself. I was happy with Rebel. Do you understand that? A man made your daughter happy. And I want to make him happy, too. I want to be with him!"

"You'll let that man drag you into the gutter, and you'll get what you deserve," her mother hissed.

How could Minnie explain the look in Rebel's eyes when he rescued her? The way he'd held her so tight before the police had dragged him away.

I'll keep eyes on you. You'll be safe until I get out. It's alright, darling. I'm so sorry.

"He loves me," she said.

226

Her mother laughed. "You really have lost your mind. Men don't love nothing, and *these* men will never *love* a black girl from down the mountain. But I'm tired of telling you that. You should go be with that man and see what happens. Go be with him! And see how he drops you like a hot potato when he's used your ass up!" Ms. Brown sank into her dining chair, her knees shaking. "When we were younger, these McCall men made our lives hell. You remember, Veronica?"

"It's true," said Mrs. Victor, nodding solemnly. *She's loving this*, Minnie thought. Minnie and her mother rarely came to blows about anything. Never, in fact. Minnie's tactic had always been to shut up and let Mama run herself down. But no more. She didn't want to hear another word against Rebel.

"Rebel's father was a demon," said Ms. Brown. "He kidnapped a girl and kept her in a basement for years. We were all afraid of him."

To think that creature had raised Rebel. That half his blood flowed in Rebel's veins...

"Rebel isn't like that."

"Says every woman about her man," Mrs. Victor tutted.

"Don't try to convince her, Veronica," said Ms. Brown bitterly. "I wash my hands of that girl. Do what you want, Minnie. You'll always do what you want."

MAMA WENT TO LIE DOWN WITH A COOL CLOTH ON HER HEAD, and Mrs. Victor said her goodbyes. Minnie passed The Photograph on her way to the kitchen. As a child she always thought of it as The Photograph. It was the only picture of anybody Mama kept in the house. Mama had no family. An aunt had raised Ms.Brown, then died and left her the trailer she now lived in. Looking inside the home, nobody would suspect Ms. Brown had a daughter.

The Photograph was a framed photo of Betty Brown herself, taken when she was even younger than Minnie. Mama had the same mole under her eye and sweetheart face, but she'd been strikingly more beautiful. In another era, in another place, she might have been renowned for it. The only flaw in her doll-like appearance was a cold narrowness to her gaze that, Minnie knew, would only become more pronounced over the years.

Ms. Greaves intercepted her at the front door. "Where are you going, baby? You want some alone time, is that it? You've had a bad day."

Mama did not deserve her friends. "I'm just need some air."

Immediately Ms. Greaves dug into her purse, hunting for her keys. "You can take my car, baby."

"Oh, no. I couldn't." Regrettably, her car was still in Rebel's junkyard on Flat Hill. Insurance still dragging their feet. With her luck, she didn't want to risk somebody else's vehicle.

"You can pick up my pralines from Miss Rita for me, then get us something to eat from Ben's," Ms. Greaves said, giving Minnie the excuse. The older woman hesitated only a moment. "Take your time. But stay on this side of town." Her eyes filled with tears. "I'm just glad you're okay, baby."

. . .

MINNIE DROVE TO BEN'S HOT CHICKEN. SHE FOUND SHE needed to talk to someone who knew Rebel. Word of the incident had reached Ben's ears hours ago.

"His father lived?" she asked.

The last she'd seen of Rebel's father, he'd been facedown and motionless in her backyard.

"It'll take more than a bump on a head to kill Duke McCall," said Ben.

"What about the other man?"

"Dead."

Minnie stared hard out the window, aware that Ben was watching her closely. Dead. Would Rebel go to prison for it? Her blood chilled.

As if he'd read her mind, Ben wiped the counter down with more force than was necessary. "I never knew a McCall to take jail over a little thing like shooting somebody."

"Rebel isn't one of them."

"Why, because he's messing around with you?" Ben said sharply. "You're wrong. And you should know better; you grew up here, Minnie. You know how it goes. Maybe I can cut my nephew some slack for jumping after that fast little girl, but a grown woman like you should have known better. You brought all this trouble messing with that man."

Will I have to go to court? Prove it was self defense?

Ben went on, "That's why I told Junior he better finish with that girl. Those men walked into your house and did that to you. Imagine what kind of hell they'd raise over their lily-white baby seeing Junior. I told Rebel as much, but he never took me seriously. Well, I'm putting my foot down. They ain't gonna turn my nephew into Emmett Till."

Ben wrung his dishrag in the sink, the steaming water not affecting him at all. "Eat something, girl. You look like a haint," he said grumpily. "What you want?"

She wondered what Rebel was eating in jail. "I'm alright. I ate at home."

He pointed at her. "Stop worrying about McCall."

"What do you know about his brother?" Minnie asked, taking a chance. Ben knew everything about everybody, but he didn't gossip. Unless compelled by his own instinct to reveal a piece of information, like he'd done with the Ruthie story, he kept it shut.

"Which brother?" he hedged.

"Roman McCall."

"Is that the one Rebel found you with?" Ben said mildly.

Minnie clenched her teeth. *So is that it? They think I was stepping out on Rebel with his brother. Maybe even his father, too.*

But Ben continued, "They call him Gypsy. He don't come around to this side of town but I seen him once or twice. Big bastard. Mean as a pitbull. He runs their business down the mountain."

230

"He looks mixed."

Ben snorted. "And I'm Chinese."

"He's got black hair and eyes. I swear, the man's got some blood, Ben."

"A pair of dark eyes don't mean nothing," Ben said, giving her a sidelong look. "I seen white people who look like him all the time, 'specially on the other side of the mountain. They used to have a word for 'em back in the day. Melungeons."

"Do you think he's really Katie's father?"

Ben smirked. "What does Rebel have to say about that?"

"He loves her no matter what. Roman wanted to be her father legally."

"That's their own business."

"But what do you think?" Minnie refused to let him wriggle out of the question.

"I think I'm going to keep minding my business."

TWO DAYS LATER, A HARRIED MINNIE GLANCED UP FROM HER reports to see Lola waving her urgently into the waiting room. Another runner? She pushed back from her desk and hastened through the adjoining door.

She stopped in her tracks. Rebel stood there, wearing the same bloody clothes they'd arrested him in. Which told her he must have walked directly from the jail. He rose stiffly from the chair when she emerged. Five days' growth of beard put golden shadows on his face. Both his eyes were blackened.

"Hey darling," he said quietly. "Let's talk outside."

Minnie quickly followed him out; she didn't want Lola overhearing.

He held the door open for her. Minnie stepped out into the fresh air and moved to the side of the building, away from the transparent glass.

He took her hand gently, a questioning touch. She gripped it. Immediately he hauled her into his arms, holding her tight around the waist and shoulders. His nose buried in her hair. She stroked his broad, muscled back, feeling hazy with pleasure and relief. He groaned in happiness.

"What time do you get off?" he asked, voice rough.

"In three hours. Lola is driving me home. Did you walk all the way here?"

"Yeah. Your spot's close to my house, remember? Figured I'd see you first."

She let go a breath she hadn't known she'd been holding. So did he.

"I wanted...You're alright, then?" he drew back, scanning her face carefully.

No concern for himself, as usual! She gripped his stained T-shirt. "Of course! But are you alright? I asked about your bond–"

"Larry took care of it. I ain't hurting for money, Minnie. These things just take time." He tugged at her chin. "It was alright. I'm fine."

She babbled, "I was so scared. I told the police you were just trying to help me but they didn't believe me. They thought I had invited those men, that I was playing you."

"I know."

"You never believed that, did you?"

"Not for a second." He tugged at a little curl next to her ear.

She grabbed his wrist. "Did they tell you about that man? The man you shot. He's d-dead."

Rebel's eyes narrowed. "I know. Bubba. He was a cousin. One of the Snatch Hill McCalls. I ain't sorry for killing him, and I'd do it again."

His words made her shudder. How had it all gone wrong so quickly? Just a few nights ago she'd woken up in Rebel's arms feeling happy and safe.

She smiled up at him, trying to put on a brave face. "Your nose is broken."

"Yeah, Roman popped me good. How's it looking?"

He turned his head for her, lips curling with amusement.

"You look a little dangerous." She leaned in and sniffed. "You need a shower, honey."

He raised his armpit to his nose and made a face. "Are my ripe odors unappealing to the lady? I pray beg her pardon; they had no soap in there."

She smiled. "I've smelled worse." Maybe she was a cave-woman, but even the strong odor on Rebel's clothes attracted her.

He cupped her chin. "Nobody tried anything while I was gone?" A very subtle edge to his voice.

"No," she assured him. It was the truth. Since that disastrous Sunday morning, Minnie hadn't heard a peep from Roman or Duke McCall. But she still hadn't been able to return to her trailer. For one thing, the place remained an active crime scene for 48 hours. Even after the investigation ended, she just couldn't lay her head where she'd been assaulted and nearly raped barely a week ago. She couldn't do it. Being alone terrified her so much she'd been sleeping at her mother's place– for now, the lesser of two evils.

"I don't want to hold you up," Rebel said after a pause. "You're busy here."

"You need to rest," said Minnie firmly.

"I'm fine. I ain't made of sugar."

"I have a cot in the storage room. Rest up until I'm done." She didn't want to let him out of her sight.

"And then you'll come to my place," he said, taking her hand. It wasn't a question.

She nodded. "Of course."

His fingers pressed into her skin. "Nobody came to bother you? You're sure?"

"Nobody, Rebel."

He inhaled. "Your mother? Is she alright? How did she react?"

"Maybe we'll talk about that later."

That seemed to appease him, and he followed her inside again. She led him to the back room, past Lola and the box puppies and the overnighting pets, and unfolded the cot while he swayed in the doorway. When an animal was in very critical condition, sometimes Minnie slept in the clinic to keep an eye on things. She was happy to have the cot, though Rebel was a little too tall for it.

By the crack of light from the hallway, she rearranged some boxes and laid out the camp bed with a pillow and a thin blanket.

Rebel sat down on the edge and caught her hand. "Wait."

"What is it?"

He fought for the words. "Minnie. It's all fucked up. I'm so sorry."

"It's not your fault."

"I just– don't say that." He exhaled harshly. "I need to make it right. I fucked up bad. I let you walk right in there. You're my woman, and I didn't protect you."

"What?" Minnie gaped at him. "Rebel, you killed a man for me."

"It shouldn't have even come to that."

"You saved my life."

"I let you walk in there alone."

"You had to get to Katie."

"I just– I had to protect you, too." Rebel clenched the edge of the cot with his fists, his gaze fixed on the floor. Every part of his big body seemed to be vibrating with rage.

"Rebel..."

"You came to me, and it was like lightning, Minnie. What's a woman all educated and sweet like you doing with a man like me? I wanted to show you all the best of me. Now I don't know...I don't know what will happen."

He scuffed his boot on the floor and looked away. But when he caught her eye again, he'd pushed down the strong emotion and was smiling...Smiling so he wouldn't worry her. "Leave me in here. I'd like to rest for a minute. I can listen to you moving in there, doing your thing, and it makes me feel like I can rest."

She leaned down and kissed his forehead. "Let me know if you need anything."

"Just you," he said.

"You'll have me soon."

"Good," he said.

She shivered.

REBEL DIDN'T PLAN ON SLEEPING A WINK UNTIL HE HAD MINNIE safely in his house with a shotgun in reach. He pushed the door of the supply closet ajar so he could listen out for the front door.

236

Alone in the darkness, Rebel rolled over on his back, forcing down his turbulent emotions. Four nights in that hole, four days of hell, not knowing if Minnie was hurt, if she'd left town, if those bastards had really raped her. Pinned her down and shoved their dirty cocks into his woman. Hit her, made her bleed. Rebel replayed the whole thing over and over from the moment he'd seen Minnie bolting out the door naked, an expression on her face he hoped to never see again. His heart had nearly fucking stopped. The way she'd screamed his name, fallen into his arms and cried like a little lost child.

The rage that followed...Hot saliva filled his mouth, remembering it. He could still feel the resistance of the trigger against his finger, see his cousin crumple to the ground. He cracked his fist against Roman's jaw again and again in his head. The dreams were worse. Every night in that cell he'd had the same nightmare. Minnie lay out of reach as he hunted for his gun in the tall grass, but never found it. While he searched, his father and brother and cousin raped his girl again and again, fucked her until she stopped screaming, stopped moving, and all he could do was paw at the grass like an idiot for a weapon that never appeared. Was he losing his mind?

He turned over again, digging the heels of his palms into his eyes.

Jesus fuck. The fact that she still could stand to look at him...She should hate him. He was part of it– those people were his family...The whole crime of having the girl, in his father's eyes, was the fact that she was Black. It was just like Minnie had said. And Rebel had been cocky. He'd always known his family were bonafide racists, but there was a code, surely. A line not crossed. A man's woman was off-limits.

Pa was provoking him. Daring him to retaliate. Going after Minnie had been an open act of war.

From Pa, a move like this was not all that surprising, much as he'd like to deny it. Roman, though? That one hurt. He and Roman despised each other, but they were brothers. Rebel could never hate his brother. Whatever lay between them, he'd always supposed they would work it out eventually.

Roman was not supposed to help their father fucking gang rape Rebel's woman to send a message.

Again he saw Minnie bolting out of the house in her panties. She said nothing had happened. But what if...

Fuck. *Fuck!*

The more Rebel thought about it, the wilder his rage became. He'd paced the cell like a trapped mountain lion, nothing for his anger to do but build and build and build. He knew they were only holding him at his father's request. If Duke wanted him out, one phone call would have done the trick. They kept him in there to send a message.

Thank God Minnie was alright.

To crown it all, Roman had actually called him in prison. Rebel had tried to hang up, but the warden gave strong hints that he would deeply regret doing so. Roman paid to make sure Rebel stayed on the line.

"Katie found the envelope with the results," Roman said. "She went to your house and found it. She gave it to me but I ain't opened it yet. I don't know if Katie wants me to."

"Right."

"Reb...I'm sorry."

"Alright."

"Reb. I would never have hurt her."

"If you're gonna lie—"

"I swear I didn't know Pa would be there. I ain't lying."

"Why the hell were you there at all, Roman?" Rebel said between his teeth. "Why were you in her house?"

"I stopped Pa from hurting her. Twice. When they locked you up he was ready to send more men after her. I talked him down, Rebel. I told him to wait until we could all talk together."

"I'm done talking."

"He made a mistake, Reb. Just don't go after Pa before we talk," his brother said. "Can you promise me that?"

Rebel couldn't believe it. "You fucking serious? A *mistake*? How can you defend him?"

"You knew what would happen if you messed with her. You know how Pa feels about crossing that line," Roman growled. "You put her in danger—"

" You want a promise from me? I promise to give you a cold bullet if you or Pa lay a finger on her again. You can tell that to whoever needs to hear it. The girl is mine."

"Then you'd put a woman above your brothers. We need each other for what's coming."

"What's coming, Roman?"

"I can't say on the phone," Roman said, frustrated. "Fuck, Reb, it weren't supposed to end like this. Just don't make smoke with Pa until we talk."

"I promise nothing. Don't call me unless you want an encore for that ass-whupping I gave you on Grace Hill."

"Reb, please—"

Click.

REBEL STARED SIGHTLESSLY INTO THE DARK, MAKING OUT THE shapes of boxes and packages. He took his mind back to the night he and Minnie spent together before everything went to hell. He put it together one piece at a time, which calmed him, the way it had done for the last four nights. The dancing. Soft barn light on her face. Her shy smile. The way she'd gone loose and submissive in his arms. Her hands in his hair, her eyes so full of adoration it drove him insane with lust. Her quiet moans as he sank his fingers into her wet, soft warmth. She was innocent. Golden. Perfect.

He'd nearly ruined her.

Never, he thought. *Never again.*

. . .

240

THREE HOURS LATER, MINNIE PEEKED INTO THE STOREROOM AND was not surprised to find Rebel awake, sitting on the edge of the cot, his fingers laced on the back of his head. It was obvious he had been in here just torturing himself, not resting at all.

She sank to her knees and kissed his cheek. "Stop thinking."

He pressed his forehead against hers for a moment, then got to his feet. "I'm alright."

"Let's go, then."

He nodded. After carefully folding the unused blanket, the cot, and tossing the pillow back on the shelf, he followed her out of the room.

When they passed the puppy cages, Rebel stopped. "What's wrong with that one?" he said, pointing at Nemo.

The puppy blinked at them warily. His littermates were nearly twice his size.

"I've done everything I can," said Minnie, poking a finger through the bars. "Hi Nemo. Good boy." Nemo nosed her finger for a moment, but settled back weakly in his bedding. "He was the worst in the litter. I think he'll pull through, but sometimes they don't. He had a lot of parasites, from fleas and ticks. It made him very sick," Minnie explained.

"He's so small. Does he belong to anybody?"

Minnie shook her head. "Some lady dropped them off in a box. If he gets better, I'll have to find a home for him."

Rebel considered the dog. "I'll take him," he said.

"Really? Are you serious?"

"I always wanted a dog. Don't give him to nobody else."

Minnie hesitated.

"What?"

"I'm not sure that's a good idea, Rebel."

"Why not?"

"What about the trial?"

He looked at her sideways. "I hadn't thought of that."

"Maybe I can keep him for you," Minnie said quickly. "Until it's all over with."

"Don't put yourself out. It's alright."

"No. I want you to have him. I think you'd be the perfect owner. You seem like a dog person. "

Rebel smiled. "Thank you. I think." He put a finger through the bar and the puppy nosed it weakly.

"Poor little bastards," Rebel murmured, looking at the others.

"They'll get adopted soon," said Minnie reassuringly. Was he thinking about jail? He'd spent the last few days in a cage himself. "And we'll take them on walks when they're stronger. I wish I had more help here."

"Katie could help you. She loves dogs."

Minnie hid a skeptical look. She didn't want to go near Roman McCall's daughter with a ten-foot pole.

Rebel stared a moment longer at Nemo, then looked around at the room. Though every cage housed an animal, it was very neat and orderly. "How do you afford this place?"

"I barely afford it." She shrugged. "We get donations, but ever since word got out I take in just about every animal, we get overwhelmed easily."

"You need more help."

"It'll come in time. I've only been open a year."

"If you ever need anything, you ask me, alright?"

"We do fine, superman," she teased. "All I need is a night alone with you."

He looked down at her through his lashes. "Good thinking."

TWO MILES LAY BETWEEN MINNIE'S OFFICE AND REBEL'S HOUSE. They took an old footpath through the woods, up the hill. The pollen-heavy air stirred her hair. Honeybees twirled among looping trumpet vines, and yellow finches chased each other through a canopy of wild lilacs. Butter-yellow sunlight spilled through the trees, dancing across Minnie's upturned face. Spring had arrived, in a wild erotic frenzy, pulsing with heat and life. But still an icy shard of fear burrowed towards her heart. If he went away for murder, these golden moments might be the last ones she shared with Rebel.

Eventually they stepped through the trees onto a wide field brimming with buttercups. Minnie's breath caught.

So beautiful! A crooked fence marked what she assumed was a property line, and Rebel ducked under it, turning to help Minnie over.

"Is this your land?" she asked.

"Yep. I got about five acres up here. Top of the hill. Look, you can see Main Street and the courthouse from here." He pointed.

"Where's your house?" she said, turning away from it. She didn't want to think about the courthouse.

"This way."

She hadn't yet seen Rebel's place in the light of day. It was a small hunter-style cabin tucked in a copse of Loblolly pines. They walked up a quiet two-track driveway buried in the trees. Rebel fished the spare key from inside a tree hollow and let Minnie in through the side door.

As they crossed the threshold she saw him visibly relax. She could tell everything that had happened was weighing heavily on Rebel. And he was trying to hide it from her.

"I'll make something to eat," she said, setting her purse down. "You're probably hungry."

"I don't keep much food in here."

"I'll see what I can do."

He kissed the top of her head. Her heart fluttered. "Make yourself at home, baby," he said.

They stood in the living room. It looked like the inside of a hunter's cabin, but more modern, and with a surprising amount of art.

Sap had beaded and hardened in between the boards on the walls and floor, and the whole place was infused with a cleaner, sharper version of the scent that clung to Rebel's clothes.

It wasn't very big. But the rafters soared, and the open plan stretched on to the kitchen and narrowed off towards the hallway with the bedrooms. The house was attractive, surprisingly neat, but it felt a little lonely. She wondered if Rebel liked it that way. Something told her he didn't.

The sound of water running interrupted her staring around. Rebel was brushing his teeth.

Prepared to make good on her promise, she crossed to the kitchen and opened the fridge. A lonely bottle of mustard quivered on the shelf. Next to it hunched a shriveled loaf of sliced bread.

Cupboards? Nothing but a value-size tub of grits, white flour, and peanut butter.

Rebel hadn't been lying about the cooking.

Food later, then.

She entered his bedroom.

Steam escaped the crack in the bathroom door. The last time Minnie had been in here, she'd spent the whole night in his bed. The bedsheets were still knotted from their play.

Rebel's room was small and neat. An alarm clock. A spiral-bound car manual opened carelessly on the bureau. She nosily opened one of his drawers and unleashed an eruption of socks.

Shit!

As she guiltily tried to stuff the socks back in, she uncovered the corner of a pointy, flat object. Apart from the manual, she hadn't seen a single book in Rebel's house so far. He'd told her once he could barely read, had dyslexia. No, not a book, she realized, lifting another pair of socks. An album.

She fished the thing out before she could stop herself. What kind of memories did Rebel want to hold on to?

It became clear immediately that the album was old. Minnie smothered a gasp at the very first page. Rebel's face stared back at her with cold, piercing eyes...But it wasn't Rebel. It was...his mother?

Adeline McCall.

The girl didn't look older than seventeen. Her eyes were wide and rimmed with dark circles. A large bruise flowered in the inside of her elbow. *Help*, she seemed to be saying. The photo unnerved Minnie.

Next came a picture of the four brothers: Ross, Rebel, Rain, and Roman. Roman, the oldest and tallest, stood over his brothers protectively. His foreign features hadn't settled; he just looked like a cute kid. Rebel held the toddler Ross by his shoulders. Rain was asleep.

Conscious that she was snooping, Minnie hurried through the rest. Mostly just random pictures of the brothers at formal events, and then a couple snaps of Rebel and Katie.

Frowning, Minnie flipped back to the picture of Rebel's mother. Sometimes a man's daughter resembled his mother or other female relatives. But Katie and Adeline didn't look remotely alike.

You're reaching...Katie doesn't look like Roman at all. She's obviously Rebel's daughter.

"Minnie?" Rebel called from the bathroom.

She stuffed the album back and shut the drawer. "Y-yes?"

"Get in here."

She could barely make out him through the clouds of steam. He leaned against the wall, still as a rock.

"That you?" he said, not opening his eyes.

"Uh huh...Do you need something?" He was breathtakingly sexy.

"Yeah. You. Come here."

She slowly stripped down. His eyes opened, feasted on her. She stepped under the spray. Water flattened her natural hair, sluiced off the points of her breasts, down her brown stomach, to the curly thatch between her legs.

"You're so beautiful," he said.

I'm naked in the shower with Rebel. She hovered away from him, squeezing her eyes shut and turning her face to get blasted by the water. Her heart was pounding hard. He stood completely naked in front of her, and her body with all its curves and flaws was totally on display for him. He could see the darker skin on her kneecaps, her love handles, her big breasts.

"Look at me," he commanded. She did. Burning, hungry eyes. A very hard dick. He towered over her. "My girl." He pulled her close; his hands cupped and kneaded her ass. Exhilarating. She wanted to open her body for him, to take him inside her deep.

He guided her hips against his, packing his erection against her stomach. Pre-ejaculate wept into her navel. *He's hung.* Warmth came down thick and sticky between her legs. Her body, preparing itself for him.

"Stay tonight," he said. It wasn't a question.

Yes...

"Good girl...My girl..." His lips found hers, his tongue breached into her mouth, hot and possessive. She gasped. They invaded each other. Rebel groped and pawed her ass like he couldn't get enough of it. "Why haven't we fucked yet?" he growled.

"Let me wash you first," she said hurriedly, pulling away.

With a groan he let his arms fall and patiently waited. She took her time, torturing herself. Rebel was an extremely beautiful man. Tall and toned, his arms banded with muscle, hands rough from manual labor. Gold hairs on his legs, big, arched feet...Strong calves, thick thighs, every inch of him solid and male and unyielding.

She knelt at his feet under the water, tilting her face to his. The hand holding the loofah stilled. Soap bubbles ran down her arm over her breasts. His long, thick dick jutted out against her cheek. Two veins surged up the sides.

It's more of a dusky rose, I'd say.

She washed it too, and cupped it in her hands as the soap sluiced off. But the act made her nervous, and she had no idea what she was doing, really, so she let go...

His flat stomach shuddered. He grasped his cock in one big hand and stroked himself. His balls drew up, plump and heavy and dark against the thick meat of his inner thighs.

Minnie felt a powerful urge to put her mouth on it.

And then Rebel cupped her head and the urge became a burning need. They stared at each other, Rebel leaning on the shower wall with his elbow, Minnie on her knees, both breathing hard.

"You don't...have to."

But she wanted to.

"Show me how you like it," she whispered.

He nodded, cupping her chin so her head tilted up. Holding himself out to her, he pressed forward against her lips. She opened her mouth, a slave to his silent command. Her lips closed on the silky heat of him.

Pre-ejaculate rolled over her tongue.

"Oh, fuck..."

She pulled away. "Is that good? Am I doing it right?"

"Yeah...Come here. Come here."

Rebel fisted the back of Minnie's head, gathering her hair the way he always had longed to do, in a big handful. He stroked his smooth cockhead over her lips. "Open for me, angel."

He rocked his hips forward. Her eyes shut and she breathed through her nose, stroking him with her tongue, her lips, and then her hands. She looked stunning.

"You're so good," he mumbled, thumbing water from her streaming eyes. He thrust a little, and she gasped, pulling away. He slowly guided her back. "You're so good. Good girl. Take my cock...Take care of me." He showed her.

One of her small hands worked up his length. His face tightened, eyes darkening with lust. Impulsively she reached up and cupped his sack, which was heavy and full. "Fuck..." His head fell back.

Minnie learned how Rebel liked it. He liked his hand clenched in her hair, his hips rocking hard. She moaned and stroked him faster, her clit throbbing, needing to be touched.

Should I touch it? Selfish...

Experimentally she trailed a finger down and found herself shockingly wet. She slicked a hand through her arousal, rubbing on the exposed bud of her clit.

Rebel noticed. "You touching yourself?" he growled, jerking at her head. Her mouth still full of his veined dick, she nodded. *Stroke...stroke...* "Good," he said, eyes hazy. Her pussy throbbed and in that same moment his dick worked past the barrier in her throat.

"Fuck." Rebel panted, losing all control now. "How– oh God almighty, don't stop it." He bowed over her, his touch growing rougher, his hips bullying her into the wall of the shower. "Minnie. You want to know how I like it?"

She nodded through her spit and tears.

"I want you to take my nut." He fucked her mouth. "Don't...swallow it. Just take it." She could barely breathe, but it felt wildly erotic to let him deprive her of air, of life, while he took his pleasure from her mouth faster, rougher, harder...She nodded.

With a strangled yell Rebel came, holding her firmly on his cock. Semen flooded to the back of her throat, spilling down her lips and chin. A lot of it. How could one man have so much? Rebel braced his forearms on the shower wall, his hips shuddering and jerking as he emptied his balls inside his woman's mouth, emptied them down to nothing. Indulging himself, he held her head in place for a moment, fingers hard against her scalp. She gagged and with a grunt he gave one final pump. "Good girl," he gasped. "Fucking Christ...So good...So good." He waited for her to start whimpering again before he withdrew his aching cock. Then he grabbed her chin with all his fingers, forcing her to open up and show him the hot cum he'd dumped into her mouth. The blazing look in his eyes brought Minnie to her feet, stumbling against him.

"Swallow it," he commanded, staring into her eyes.

She did. Every drop of McCall seed.

"Minnie!"

Rebel's cheeks were scarlet red, and instead of quelling his lust, she'd doused it in gasoline and lit a match. With a growl he curled forward, smashing her body against his and capturing her lower lip between his teeth. The water shut off, somehow. They tripped across the floor, Rebel's mouth branding across her skin, Rebel's hands cupping and squeezing her tits, her ass. She whimpered when the mattress caught her fall, and again when he covered her body with his, resting his weight on his arms.

"You alright?" he said, lifting wet hair away from her face. His knees caged her body underneath him. The thick root of his cock dipped against her inner thigh. The violence of his lust for her was undoing him. She felt the same.

Her eyes were watering and her lips felt plump and bruised, but she'd never imagined these sensations would be so delicious. "Kiss me," she said.

Rebel bent his head to suck her breast and the tip of his cock kissed the unprotected entrance to her pussy. She jumped.

He pulled away, a question in his eyes.

She said quickly, "I'm just scared."

"You're scared?"

She nodded. *I've never had sex.* "Was it too much just now? You can tell me," he said, frowning. "I was too rough?"

Her nipples beaded as the water cooled on her skin; she shivered. "No...I'm just..." He'd stop. If she told him the truth, he'd stop right now.

"I'm not real experienced," she hedged, touching his lips with a shaking finger.

"I know that, Minnie."

She winced. Was it that obvious?

"You said you never sucked dick before."

Oh. Right.

"Did I do it right?" She whispered.

"Honey..." He laughed and tugged her against him, hiking her leg over his waist. Again his cock slid against her cunt. He spoke right in her ear. "Did you like it?"

"I did."

"You were perfect." His middle finger dipped inside her channel. She gasped but curled up to meet it. "It's alright," he said raggedly, speaking slow and soft. "I got you. So tight...got to prepare you for me."

Another finger joined the first. They slicked in and out of her channel, skimmed over her hole, the thick nub of her clit. "Think I can get you off just doing this?" he murmured wickedly. His fingers hooked into her G-spot.

"Oh my God," she said.

REBEL WAS GONE. *GONE.* HE WAS HARDER THAN HE'D EVER BEEN in his life and he was going to fuck Minnie for the first time. Every time she rocked into his fingers he felt her wetness slick on his palm. The greedy male instinct demanded a hard and messy fuck. He had to claim her. Mark her. He had to use her body over and over...

He thrust his fingers hard inside her, twisting them, and she started shaking with abandon. She gripped his arms hard. "Rebel!"

He was losing his mind. One moment he felt like a ravenous dog, wanting to rut into Minnie and spend himself deep, just fucking her until she was sore and aching and crying him off her. The next, he wanted to take his time kissing every inch of her deep brown skin, romantic-like, slow and tender.

He blinked down at her, circled in his arms, and wondered how she could be real. Thick, gorgeous black hair pillowed under her head, framing her doll-like face. He inhaled her scent: freesias, lavender...honey.

Her large breasts splayed over her chest, nipples dark and big and tender for him. Then lower, her silky stomach quivering as she came apart, his thumb pressing on her clit while his second and third fingers delved where she was hottest.

He removed his fingers and squeezed her hips possessively...Wide and solid, just how he'd always liked his women. But there wouldn't be another woman for him after this. He knew it in his bones.

"You're hard again," she whispered in her soft, innocent voice.

No shit. Instead of replying, he dragged her thigh up higher and fit his cock at her entrance. *Thrust. Fuck.*

"Rebel," she gasped.

Just fuck her.

Resisting the wicked urge to just push into his woman unsheathed, and to hell with the consequences, he rolled off her. Took a rubber from the nightstand and tore it open with his teeth. He'd make her put it on for him next time...He rolled the rubber down...When he looked back at Minnie, she'd gone tense.

The outrageous notion came to Rebel: *Is she a...virgin?*

Well, now would be a good time to say something. But Minnie didn't say anything. She just relaxed, taking him back into her arms and laying a kiss on him that made his toes curl.

He kissed her back, the luxurious haven of her warm, sweet mouth robbing him of thought. He knew he'd never get tired of kissing her. He nudged apart her knees.

A drop of sweat quivered between her breasts. Her eyes were dark as jet. Skin so soft... He lined himself up.

"Relax, alright?"

She inhaled...He pushed.

She gasped, squirming under him. Uncomfortable. "It's okay," he said through gritted teeth. "Take a little more, babygirl."

Another thrust. She came up off the bed, her sharp cry cutting through his bliss like razor steel. His hips rolled towards her almost automatically, wedging himself deeper. His vision blurred. Minnie was so damned tight... His mouth watered, balls ached, needing to pump inside her. Fuck, he wasn't even all the way in. Pleasure shot up the tip of his dick, and he tried to withdraw.

"Don't stop," she gasped.

"You okay? I know...my size..."

Fuck her. Make her take it. She's your woman; she's got to learn.

"N-no," she said. "It's n-not you. It's me."

God almighty. He leaned back and looked her in the eye. Her breath caught. It hung between them, unspoken.

But he let her have her pride. Just as he was going to adjust her, she hooked her legs behind his thighs and forced him deeper. "I want it," she whispered. "Don't stop. Please don't stop." She tried to tilt her hips, brutalized by his size but desperate to accommodate him.

Stop. Think. God, how could he think, when he was nearly balls deep inside the woman he'd dreamed about night after night? He looked down where his pale cock was about to disappear inside her. *Say something.*

"We shouldn't..." he began hoarsely. *Shouldn't what?* He had no idea. "I just need you to fuck me, baby," Minnie whimpered.

His cock jumped inside her. *Fuck it.* He seized her hips, forced them into the angle he liked best, both hands spread wide on her thick ass. He pinned her to the bed with one brutal thrust.

She gasped.

"You okay?"

"Yes," she panted. "Don't stop."

He bit her neck and kissed it. Pain to pleasure.

256

"It doesn't hurt," she said.

He kissed her mouth, kissed her so fucking deep and hard she kissed back and bloodied his lips. She was squeezing the life from his cock. His thrusts became loose, aggressive. She moaned and writhed and he had to pin her down. *Good girl. Fight me for it*...Minnie a virgin...Her first time...She'd given it to him...She was his. His alone. Blind with lust, he found his own pleasure building like a storm. This was insane.

A low moan wrenched from Minnie's throat, and then another. Her eyes were wide, wild. She gripped his ass. "Rebel!"

She could get off like that just from his cock in her pussy; Rebel held her down and fucked her like she'd asked, just fucked her, until he felt it building hot and annihilating in his balls, and her breasts with those damn purple nipples were bouncing and rolling, and he saw the love bites he'd sucked against her neck and he felt her squeezing and clenching and soaking his cock with everything she had.

Rebel jerked Minnie up so she was straddling him and he fell back on his ass. He wrapped his arms around her and buried his face in her breasts. From below he pumped into her deep. He held off, teeth clenched, until she began to shake and writhe against him, her orgasm starting the spiraling explosion of his own. He didn't recognize his own voice. Face buried in her incredible breasts he cried out and filled the condom, wishing he could somehow keep coming forever, holding Minnie down to receive his seed. It dragged out even still, every thrust emptying him until there was nothing left to give her.

CHAPTER 16
THE WHOLE TOWN KNOWS

"Y ou should have told me." Rebel plumped her breast with his hand and sucked lazily on the dark nipple.

"I thought you wouldn't want to do it if I told you."

"I came at you like a wild thing..."

"Maybe I liked it."

"How come you never did it before? It ain't a religious thing?"

"Not really..." She blushed, partly because Rebel's thumbs were tracing her nipples. "I did want to wait for my husband, at first. Be a good Christian girl."

"So are we going to hell 'cause we ain't married?"

Minnie bit her lip guiltily. "I'll talk it over with God."

"Let me know what he says." Rebel let himself fantasize about marrying Minnie. Her in a white dress, done up in lace, waiting for him at the altar.

Minnie pictured Rebel in a button-down, tall and handsome, giving his vows as his intense green eyes stared into hers. Rebel sliding a ring on her finger, her small hand tiny against his large rough fingers...

"So what did you think of my house?" Rebel murmured.

"Oh...I liked it."

"Lonely, ain't it? It was built on old foundations. House before it was a hundred years old, or more."

"Did you build this place?" Minnie asked, cued by something in his tone.

"Uh huh. Well, Larry and my boy Chick helped. We did it in four months over the summer 'round the time Katie came to Florin. We was drunk as catfish, but we got her done. The roof don't leak. That's the important thing."

"That's incredible," said Minnie, impressed.

"It's too big," Rebel confessed. "I guess I planned to start a family in here but never got around to it."

"Would you ever want to get married?" She asked Rebel lightly. "At all, I mean."

"I ain't against it," was all he said.

They lay in his bed, the sheets damp and tangled, her body curved against his.

"What about you?" Rebel asked.

"I would."

"Is that why you freaked out the first time I kissed you on the lookout?" he said. "You'd barely done anything with a man before me, hadn't you?"

"Basically nothing."

His arm tightened around her jealously. "What's 'basically'?"

"Touching. Dry-humping."

He shook his head. Then he laughed to himself. "You were mad as a hornet that first time I kissed you."

Minnie cringed. She'd given him a harsh and sudden rejection after a whole morning encouraging his flirtation, kissing him, letting him into her panties.

"I was afraid of what people would think, seeing us together," she admitted.

"And now the whole town knows," he mused.

"Yes," said Minnie. "Now the whole town knows."

"And?"

"The whole town can mind its business."

Rebel murmured, "I'll do whatever it takes to have you. I won't let anybody hurt you again. If I have to start a war in this town over it, I'll do that, and everybody else be damned. I promise you, Minnie, you're safe with me."

The force of his words scared her. "Maybe you'll change your mind, Rebel. We haven't known each other that long. I just wonder..." *Say it.* "I'm afraid I'm making a mistake."

"This don't feel like a mistake to me. You're the woman I want. And I feel in my heart that this was meant to be. I got no problems saying I want to fight for you."

"I'm hoping it won't come to that," said Minnie nervously.

Rebel didn't say anything.

Then, a while later, "It feels like I just stepped out the door on the first day of summer, and warm sunshine is beating right down on my face."

"I'm glad I met you," she whispered.

He tucked a curl behind her ear. "I don't mean to scare you with all that talk. All I'm saying is I want you, darling. That's all. And I aim to get what I want...That's if you'll have me."

Her heart melted. A part of her felt this was all too good to be true. But her connection to Rebel felt like the deepest, most honest instinct she'd ever experienced.

"Of course I'll have you," she said.

He grinned. "For the record, we'd make some beautiful young."

"Babies? Oh my goodness."

"I'm thinking five or six."

Five or six! Minnie gently reminded him, "I'm not twenty, Rebel. I only got gas in the tank for two. Maybe three."

He nodded. "We'll have to start soon, then. Or adopt another four."

She laughed. "You are crazy."

Her thigh brushed his semi-hard dick and he grunted. He cupped her ass and kneaded it. Minnie watched blood slowly fill his cock until it stood out hard and distended against his navel, a smear of pre-cum leaking from the tip.

"Let's start now," he said.

"Boy..."

LIKE THIS, REBEL THOUGHT, HOURS OR MINUTES LATER. *ALWAYS like this.* Covered in sweat, he fucked into Minnie's slick heat, her tits chafing on his chest, her eyes glazed. The sheets were damp and coming off the bed. His knee dug into the bare mattress. Some of her woman's cream was on his chin. The salt of her body was in his mouth.

They'd been fucking all night. He'd lost count. He just kept getting hard. Minnie kept getting wetter. Get hard, cum inside her, get hard again. He'd never get enough of her. Every single time felt like the first.

She came again, her cries sweet and her body twining around his. Her thighs gripping his waist. Her hips jolting into his no matter how hard he plowed her, greedily trying to take more of him. Groaning, he fondled her heavy breasts.

Lord, he wanted to marry her. He wanted to breed children on her. He wanted her pregnant, he wanted her just like this, young and sweet and his, he wanted her...he wanted her...He'd kill for her, die for her.

He wasn't a man anymore, just an animal, a beast with a hungering need to breed its mate. And Minnie was his woman, sure as God intended. She started coming, her cries hoarse, because he'd wrung so many out of her already.

"Rebel, baby please…"

I love her.

"Come here," he gritted. "Come here, babygirl. Get it from me."

"Yes, baby," she cried.

He seeded into her deep, crushing her under him, crushing her close, and the endless yield of her flesh sent him rocking into a whole new world of bliss. She sobbed his name. He saw colors he'd never dreamed of explode, like a shattered light, into cool and glittering dust.

CHAPTER 17
LUCKY'S WARNING

Mister John Lucky was the Sheriff of Florin County and the first "foreigner" to ever wear the badge. Though only from Charleston, not exactly Timbuktu, he was a complete alien to the mountain, and very proud of that fact.

The man had come to power under unusual circumstances. For years, Earl Jackson Jr. had worn the silver badge. But one morning while enjoying his daily breakfast of fried chicken, cheese grits and pineapple juice, the old Sheriff's heart tragically gave out. The town voted on a new man, James Craw, a few days later. A week after that, Craw resigned and fled the mountain with his entire family. There was another election, better rigged this time, and the badge was finally given to John Lucky, the Charleston man, where it had remained ever since.

Lucky's Carolina accent was in Rebel's book one of the worst offenses about the man. He laid it on thick as gravy on a biscuit. He said things like *I declare* and *Good Gracious*

Lord. He was a fusty man, too; he never let a single scuff disgrace his boots. Rumor said he'd gone to Harvard.

"I declare," said Lucky, coming up the hill. "What a splendid morning, isn't it? How are you holding up, McCall?" Lucky was older than Rebel by a year.

"Morning," said Rebel shortly.

"I bring good news," said Lucky, smiling.

"Is that so?"

"It is indeed. I come to tell you that your cousin's death was officially deemed an accident by the coroner. A self-inflicted gunshot to the chest."

Rebel looked up. "I see."

Lucky shrugged. "And it would seem the murder weapon in question has mysteriously vanished. So there won't be a trial. The law has declared you a free man, McCall."

Rebel glanced back into the Jaguar's engine, carefully controlling himself. "Well, thanks for bringing it to me, Sheriff. Taking time out of your busy day to reassure me. Very generous of you."

"Surely that can't be all you have to say for yourself," the Sheriff prodded in the same cheerful tone.

"Who did the autopsy?" Rebel grunted.

"I think you know who." Lucky paused. His cheerful tone dropped. "And I think you know it's bullshit."

Rebel straightened up. "Oh, really?"

"Perhaps Bubba McCall's death was no accident," the Sheriff said. Rebel said nothing so Lucky continued, "Perhaps the Brown woman invited those men to her house. Then you showed up in a green rage, with intent to kill, and shot Bubba McCall in the chest." Lucky's gaze dropped to the wrench in Rebel's hands.

"She invited them, you say." Rebel turned the wrench over and over. "You calling her a whore?"

"Merely repeating a theory."

"I dare you to repeat it again."

Lucky's lip curled. "You're still with her, I hear?"

"That ain't your goddamn business."

The Sheriff tensed. He didn't want to enrage Rebel, but if he turned tail at every ornery McCall, he might as well hand in the badge.

"You must understand how it looks, Rebel. "

"I don't care how it looks." Rebel set down the wrench. "I got a right to that woman without the whole fucking town trying to break down her door. Why is that so hard to understand?"

"May I make a suggestion, McCall?"

"You'll do it anyway. What?"

"Leave town," said the Sheriff.

"Excuse me?"

Lucky shrugged. "Your father won't stop until that woman is lying on a slab. And all the corrupt coroners in the world won't bring her back."

"You speaking as his mouthpiece?"

"I'm speaking as Sheriff."

"My woman never led nobody on. He attacked her unprovoked. I don't intend to let that stand, Sheriff."

"There's two sides, and there's the truth, they say," Lucky mused. He circled the car Rebel was working on, conscious of the rising hostility from the taller man. Lucky gestured to the car, if you could even call it that. The thing looked nearly gutted, the parts spread out on the cement floor. "What's this?"

"Old Jag. I'm fixing it for...a friend."

For his woman, Lucky guessed.

"Is it a gift?"

"Could be."

Definitely his woman.

Lucky scratched a spot on the hood with a fingernail. "I assume you'll repaint it."

"Obviously," said Rebel through his teeth. "Is that all, *Sheriff*? I'm running a business here and this ain't teatime."

Lucky clasped his hands behind his back and faced the tall McCall. His expression became serious. "You start a war on this mountain over some woman, you're gonna get more than you bargained for," he said. "So tread lightly from here on, McCall."

"Is that a threat?"

"Consider it a warning." Lucky shrugged. "Between you and me, more eyes on the mighty McCalls might just be more than they can stand right about now. Don't make any more smoke on this mountain, or somebody's gonna come up here looking for a fire. Understand what I'm saying to you?"

"You mean the Feds?"

Lucky examined his reflection in the Jaguar's tinted window. He fixed a stray curl as he said, "Let's just say that change is coming to this mountain, and sooner than you think."

"You told my Pa this?"

"No."

Rebel wiped his hands on a filthy rag, saying nothing. His glower looked contemplative. Despite his rugged looks and limited vocabulary, this McCall wasn't a fool.

"Get your house in order before the big boss gets home, McCall. That'd be my advice." The Sheriff tipped his hat. "Have a wonderful day."

"They cleared you of the charges?" Minnie exclaimed. "Then why do you look so serious?"

"Just thinking." Another lie.

Minnie sighed and settled back in the seat. "Long day today. We got homes for all the puppies now, thanks to you. But somebody dropped off a box of seven kittens. Can you believe that?"

"Oh, really?" He said, distracted.

She bit her lip and looked at him. "You're alright, Rebel? Is something wrong?"

"I'm fine, darling."

Back at his house, he wasted no time getting Minnie into bed . She had worried about the trial more than he had, he reflected. Maybe he knew deep down it would never come to that. No matter what, he was still a McCall in Florin.

He peeled off her clothes, laid her out on her back while he knelt on the floor. He wanted to taste her, take her sweetness inside him and purge the ugly stress of his day with her pure essence. He sucked directly on her clit until she gasped and dug her heels into the mattress, thrusting against his mouth. "More...Harder..." she gasped. He obliged her, and just as she started coming he rose up and took his dick out and pushed inside her.

She whimpered, going soft in his arms, but her eyes narrowed with pain. He rolled over with her, making her kneel over him, panting. Her brown breasts swung at the perfect height for his lips, her nipples like two summer cherries, juicy and sweet. He groped them blindly, sucking hard. She moaned and twined her hands in his hair, a thing that always drove him crazy. She twirled her hips up and down in a sinuous, slow dance. If his cock slipped out, the cool air kissed it for just a moment before

Minnie's cunt claimed it again. She didn't even use her hands.

It was like a fight. The more she tried to make love to him, the harder he fucked her. He let her be sweet. Think she'd won. But just as cum started climbing up his dick he wrenched her hands behind her back, pulling out of her and flipping her facedown.

"Rebel, wait—"

"Just take it." He thrust into her roughly.

With a cry of surrender her head and shoulders dropped to the mattress. Her back arched and he slid inside her, one solid hot spike that seemed to touch the back of her throat.

"Yes," he growled.

When he came his fingers dug so hard into her ass Minnie had to grip the sheets to keep from howling. He pulled out of her, his cum spilling on the sheets and trickling down her thighs. She was on birth control; he'd been tested; they didn't use condoms anymore.

Minnie heard her man breathing hard, like he'd just run a great distance. After a moment the bathroom door slammed. Running water. Then he returned, and a warm wet towel pressed between her legs.

He cleaned the trails of his burning seed off her slowly, gently. He passed the towel between her legs. Then he left the room.

After she collected herself she went out to meet him on the porch. Facing west, it captured a full view of the setting sun. Rebel leaned on the railing, dragging at a cigarette held between trembling fingers. Since she started staying at his house he hadn't touched one. Until now.

His eyes avoided hers. "I was rough on you."

"We can talk about it, Rebel."

He nodded. "We got a problem, Minnie."

"Okay." She leaned over the railing, anxiety clawing up her throat. Luckily, Rebel wasn't one to beat around the bush.

"I'm having second thoughts."

She froze. *Keep calm.* "Oh," she said. "About...us?"

"No. Yes. I mean, not really."

"Is this about Duke?" She realized what was bothering him. "He got you off that sentence, didn't he?"

"Yeah."

Though she'd expected it, Minnie's gut clenched. She didn't like McCall holding that over Rebel's head.

Rebel said, "I feel like I have a chance to screw them over big time. I feel like something's coming that will turn this whole mountain over. But it's all uncertain..." His eyes went hazy. "It's driving me crazy. How am I going to protect you?"

"It's been weeks since it happened, Rebel. They haven't tried anything so far. Maybe they'll leave us alone..."

Rebel shook his head. "I don't think so. He's just biding his time. Something's brewing out there, Minnie."

"We agreed we could handle anything that comes," Minnie said. "We promised we would face it together." She had never heard Rebel sound so bleak and frustrated.

"I know, darling." He leaned over the railing. "I know."

"So what now?"

"We could leave Florin," he said, surprising her. "Go down to Rowanville. I got money put away. We could start over. Try something out for a while."

"No." She was never giving up her animals, her patients, no matter what. She clutched his arm, trying to make him listen. "No," she said. "Florin is my home, same as yours. I don't like what your family does, or what they stand for, and I'm fearful every day because of what they did to me. But—"

"Your nightmares," interrupted Rebel suddenly, a cloud passing over his face. "What are they about? Sometimes you call Roman's name. You said he never did anything to you. Are you sure?"

Minnie opened and closed her mouth. She had never told Rebel the extent of what went down in her trailer. How Roman made her kiss him. She suspected if she did, Rebel would do something irreparable to his brother.

"I'm sure, Rebel," she said quickly. "Listen— I have a business here. A life. A mother to take care of. I have...you." She added softly, "I know you love it here."

"I'd rather have you than Florin."

"We can have both. We can try. If these rednecks want to kill me, then they can try! But I won't be running scared." Her brush with death and torture had changed her. She found a piece of iron in herself that wouldn't bend, and it was this: nobody would stop her from making the life she wanted. Nobody, not even the McCalls.

Of course, maybe it was foolish. Maybe her growing suspicion (helped by Rebel's cryptic words) that the great house of cards was going to come crashing down was wrong, and the McCalls would find some horrible way to end her life. Or Mama's. Was her defiance selfish?

How could it be selfish, to stand up for the right thing?

After all, nobody ever *stood up* to the McCalls. They were just a part of life on the mountain. So omnipotent that Minnie had known nothing about them until she met Rebel, even if they controlled everything. So powerful they could change the law. *Become* the law.

"We may have a little rebellion here," said Rebel, watching the glint of determination in his woman's eye. "But there will be a price on that, and I ain't sure I want to pay it in your blood. Or our children's."

"I want to fight. I'm not afraid, Rebel. Honestly."

"My little braveheart. Come here."

She stepped into his arms, pressing her nose into his bare chest. He kissed her head and said, "If we had young, I'd want them to know their parents ain't cowards." His big hand slid across her stomach. "It'll be as you say, Minnie. We'll stay."

"I just know it will work out," she said softly.

"I hope you're right." He paused. "But if it comes to blows between me and my family again, promise me you'll let me handle it my own way. Trust me to always take care of these things. To always take care of you."

He'll always protect me. After a moment, she nodded.

He turned her against the railing, tucking her firmly against his chest. Their naked skin slid together. Though the sun was sinking, the afternoon heat remained, and a flush of sweat beaded on Minnie's collarbone. Rebel's big gilded body wrapped around her, holding her in a loose embrace against the railing.

Don't stand in the sun. You want to get even darker?

Sorry, Mama. Don't care.

THE HILLS TURNED GOLD, AND THEN THE COLOR OF RUST ON A wagon wheel. The sun ducked behind the spine of the mountains. A cardinal trilled in the magnolia tree. At the bottom of the hill, a family of white tails darted over the fence. The road wound on, down dark hollers and roads like sunlit rivers, on and on through the mountains, forever.

"This place is beautiful," Minnie breathed.

"It's old Aberry land," Rebel murmured. "Inherited it when Pap died— that would be my mother's father. He was a good man. Left a piece for all us boys, even though I was his only real blood. I sold some to open my shop. If you go down that hill there, you'd get to Roman's. Rain's is that way...Ross is over there."

"You think one day you'll all live together up here?"

"That was Pap's dream. You like this place?"

"I love these mountains," Minnie said. "I could never live anywhere else in the world."

"How about livin' here, then?"

She shivered and put her hands over his, where they clasped across her stomach. "I'd like that."

They stayed there standing, saying nothing.

"One day we'll be just dust blowing over the tops. Going wherever we want," he said.

"To Ben's Hot Chicken."

Laughing, he pushed her loose hair back from her neck. "It's Saturday night."

"Yes..."

"Wanna go dancing?"

CHAPTER 18
EPILOGUE 1

The cool fizz of champagne made Minnie sneeze. She took another sip. "I stand corrected. This is delicious."

Rebel ripped a piece of bread in half and began slathering it with jam. He put the whole thing in his mouth. "Still can't believe I tasted champagne before you did."

"When was the last time you had champagne?"

"When the Cowboys won."

Minnie kicked off her slippers and dug her toes into the warm grass. Pollen traces danced through the air. The wind ruffled through her summer dress.

Rebel was stretched out on the blanket, resting on one elbow and staring down the hillside.

Nemo slept on the blanket, his leash firmly fixed to Minnie's wrist. Even though his mange healed into a sleek brown coat with four white paws, it took him a while to gain strength. It had been Rebel's idea that a little sunshine would do Nemo some good. Rebel let the dog run around his shop and took it on walks, and sure enough Nemo improved. Man and dog were now in love, never to be parted.

"I saw your mother this morning," Rebel remarked.

Minnie stiffened. "What did she want?"

Since that horrible fight in her kitchen, she and Mama hadn't spoken to each other. Minnie still sent her the weekly checks, and knew that her mother cashed them. But they hadn't exchanged a word.

"She wants you to come back to church."

The Incident at Minnie's trailer was still hot gossip. Mrs. Mabel was running around giving a reenactment of the scene to anybody who would listen.

She didn't have nothing on but her drawers!

Now Mama wanted her back in church? So everybody could point and whisper? Harass her about Rebel?

Hell no. At least...not yet. She cast a guilty eye at the sky. She had God to thank for meeting Rebel. And thanks to him, these last few weeks as town pariah had been the best of her life.

AFTER SHE CLOSED UP THE CLINIC FOR THE EVENING, AND REBEL finished at his shop, they took long drives through Florin. They sped down roads she had never seen, over secret hills that ended in stunning views of the peaks. They ate ice cream in the middle of the night. They talked about everything.

In Rebel she found a passionate man of fierce devotion. He showed her his world, the secret parts of the mountain that only a McCall would know, surprising her with his knowledge of the forest, its plants and animals, its seasons, its moods, and so much more.

He watched every episode of *Preacher Man* with her, and all seven movies. He concurred that it was a masterpiece, but did not think Jackson Creed was "a dime".

One afternoon he stopped by her hospital with his truck full of tools. He demanded Minnie list out things she wanted fixed. Her embarrassed hand-waving went ignored. In one week, while balancing all his clients and some other "secret" project behind the garage, Rebel found time to come up to the clinic, repair the roof, clear the gutters, caulk the toilet, replace the taps, change the light fixtures, tune the air conditioning, and displace a hive of bees from the vents. Watching Rebel handle the swarming mass, calm as if he was moving a pair of shoes, was the sexiest thing in the world.

She insisted on paying him. Offended, he refused. That had been their first big argument.

And then...

A week later, he drove her halfway down the mountain to Larry's garage, which she'd never visited before. In between piles of scrap junk sat vintage cars in different stages of decay and repair. Larry showed her the only car ready for sale: a fully restored 1984 Jag. Emerald green.

"You can get it for three grando," the redheaded man told Minnie cheerfully. She didn't miss the sidelong look he gave to Rebel, who pretended to be inspecting the engine.

"I...Really?" The car was worth probably ten times that.

"Yup," said Larry.

Minnie took Rebel aside. "Is this car stolen?" she asked from the side of her mouth.

He grinned. "Larry only steals from the government."

"This is a luxury car... The repairs will cost a fortune," she argued.

Rebel patted her ass. "Now if only you knew a good mechanic."

"You're unbelievable." She shook her head. "Is this what you had under that tarp in your shop? Is this the big secret you've been working on?"

His green eyes widened innocently.

One more attempt to talk herself out of it. "Rebel, I need something more practical...I can't put animal crates in that."

"I see your point," said Rebel. His voice lowered conspiratorially. "But if you buy it for three grand, you can sell it for, I'd say, about eight times that?"

"You wouldn't care if I sold it?"

He shrugged. "It'll be yours. Just don't take a sledge-hammer to the windows if I piss you off, alright?"

Her heart swelled with love for him. She kissed him on his blonde-stubbled cheek. "I'll never sell it," she whispered.

And she never did.

. . .

MINNIE TIED NEMO'S LEASH TO THE PICNIC BASKET AND crawled over to Rebel, landing heavily on top of him. Her hands slid under his T-shirt and stroked his chest. His steady heartbeat calmed her down. He chuckled and nuzzled her close. He trailed his hands up her sundress, over her ass.

"You got pollen in your hair and grass on your dress...You look like a real country girl."

He rolled her underneath him and slowly peeled off her sundress. She'd worn it for him. He loved her in skirts and dresses as much as he loved her in her scrubs with her hair all mussy from a long day.

He pulled her panties down. They landed somewhere in the grass. Breathless, Minnie lay there on the blanket with her hands over her breasts. Sunlight caressed her skin with a gentle, warm touch. Rebel's touch was warm, but not gentle.

"I love seeing you like this," he murmured, his green eyes feasting on her, his palm groping her breast. "Naked, bare, open for me. So beautiful..."

Her knees drifted apart. He hauled her against him until the stiff fabric of his jeans compressed her clit. After rocking and nudging her with it until she was panting, ready, Rebel unzipped and freed himself. She splayed a palm flat on his hard stomach. Behind her man, the Blue Ridge mountains ran on endlessly. He slid in deep, his thick shaft stretching her. He groaned.

"Baby," she panted. "Oh, baby. Yes...Yes."

I want his child.

"Couldn't be...Anybody else for me." His jeans stretched tight over his thighs as he took her again and again and again. His balls slapped her ass, sticky with their mingled arousal.

"Yes." She held onto his shoulders, cupped his face. "I love you."

Rebel's cock pinned her down in hard, almost violent strokes. "Always," he panted. "Say it's always."

"Always..."

She tilted her hips and took him deep, running her hands up his back and into his hair until she felt his muscles clench. His balls tightened up and he came inside her, hot and thick, spilling out onto the blanket, streaking on her thighs. Her cries became just another part of the wilderness around them.

"I love you."

EPILOGUE 11

As Katie McCall passed her father's bedroom, she paused and listened. No sound passed through the heavy pine door. She could see nothing in the dark, not even the glow of his reading light. Slowly she reached for the envelope in her overall pocket, meaning to slip it underneath and continue briskly towards the back stair.

"Katie?"

She froze, her heart pounding so loud she was sure her father could hear it. She turned, hastily tucking the envelope into her pocket.

"D-daddy?"

Roman stood in the hallway. His enormous physique created a void in the darkness. She took a small step back.

"You're awake?" she said stupidly. Her father could go days without sleep, but when he did, he crashed for hours and nothing but the rapture could wake him. That was why she'd told Junior it had to happen tonight. Once her father went into his room, he wasn't supposed to get up and start prowling the house like a haint.

"I thought I heard something," Roman said, fumbling for the light. He winced when it flicked on. "You alright?" He said gruffly.

"I'm fine." *Go back to sleep, old man.*

"I heard somebody crying," Roman said. He rubbed his face. "It sounded...I don't know. Why are you dressed up?"

He'd noticed. The lie jumped to Katie's lips immediately, but sometimes her father's penetrating black stare threw off her game. "I'm goin' on a walk," she said, trying to sound cool, like Mama used to when talking to an annoying boyfriend.

"It's nine o' clock, girl. You ain't walking nowhere at this hour."

"Uncle Rebel says I can come over."

"Does he." Roman scowled. "I'm surprised he still has the time to entertain you, these days."

Katie bit her tongue. She was angry at Uncle Reb, but didn't like when her father talked bad about him.

"Anyway, you ain't going. It's too far," said Roman finally. Rubbing his bare chest, he turned towards the kitchen.

Katie bit the inside of her cheek in frustration. Great. She might be here for hours waiting for him to crash again. The whole plan could be ruined because her father just had to quit the only reliable thing about him at the worst possible time.

She had no choice but to follow and keep him in her sights. She glanced at her watch, the glow-in-the-dark dial showing she had better get a move on.

In the kitchen Roman poured himself a bowl of cereal and leaned over the counter to eat it. He moved slowly. He had a bone-weary look that she'd been seeing a lot of lately. But she didn't have the time nor will to worry about her father sending himself to an early grave.

Saint Roman. Daddy's mission in life was to make his family of crazy hillbillies seem respectable. It was a full time job on top of his other full time job of running McCall's Supply and Feed.

He moved the spoon around the cereal bowl. People called her Daddy handsome. Even the girls in school had fits over him, which was so gross.

"Come," he said. "Sit down."

"Do I have to?"

"Sit."

"Okay." She edged into the seat.

"You weren't going to Rebel's, were you?" he said mildly.

"I was."

He sighed. "I wish you would just tell the truth."

"You ain't ready for the truth, Daddy."

Sometimes Katie's mouth moved faster than her brain.

"Maybe you're right," her father said.

She stared at him. "What?" She asked.

"You just showed up here one day, Katie. I didn't even know you existed. If you'd been a boy, maybe–"

"I'm sorry to disappoint you for bein' a girl," Katie said stiffly.

"I mean to say, when you were little, I should have been there. I should have seen you grow up, made to know you. But you were all the way in Tulsa. I had no idea you even existed. I'll never know why your mother..." His jaw clamped shut.

"Why she was such a whore?"

He ignored this, as if he hadn't heard it. Or as if he'd heard it too many times.

Roman said, "If I'd known you sooner, it would be different. We'd maybe have trust between us. You wouldn't have to lie to me about where you're going and who you're seein'."

She wanted to hurt him. "Uncle Rebel never saw me grow up, neither. And he never treated me like some Amish girl that don't know her ass from a microwave."

"Rebel spoils you."

"He never took a switch to me, though."

Roman flushed. Four years ago, at his wits end with Katie, he'd resorted to the old country technique of getting wayward young to mind. The first strike of the belt felt like fire across her legs. Even trying to use the smallest

286

fraction of his strength, Roman overpowered her. Katie screamed her head off, but again and again the belt came down, the torment going on without stopping. She fought him with everything she had, fought him like a wildcat, but he just kept coming at her and finally she just gave in to the punishment. The devil was, she could never remember what she'd done to earn herself the beating, but she sure as hell didn't forget it.

Katie had been whupped before by Mama, but it had been years, and Mama wasn't half as strong as Roman. Besides, getting a whupping at ten was a little different from one at *fifteen*.

She had limped to the bathroom and wet strips of toilet paper to plaster on her stinging flesh. As she soothed herself, she unhooked the slats on the bathroom window and looked down at the monster, her father. He sat alone on the porch, covered in sweat, squeezing the life from a bottle of corn liquor. He stared at nothing, but it was as if the *nothing* held something horrible inside it. Glass-eyed, he drank and drank all night, just sitting there.

He never apologized, but he never beat her again.

She'd never told Uncle Reb.

"You made me out to be just like Mama," she accused him bitterly. "You punished me for what she did to you. She embarrassed you, didn't she? You never forgave her for that."

"You're right."

She was speechless.

287

"I can't ask your forgiveness for it yet," Roman said. "But I want things to change, Katie. These days I'm so caught up in what's happening down the mountain. But it won't be for always. When that's taken care of, I can start being a better Pa to you." Her father looked down at her. "Maybe we can go to New Orleans, eh? Just us two."

"That would be nice," she forced out. Had he been drinking? She leaned in to sniff, but all she smelled was his sandalwood soap.

"I haven't been drinking, Katie."

She almost wanted him to be drunk. To say she was just like Mama, to call her willful and stubborn and childish. To threaten to marry her to his creepy holy-roller friends if she didn't get some behavior in her uppity, miss-ish head. Who was this man sitting in daddy's kitchen, apologizing and making amends?

"Daddy..." Katie realized this might be the only moment she could ever bring this up. "Daddy, won't you work it out with him? Uncle Rebel?"

Roman shook his head. "I don't think there'll be any working out this one, Katie."

"He'll forgive you." In truth, Katie wasn't sure. Uncle Reb was an easygoing fella, but he didn't like to be fucked with.

"I didn't open the envelope yet," said Roman.

For a stupid moment she thought he meant the letter in her pocket. But he was talking about the results from that ancestry test Uncle Rebel had done. A thrill went through her. "Why not?"

"I..." Roman hesitated. "Maybe this conversation ain't for now."

Katie glanced at her watch again. Junior must be losing it. She had to get out of here.

"Christ, I'm tired."

"Why don't you just take a sleeping pill?" She suggested.

"They don't work no more. I don't want no drugs."

"You should go back to bed, Daddy."

"Do you love me, Katie?" He said.

"Um...I...Yes, daddy."

"You're the only one, then." He turned away from her and put a hand over his face. His shoulders shook, but he didn't make a sound. A long minute passed. She stood there frozen, just staring at his bowl of uneaten cereal. Daddy always bought the healthy kind that tasted like junk. He never even let her put sugar on it. Parts of the wheat squares were dissolving into the milk.

"Go on," her father said in a low voice. "It's alright."

"What?"

"Go on about what you were doing." He cleared his throat. "You going to Emily's? You need anything? You need some money?"

"I–yes."

"My wallet's over there. Take whatever you want."

What is happening?

Katie plucked the wallet off the dining table. Her gaze flicked over the China settings, sparkling clean, like everything in her father's neat-as-a-pin house.

When she first came, Roman insisted they eat every meal at that table. Together, as a "family". But he'd never felt like family to Katie. He was just somebody the law said she had to live with.

Uncle Rebel felt more like family. Somebody you could trust with all your secrets. Somebody who never judged, just listened. A nice man, the kind her Mama should have been with.

She glanced at her father. He was still hunched over, holding his head. Did he look thinner?

Migraines often laid him up for days. Katie had googled the pills in his cabinet. She knew what they were for.

She felt guilty, but only for a moment. To start feeling sorry for the man and listening to his woes would mean she'd officially lost it. But if he was offering up some financial compensation, why decline?

She picked up the wallet, initialed R.E.M— what did the "E" stand for? She'd never learned— and opened it. The old thrill tingled up her hands. Daddy's wallet. She'd pilfered it many times to go a-larking, but this wasn't some sneaky run down the mountain for beer and weed. Her fingers hovered over the bills, counting. A whole baseball team of benjamins peeped up between the leather folds. Holy smokes. It looked to be well over a grand. What in creation was he doing with all that money?

She emptied the wallet. Daddy didn't even raise his head.

"Are you...okay?" she asked, mostly to make sure he hadn't seen her stuffing that wad of money in her pocket.

"Yeah," said Roman. "Go on. Go have your fun, darling."

"You're really letting me go?"

He nodded. "Just don't be gone too long."

"I won't," she said.

She left through the back of the house and hurried down the hill. She cut through what Uncle Rain called Fairy Wood, taking the old path he had shown her once. The letter to her father was still crushed in her back pocket. The things she'd written now seemed childish and simple. She didn't really mean them...

Ugh! Would she listen to herself?

She reminded herself that she hated him. The man was an arrogant pig. He thought girls who went out and had a good time were just cheap whores. It really ground his guts that she was bad at school, and he always bitched about how she could be so dumb when her mama had been so smart. As if school meant anything when you already had money.

Also, he hated black people, didn't want them on his mountain. That was so annoying, because it meant she couldn't take Junior out anywhere. She had to beg Uncle Reb to let her see him, and Uncle Reb would only do it if he could give a boring lecture about taking things slow with boys. Treating her like she was dumb as an ear of corn.

She was glad to be leaving them both. Glad to be running off with Junior, who would do anything for her.

Katie knew what she was doing. Compared to Mama's hard-back Tulsa guys, Junior was easy as a peanut. He weren't different just because he had darker skin. If anything, she liked the way he kept admiring her hair and eyes. It made her feel pretty as a magnolia, and soon she had him nodding to every word she said. Once you got a man to that point, Mama swore, you could make 'im do anything. Mama had been right about that. About a lot of things.

Yes, Katie thought, taking the image of her father slumped over his cereal and shoving it deep inside the locked, rattling box in her chest. Yes, she was better off now. Junior would help her get off the mountain, and lickety-split she'd be back in Tulsa with the rodeo gang, living life the way it was meant to be lived.

Poor Junior. He really didn't know what he was getting into. She would make him see how amazing Tulsa was. All in good time. At any rate, she was sure she could at least get him all the way to Little Rock before he bailed. Getting him to take her off the mountain was the most important thing.

Uncle Reb would say she was just using Junior for her own schemes. He'd say she was being selfish. He'd tell her to wait until she was old enough. Uncle Reb could always spin something she did to make her feel terrible and guilty. But since he'd decided to shack up with that woman and drop Katie like a hot potato, what Uncle Reb thought weren't the least of her concerns anymore.

As for that stupid DNA test...Only her uncle and her father cared about that now. It didn't make a lick or difference to Katie. Surely Uncle Reb didn't even want her. He'd sat on those results for months without telling anybody.

But worse than that, worse than ditching her for some fancy-talking animal doctor, he broke his promise. He'd said he would talk to Junior's uncle, but never did. It wasn't fair. So *he* could run around with a Black lady, but didn't want her with Junior?

Screw him. After the fight at his woman's house, he'd tried to talk to her. She ignored his calls and told daddy she didn't want to speak to him. Roman had been all too happy to shove that in Rebel's face when he came to the door. So he stopped coming. Her laughing, happy uncle took his happiness to somebody else. He was in love with that woman, didn't care about nothing else. Somebody said they saw him at the hardware store in Rowanville with enough lumber to build a second house. Maybe that woman was going to run him broke.

Katie blinked away her tears. Let them have their fun in Florin. She'd be long gone by the time anybody stopped to give a thought to her. If they ever did.

Junior had parked exactly where she'd told him. She could see the moonlight reflected off his headlights; the car was off. Nothing stirred inside the little blue sedan that held her future. She thumped on the driver's side window.

Junior jumped awake and came out of the car. "What took so long?" He grumbled. "You said you'd be out of there fast."

"Nothing. Just got us some money."

"What money? You serious?"

"Yeah," she said coolly. "Got about a grand right here."

"I told you I had it covered," said Junior angrily. He meant his three months of savings from working at his uncle's, a measly seven hundred dollars.

Neither of them had bank accounts, so they'd have to rely on cash until Katie turned eighteen. Katie didn't mind roughing it. In Tulsa, when Mama was in between boyfriends, they often did without. But Junior was kidding himself if he thought a couple work checks would float them in the early stages, when everybody would be out hunting for them.

"Look, Katie, I don't hold with stealing," Junior argued. "Running off is one thing, but stealing—"

"He gave me the money, stupid." Katie slipped into the passenger's seat and after a moment Junior climbed in too.

"He *gave* it to you?"

"I'll explain later, alright? You gonna run off with me or not?" she snapped.

He hesitated. "This is the last chance we have to back out."

"Don't be chicken. You agreed to do this."

Junior shifted on his feet. "Yeah. I know."

She felt a wave of pity for him. Poor Junior, he'd never been off the mountain in his entire life. "It'll be an adventure. You'll see." Katie stepped up to him and hugged him round his waist. Junior liked when she did that. "Imagine all the hotels. Them nights under the stars," she purred. "Nobody can stop us doin' what we want. We can get to know each other even better, right?"

She trailed her hands up his sinewy arms. He shivered against her, then stepped back, sidling against the car. "I just mean, my uncle ain't been feeling too well...It was hard seeing him tonight. Leaving him on his own...I don't know. It feels wrong."

His guilt just made her own worse.

"So? Why do you even care? He doesn't want us to be together. He's a racist, just like my daddy."

"Yeah..."

"Don't get yellow on me, Junior. You got to man up about it. You promised me we'd be together, and this is the best way. You agreed, remember?"

"I ain't yellow, Katie. You know that."

"Good," said Katie. "Then quit moaning. We got a lot of ground to cover."

They drove off the mountain into the jaws of the night, down the winding roads, past the sleepy hollers, the old mills, the bald-faced hills of pasture like chips of dark turquoise on the breasts of the distant, darker hills. They drove until the road was nearly swallowed by forest, until every light of human civilization disappeared. They crossed into Burn Mountain. Junior didn't say anything. He wasn't much of a talker. Slow and dependable, that was Junior.

Leaving the driving in his hands, Katie cranked the seat back and snuggled down with an old quilt she'd taken from the closet. *For my Roman* was embroidered on the back of it in red thread. Weird. The thing looked old and musty, but she'd been in a hurry packing. And it smelled of sandalwood, which wasn't so bad.

Mmm...So cozy. She dreamed of Tulsa. She dreamed of greasy dollar bills and cigarette smoke, whiskey sour and music playing all night long. The good old days, when Mama had the number of the rodeo boys, and a few other numbers besides, to make every day and night just riots of fun.

It was the peak of life, them parties. Adults boozing, Katie and the other kids playing Cowboys and Indians between the trailers, trying to wake up the drunk people that dropped like flies when the night ran long. People got drunk and fought. It was funny to see 'em stumbling around and falling in the mud.

And Mama was always the center of attention. Everybody knew her. Eileen didn't give no fucks. But sometimes it got her in trouble. More than once Eileen and her daughter had to flee the scene, leaving everything behind, on to the next corner of Tulsa. Whenever Tulsa got too hot, the pair could always split to Granny's house and wait it out.

They were headed there now. Granny's house. After Eileen died, the old bitch kicked Katie out, sent her back to the hillbillies she'd come from. Katie had never even heard of Florin. But apparently her Mama's daddy came from there, and that was where Katie's Pa lived. Eileen had known all along about him, though she pretended like she didn't.

Roman. Her Pa. He was redneck-rich, drove a truck that the rodeo guys could only drool at. Eileen even had pictures of it. Her cousins in Florin had acted as her spies, keeping her up on everything Roman did. Those cousins never told Roman where Eileen was. They never told him about Katie.

But after Eileen was buried Granny learned the truth. The old bitch nosed through Eileen's things and found her proof. She wasted no time calling the oldest McCall brother and telling him the whole story. He demanded custody, and Granny gave it, since it had been her plan all along. She ignored Katie's pleas.

"If I keep you in this house, you'll turn into a whore just like her," Granny replied. "And I'm too old to deal with that bullshit."

That still stung, years later. But Katie would see to the old bitch, oh yes she would. She'd bet dollars to donuts the woman still kept that stash of money under her mattress. That would do plenty for her and Junior. Maybe when they got to Tulsa they could ditch this little rust-bucket and get a real set of wheels...something to take onto the strip...Did Junior know how to race cars? Nevermind... He'd learn. She hadn't told him about her plan with Granny. Better not reveal too much at once. Junior was fraid-ish. Full of country notions about honesty. He'd only make a fuss about nothing.

Katie smiled at him lovingly. She was glad they hadn't broken up. It would have been a real bummer trying to find somebody else to get her off that wretched mountain. Nobody was sweet as Junior. Nobody listened so well.

As the runaways passed the Tennessee state line, morning dawned across the Blue Ridge, cool and hazy. Roman McCall woke to an empty house, and twelve missed calls.

He called the last number— his brother, Ross. This was unusual. His youngest brother answered on the second ring. It sounded like he was driving.

"Roman?"

"Yeah? What's going on?"

"Where are you?"

"In bed."

"You sitting down?"

"I said I'm in bed, boy."

"Alright."

"*Well?*"

"Roman, something happened."

"What? Is it Rain?"

"No. It's Pa."

"What about him?"

"Pa is dead."

"*What?*"

"He's dead, Roman."

"How? Who?"

"Somebody done went and shot him," said Ross. "No witnesses."

AFTERWORD

The next book in the BWWM Small Town Saga will be *Small Town King*. It will pick up after the events of *Small Town Rebel*.

Don't miss it!

Sign up to the email list for more dark and sexy BWWM from Marion Meadows, weekly newsletters and general tea on upcoming books : Click Here to Sign up

Get text message updates on books, sales and discounts here: https://slkt.io/VlQ8

AFTERWORD

Made in the USA
Middletown, DE
04 January 2023

21038725R00184